Cumberland Mansions

by
Eileen Mahony

Published by Wiverton Press

© Eileen Mahony 2016

ISBN 978-1-5272-0394-5

Endpapers designed by © Mary Gordon-Smith 2016

Photograph of James Dennis used courtesy of www.britishempire.co.uk

Photograph and biography of William Henry Peppiatt reproduced with kind permission of The Old Bancroftians' Association

Photograph and biography of Audley Delves Thursday © Imperial War Museum used under licence HU119113

Photograph of Sidney Davies Sewell reproduced with kind permission of Tonbridge School

Extract relating to Sidney Davies Sewell taken from the memoirs of Samuel Charles Portman Drury published in 'Stand To' courtesy of the Western Front Association

Photograph and biography of William Burt-Marshall © Imperial War Museum used under licence HU120869 and added information taken from 'War and the Breed' by David Starr Jordan

Newspaper clippings from the Daily Telegraph 1914 & 1915

'The Sunshine Of Your Smile' by Leonard Cooke & Lilian Ray

Typeset in Baskerville

Printed in the UK

Acknowledgements

My heartfelt appreciation goes to:

Theresa Smith, Gisele Kelly-Liegeois, Julie O'Hara, Lori Winters and Christine Oberman for encouraging and participating in the creation of this book.

Theresa Smith for being a central part of the original story and for discovering the 1914 Telegraph online.

Gisele Kelly-Liegeois for her beautiful illustrations that brought my characters to life and have been stored away for another time.

The 'Home Front' series on Radio 4 which inspired the start of this project.

Paul Caswell for providing the beautiful passage from his grandfather's memoir relating to Major Sidney Davies Sewell

Old Bancroftians, Tonbridge School, britishempire.co.uk, and the Imperial War Museum for permission to use photographs of the deceased relatives in the novel.

Brenda for discovering my editor and for her interest in the book.

Alison Williams for her invaluable editorial input, encouragement and understanding of my intentions for this novel

Nigel at Biddles for his generous giving of time and advice in the production process.

Declan Fitzsimons, my childhood friend, for his enthusiasm and advice in the early stages of the writing of the novel.

My dad, Peter, for nurturing in me the love of the written word, in both novel and song.

My daughter, Ella, for encouraging me in a way that only a daughter can.

My husband, Crispin, for his help with the details of the finished product and for accepting everything I do with love.

Dedication

for Crispin
who came along
someday

Preface

In August 2014, to mark the centenary of the First World War, I gathered a group of friends and together we wrote a daily episode of a fictional story set in England exactly one hundred years ago. We posted each episode on social media, and it operated like a Chinese Whisper where one episode led to another in comic and poignant ways. During the course of this, one of the group found that the Daily Telegraph was reproducing the newspaper online everyday, exactly one hundred years after it was first published.

I began to read these daily, which became not only time consuming but highly addictive. I was immersed in the world of 1914 in a way never before, even though I have read endless books, articles and poems about this period of our history. I realised I was drawn to the obituaries and the personal column before anything else. Each day the repercussions of the war were revealed as bereaved parents, spouses and siblings paid to place notices in remembrance of their sons, husbands and brothers who had recently died at the Front.

One morning I picked out an obituary at random, took a screenshot, and saved it. Here is an extract from the episode I wrote around this obituary:-

"5th November 1914, KILLED IN ACTION, DENNIS on Oct. 22nd-24th Lieut. J.O.C. Dennis, 12th Battery R.P.A. beloved only son of Mrs Dennis, 31, Cumberland-mansions, W., and the late Colonel Dennis 6th Dragoon Guards (Carabiniers), aged 26.

Edward Moresby set down his copy of the Telegraph informing him of this latest casualty. Exact date unknown. Some time between 22nd and 24th October. What on earth was going on? It no longer seemed tragic to him that these young lives were being thrown to the shells of the Germans, it was more than this. It was a disaster. And what of Mrs Dennis? Left behind. Breathing. Her husband and now her son, gone. Edward made a mental note to visit 31, Cumberland-mansions, W. when he had a spare moment."

I then began a journey with Edward Moresby boarding a train in Hastings, bound for London. He hailed a hansom cab and arrived at 31, Cumberland-mansions, W. (sic) where the maid answered the door. She showed him to the morning room where Mrs Dennis sat, and he extracted a scrap of paper from his waistcoat pocket, explaining to Mrs Dennis why he was paying her a visit. This was the beginning of Cumberland Mansions.

Seven of the characters in the novel lived, and seven are imagined, using the Personal Column as my inspiration. Most events within the novel relate directly to what I read in the newspaper, either through personal notices and obituaries or from articles and advertisements.

Throughout the book I have reproduced the exact format in the original obituary whenever the address is mentioned. I have used the present tense when the characters are inside Cumberland Mansions and the past tense when they are elsewhere, reminding us that the events outside the mansions took place one hundred years ago. My intention is to present Mrs Dennis' home as a timeless place where friends continue to meet and share concerns that they do not reveal in their day to day lives. It is a place where time and mortality do not exist.

The book is presented in two parts: the first contains the novel, the second reproduces the newspaper clippings. Both sections are organised by date rather than chapters. I have included the clippings to add historical interest and to illustrate the hazy line that lies between fact and fiction. Although I have used real people and names, my characters and the events in the novel are completely imagined. Reverend Alford was the Vicar of St Luke's in the latter part of the nineteenth century but died before my novel began; his character is taken from an interview between himself and the social commentator Charles Booth in 1899. The handwritten notebook containing this interview is kept at the London School of Economics library where it is available for public view. St Luke's, the church that is central to the novel, closed after the Second World War and is now the Sylvia Young Theatre School. The bereaved parents and sister in the novel have all been inspired by information I have gathered from their lives, but again are wholly imagined and do not intend to reflect the true character of these people. During my research I stumbled across Henrietta Barnett, a philanthropist and educator of the time, who founded Hampstead Garden Suburb and whose legacy is well worth further investigation. I also discovered Arthur Pearson and the Regent's Park hospital for blinded soldiers, now largely forgotten and worth exploring in greater depth.

The centrepiece of the book contains photographs of the sons and brother whose obituaries helped create Cumberland Mansions. I have included a photograph of Mrs Dennis' late husband, mentioned in the obituary for her son, as I have been unable to locate a photograph of her son, John Owen Cunninghame Dennis, and would be most grateful if any reader is able to fill this gap.

There were many journalists risking their own lives at the Front and I have included two extracts from war correspondents in the centrepiece of the book. They evoke a realism that is hard to find in literature of the period. The question of what became of these broken men after the war is still a mystery to me; I have talked to people of the generation after them and none seem to recall a great number of disabled men in society during their childhood. I can only conclude they stayed at home and were kept from public gaze, or that they died young from the effects of the damage done to them in the trenches. I have heard stories of men with breathing difficulties right up to the late 1930s as a result of gas poisoning.

There are, of course, too many notices and obituaries in the Telegraph during this period to number. The most poignant I came across was from a lady in Hastings asking if there was a kind lady reader who may be in a position to give a home to her beautiful baby.

Beyond the obituaries and the personals, the Telegraph provides articles and advertisements through which we can glimpse our society at the end of the Edwardian era. What is most notable to me is the redistribution of wealth one hundred years ago, where ladies of the aristocracy held coffee mornings and organised various arts and crafts gatherings to provide necessities for poorer families, and indeed for the Belgian refugees. This was, of course, decades before the birth of the Welfare State. Most striking is the similarity today with our food banks and our collections of clothing and essentials for the refugees waiting in camps to be 'processed'. My mind then wanders onto the building of Trident, and I really do wonder how far we have come in the century that divides ourselves and Mrs Dennis' gatherings.

The friends meet at Cumberland Mansions on Monday every week. Each section of the novel was written exactly one hundred years to the day after it happened. I discovered, after completing the manuscript, that Armistice Day 1918 was a Monday, and this felt a fitting conclusion to my story; I plan to complete the narrative up to that historical day.

My intention is that the reader will find consolation at 31, Cumberland-mansions, W. as Mrs Dennis' visitors do, and that the memory of John O C Dennis, Audley Delves Thursby, Sidney Davies Sewell, William Henry Peppiatt, William Burt-Marshall and all the men of their generation continue to live.

Eileen Mahony

London

24th October 2016

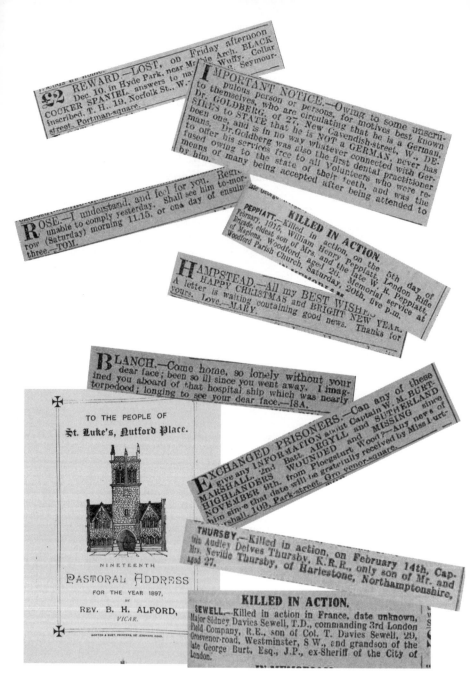

£2 REWARD.—LOST, on Friday afternoon Dec. 10. in Hyde Park, near Marble Arch. BLACK COCKER SPANIEL, answers to name of Wuffy. Collar inscribed, T. H., 19, Norfolk St., W.... Seymour-street, Portman-square.

IMPORTANT NOTICE.—Owing to some unscrupulous person or persons, for motives best known to themselves, who are circulating that he is a German, Dr. GOLDBERG, of 27, New Cavendish-street, W., DESIRES to STATE that he is NOT a GERMAN, never has been one, and is in no way whatever connected with Germans. Dr. Goldberg was also the first dental practitioner to offer his services free to all Volunteers who were refused owing to the state of their teeth, and was by means of many being accepted after being attended to by him.

ROSE.—I understand, and feel for you. Regret unable to comply yesterday. Shall see him to-morrow (Saturday) morning 11.15. or one day of ensuing three.—TOM.

PEPPIATT.—KILLED IN ACTION, on the 5th day of February, 1915, William Henry Peppiatt, London Rifle Brigade, eldest son of Mrs. and the late W. R. Peppiatt, of Maylena, Woodford, aged 26. Memorial service at Woodford Parish Church, Saturday, 20th, five p.m.

HAMPSTEAD.—All my BEST WISHES. A HAPPY CHRISTMAS and BRIGHT NEW YEAR. A letter is waiting containing good news. Thanks for yours. Love.—MARY.

BLANCH.—Come home, so lonely without your dear face; been so ill since you went away. I imagined you aboard of that hospital ship which was nearly torpedoed; longing to see your dear face.—ISA.

EXCHANGED PRISONERS.—Can any of these give any INFORMATION about Captain W. M. BURT-MARSHALL, 2nd Batt. ARGYLL and SUTHERLAND HIGHLANDERS. WOUNDED and MISSING since NOVEMBER 9th, from Ploegsteert Wood?—Any news of him since that date will be gratefully received by Miss Burt-Marshall, 109, Park-street, Grosvenor-square.

THURSBY.—Killed in action, on February 14th, Captain Audley Delves Thursby, K.R.R., only son of Mr. and Mrs. Neville Thursby, of Harlestone, Northamptonshire, aged 27.

KILLED IN ACTION.

SEWELL.—Killed in action in France, date unknown, Major Sidney Davies Sewell, T.D., commanding 3rd London Field Company, R.E., son of Col. T. Davies Sewell, 29, Grosvenor-road, Westminster, S.W., and grandson of the late George Burt, Esq., J.P., ex-Sheriff of the City of London.

TO THE PEOPLE OF
St. Luke's, Nutford Place.

NINETEENTH
PASTORAL ADDRESS
FOR THE YEAR 1897,
BY
REV. B. H. ALFORD,
VICAR.

NORTON & BURT, PRINTERS, 157 EDGWARE ROAD.

Contents

Part One

Thursday 26th November 1914

Priorities

District Judge Edward Moresby knew he should be at his wife's 'at home' to receive their guests, but he had woken with a thought in his mind that he was unable to ignore. As he stepped from the train at Charing Cross station and went onto the damp street to hail a hansom cab he was glad of his decision. More and more he was enjoying the new meaning the war had brought to his life.

The streets of London were dark and the judge was puzzled by the lack of illumination as his native Hastings was well lit. Some ten minutes into his journey he felt a sudden jolt and slipped from his seat to the floor of the carriage. He heard the driver curse. Voices and gasps were heard from outside, and Judge Moresby opened the door to a sea of concerned faces. Lying in the kerb was a young woman, no older than his daughter Freda, her skirts wet and muddy; she appeared to be unhurt.

"I say! Can I be of assistance? Dreadful lighting - can't see a thing. Let me help you up. Please, take a seat here. A ride home is the least I can offer."

"Oh no, sir. I am quite alright." and with this the woman gathered up her skirts and limped off into the night.

"I didn't see her, sir." said the cabbie. "Can't see nothing in these dark streets. They need to start lighting the streets again, sir. They say the airships will be coming over to bomb us, but I don't see no airships. I do see a lot of accidents, sometimes deaths."

The judge was horrified. People scurrying about the streets in the dead of night, rain and hail, being knocked down by horses and motor cars and goodness knows what else. He would see about this at his next council meeting. What a sorry state of affairs. He settled himself back into the hansom, having instructed the driver to go very slowly, "There is no hurry." Finally the hansom came to a gentle stop and Judge Moresby paid the driver with a generous tip. He watched as the cab trotted off into the distance, no lights to guide it or to warn pedestrians of its existence. Next council meeting. Mustn't forget.

The judge made his way up the steps of 31, Cumberland-mansions, W., and rang the bell.

"Can I help you sir?" asked the maid.

"I have come to see Mrs Dennis. I do not have an appointment but I am hoping I have something that will be of assistance to her."

The maid retreated into the hallway, there was a tapping on an inside door, whispers and movement, then she returned to the door and told him that Mrs Dennis would see him.

———

He is shown into the morning room and Mrs Dennis greets him warmly and shows him to a seat. Edward observes the slight but erect woman, offering a brave and determined face to the stranger who has entered her world.

"I do apologise for intruding in this manner, Mrs Dennis. You see, I read the obituary you placed in the Telegraph some weeks ago. It has played on my mind ever since."

Edward Moresby fumbles in his waistcoat pocket and pulls out a tiny newspaper cutting.

"I hope I haven't startled you. The truth is I have lost my own son in this infernal war. My wife has been at a loss." He pauses, gathers his thoughts and continues. "I see from your notice in the newspaper that you have also lost your only son. I am hoping I can be of assistance to you. I don't know what I can do to help, but I felt compelled to come."

Mrs Dennis lowers herself gingerly onto a chair, and sits in her own home as if she is the strange visitor and Judge Moresby the man of the house. How strong and kind and capable he appears to her. Edward glances around the room, full of fringes and drapes and porcelain ornaments, the light from outside peeping through the heavy curtains and dancing on the table where Mrs Dennis' tea service is placed.

"May we offer you some tea and a slice of cake Mr.... Why! I didn't quite catch your name...."

"Judge - um - Edward Moresby, Mrs Dennis." He thinks twice before deciding to use a more friendly approach with this lady who appears vulnerable and spent.

"Judge Moresby, a cup of tea?"

Edward puts the dilemma of formality to one side and accepts the tea graciously. As he settles himself in an easy chair near the window, he notices a crumpled and open newspaper on the table, the same paper he reads. Of course, it is the obituary she placed in the Telegraph that has brought him here, but seeing the newspaper open and in the process of being read brings a familiarity to Edward and he feels quite at home.

"I always browse the obituaries, Mrs Dennis, since this dreadful war began. I don't know what made yours stand out among the others. I suppose I saw that your only son had died, and as I have lost my only son - one of the first to die, you know - I thought I may be able to understand how you feel in some way. Do say if I am intruding and I will, of course, leave directly."

Edward doesn't mention the fact that he was drawn to Mrs Dennis' home on account of her also being a widow; to have lost her entire family! It is impossible for Edward to imagine such loss.

"Judge Moresby, I am touched that you have taken the time to come to see me, a stranger. How far have you travelled?"

"I took the quarter past six this morning from Hastings to Charing Cross. I then took a hansom cab to your door. It was really no trouble."

Mrs Dennis is lost for words. Such a long distance. The generous giving of time. This man must be extraordinarily busy in his daily life, why on earth has he expended so much to visit her?

"Why Judge - may I call you Edward?" - a slight nod of the head affirms that Mrs Dennis may do so and she continues - "Edward, how splendidly kind of you to put yourself out so. I do not quite know what to say."

Edward sips his tea and partakes of a slice of angel cake offered by the maid. Mrs Dennis sits back in the easy chair adjacent to the one in which Edward sits, lets out an almost imperceptible sigh, and retreats into her own thoughts. Edward's eyes are drawn to the fireplace at the far end of the room, and he gazes at the flickering flames that are bringing their heat across the room to where he and Mrs Dennis sit. His thoughts move back in time to the day he received the telegram telling him of Teddy's death, so soon after his arrival in France. Teddy. His only son. His first born. Eighteen years old. No word of his horse, Chestnut, who had carried him onto the troop ship at the harbour in Folkestone, taking them both off to France on a journey with no return. How Teddy had groomed his beloved Chestnut, every day. Lovingly. The excitement when they were called up to serve their country. The pride Edward had felt on the day of their departure. Yet Edward has been able to speak of none of this to his wife, Teddy's mother Frances. Everything has remained unspoken. Unspeakable.

Next to Edward, Mrs Dennis muses on her own son, John, her pride and her joy. Such a rock after the loss of her husband. They had been a small unit, sufficient nonetheless. The three had not wanted for more. The fourteen years they had enjoyed before John's father was taken in battle at the end of the Boer War had been the happiest for Mrs Dennis. She and John had awaited her husband's leave with anticipation through all those years. When he did not, finally, return, she and John had clung to one another and had worked around the wreckage until something strong and enduring had emerged. Now, twelve years later, that enduring state had changed and Mrs Dennis was at a loss. There had been no one to speak with, no one to share the burden. As Mrs Dennis ruminates in this way, she turns to Edward, dismayed at having neglected her guest so thoughtlessly. She opens her mouth to speak but stops short as she notices his gaze directed towards the fireplace at the far end of the room. She sees, in an instant, that the thoughts he struggles with as he gazes into the fire are akin to the thoughts she, too, is battling. It is at this moment that Mrs Dennis realises there are no words. She feels as if a warm overcoat has been wrapped around her and that all her worries have come to an end.

The unlikely pair sit like this for some time, possibly hours, and derive from one another the comfort they have found from nowhere and no one else.

Monday 30th November 1914

Mrs Rose Muller

Rose sat by her dressing table mirror gazing at the anxious woman in the glass. What was she to do now? And with Toby returning to the Front at the end of the week. There must be a way to make him see, to make him understand. They had been so young; and now this mess.

Of course the war had changed everything. Perhaps she should let things take their course, sit back, allow things to happen. But what if Tom decided to enlist, what then?

Round and round these thoughts spun in her brain. What seemed a good idea at one moment seemed futile and pointless the next. Rose glanced at the newspaper on her occasional table and her eye caught the Personal Column on the front of the Telegraph. That was it! She would place a message where Tom would be sure to see it, on the front page of the paper they both read every day.

What a stroke of luck that Toby read the Times.

Monday 7th December 1914

Dr Goldberg

Judge Moresby enjoys his weekly visit with Mrs Dennis, especially since the return of Wuffy to the household. Mrs Dennis was quite distraught the day Wuffy had bolted in Regent's Park; the dog had been startled by a swan attempting to peck at his ear and Mrs Dennis was beside herself when he disappeared into the distance. Wuffy had belonged to her son John, and he was the only living link between herself and her dead son. It was Edward who thought of looking in the Personal Column of the Telegraph and Mrs Dennis found her beloved dog with no trouble at all. How reassuring it is to have a man of Edward's calibre enter her life from nowhere.

For his part, Edward finds his visits to Mrs Dennis relaxing and grounding. He compares this woman with his wife: the two could not be more different; where Mrs Moresby is strong-minded and independent of thought Mrs Dennis is easy going, relaxed and pliable. Edward marvels at the contrast in these two women while they each seem able to shoulder the burden of the terrible loss of their only sons. It had not occurred to Edward prior to this wretched war that women may be made of sterner stuff than himself.

Today, however, other guests drape themselves on the sofas of Mrs Dennis' room. Dr Goldberg is introduced to Edward.

"Good evening Judge Moresby. So kind of you to contact me in this unusual manner."

"Please. Mrs Dennis is your hostess. We are all guests in her home."

It had been Mrs Dennis' idea that they contact people in this way, through the Personal Column of the Telegraph. If it hadn't been for Edward's stroke of genius she would not have had Wuffy returned. So Mrs Dennis thought it only natural to extend the idea one more step and to gather people to her home who may be in trouble due to this wretched war. And here was their first visitor, an eminent dentist from America, long settled in London, but having to prove his absence of German blood to a world gone mad. The indignity of having to expose himself in the newspaper in this fashion Mrs Dennis can only imagine. As Dr Goldberg introduces himself to Edward, Mrs Dennis observes the anxiety that tumbles out with his words.

"Of course. Mrs Dennis. Delighted." Dr Goldberg takes Mrs Dennis' hand and raises it to his lips with an air of respect and appreciation. He then drops it quite abruptly and turns to Edward.

"Judge Moresby, I must assure you I am not of German heritage. I have no German blood. These trouble makers are causing my work to suffer and are making my life quite intolerable. I am interested in my research into dentures and the improvement of my service."

Edward turns in the direction of the patient who is accompanying Dr Goldberg today. His lips are swollen, his cheeks bruised. He seems unable to speak and so Dr Goldberg speaks for him.

"Here is one of my Patriotic Patients. Rotten teeth. Lack of dental hygiene, family can't afford a dentist. The government pays me for his treatment. Now he has a whole new set of dentures and is fit to go to France and fight those Germans. If I were of German heritage I would hardly be preparing our men to fight them!"

All this is spoken in front of the patient as if he is unable to hear. Edward looks at the Patriotic Patient and assesses him to be quite unfit to hold a conversation or eat any solid food, let alone fight the enemy. Edward is familiar with dentists and their dentures from his own bitter experience. The dentures in the young man's mouth may be new to him, but Edward suspects that to Dr Goldberg they are far from new and that they may have lingered in his wooden drawers for many years.

"Sidney can't afford to pay my fees" - this is the first time Dr Goldberg has referred to the patient by name - "so the government pay for him. That way Sidney can be a soldier and I can maintain my business in these difficult times. Everyone wins."

The fact that the soldier can neither talk nor eat seems of little concern to Dr Goldberg. Neither does he seem to notice Wuffy sniffing around the soldier in a curious and excited manner. Sidney is excited about having enlisted this very morning with his new dentures. Edward and Mrs Dennis glance at each other momentarily, an ocean of understanding passing between them which goes unnoticed by Dr Goldberg and Sidney.

Edward steers the conversation on another route.

"Dr Goldberg. Sidney. Perhaps you would care to browse the newspaper here to help us find another soul in need of succour. I myself am rather taken with Rose here. She has regular entries in the Personal Column and she appears to be someone in need of support."

Dr Goldberg takes the newspaper and reads the message from Rose. While he does so, Mrs Dennis takes pen to paper to compose their request.

31, Cumberland-mansions, W.

Dear Sirs,

I would be most grateful if you would contact the lady who has an entry in the Personal Column of your newspaper on the 7th inst., and in previous editions, by the name of Rose. If she were to present herself at 31, Cumberland-mansions, W., on Monday next after ten o'clock in the morning she may find something to her advantage.

Yours sincerely,

Mrs Dennis.

Widow of the late Colonel Dennis, 6th Dragoon Guards (Carabiniers).

Monday 14th December 1914

Rose

"This is Judge Moresby. Edward - this is Rose, the young lady we contacted from the newspaper when last we met."

Edward beholds the beautiful woman before him and shows her to a seat by the fire. Before he has time to settle himself in the chair next to her, Rose brings forth a torrent of anxiety and fear:

"Judge Moresby, my children are being shunned at school, teased, and worse; and all because of their name. Muller is so obviously German. Oh dear. I simply don't know what is to be done!"

"Call me Edward, my dear." He considers talking pleasantries, getting to know this newcomer, partaking of tea; but something in Rose's demeanour prompts him to do otherwise.

"Have you considered changing their name? Something more English?" He considers for a moment. "Miller, perhaps."

"I have thought of that very name, Judge Moresby! My husband used Miller when he enlisted. But my children are known already by their name, and I don't know what it would achieve to change it. What would their father think?" Rose ponders momentarily. "Toby is in France. He wouldn't know. Besides, I'm the one living with the problem, it's of no concern to him. Oh, Judge Moresby, you must consider me a dreadful wife, and my poor husband fighting for King and Country......"

"Not at all, my dear."

Edward ponders on the idea: Muller. Miller. One simple vowel is the difference between comfort and fear. What a strange world it has become. He listens further while Rose pours out her heart regarding Toby, her husband at the Front, and Tom who was Toby's best friend who also misses him dreadfully.

"At least we have each other to lean on." Something in Rose's demeanour causes Edward to ponder on this latest complication.

"Before the war we were happy."

Mrs Dennis observes from the far end of the room whilst in conversation with Dr Goldberg. It all sounds depressingly familiar to her after Dr Goldberg's experience. She excuses herself and moves towards Edward and Rose.

"Rose, dear, I wonder if you can help me. I can't decide who to contact next, there are so many troubled people placing notices in the newspaper. Come over with me to the table and we can peruse the paper together."

"Oh, if I can be of any assistance Mrs Dennis, it will be my pleasure. It's the least I can do when you've been so kind as to invite me into your home. Listen to me go on! You would think I was the only one with a problem. Let's look together."

The two ladies move across to the table while Edward makes his way to where Dr Goldberg is sitting.

"May I join you, Dr Goldberg?"

"Why of course, Judge Moresby. Be my guest."

The irony of Dr Goldberg's words is not lost on Edward, but the dentist seems unaware, so confident is he in his station in life that he feels a sense of ownership wherever he is. Quite a character trait, thinks Edward, himself rather more reticent despite his position in society. Perhaps this is why Dr Goldberg is so ruffled by his current problems regarding his bloodline. Edward sits down and braces himself for the inevitable onslaught of Dr Goldberg's words, but he is surprised to be offered only silence. Dr Goldberg stares out of the window deep in thought. Edward makes himself comfortable and prepares to enjoy the interlude.

Over at the table, Mrs Dennis and Rose have picked out a message from someone called Mary who seems to be contacting her friend Hampstead. Rose has noticed there have been regular messages sent between these two for the past few weeks and tells Mrs Dennis this is one of the reasons she decided to communicate through the newspaper herself. Mrs Dennis asks the maid to bring her writing materials so she can write a letter to the Telegraph.

Thursday 7th January 1915

Mary

Mary was delighted to be expecting her first child and, to cap it all, a war baby. Looking back to only Christmas Eve so much seemed to have happened in two short weeks. It had been like this since the summer that now seemed years ago, at the beginning of the war. How young she had been then. Now she felt as if she could take on the world, so confident and full of vigour was she, quite unlike the little slip of a thing she had been just one short season a lifetime ago.

Dear Hampstead. Dear, darling Hampstead. How strong and dignified he seemed still, despite the bandages around his eyes and the trembling of his fingers as they lay limp on the bedsheets. At least he was out of it. That was something to be thankful for; and their baby would have a father, not a photograph of a young soldier on the mantel to gaze at. In time Hampstead would regain his sight, rebuild his nerves, and it would all be as they had planned it to be.

Mary looked back to her letter, written just before Christmas Eve, telling her husband of the good news that she was with child. She was, at first, uncomfortable sending messages via the newspaper, but she had seen the sense in it when Hampstead had explained. Now he was back from France it would be so much faster than letters that were read by his commanding officer before they arrived at Hampstead's bedside. By sending a message via

14

the personals she could collect his letters directly from his parents who visited him daily. See. He had lost none of his smart, creative mind. His sight was only one small part of this fine man whose child she carried.

Monday 11th January 1915

Connections

There has been something of a hiatus over the holiday period which has been unsettling for them all. Now with their first meeting of the new year, and the war still showing no signs of ending, there is a sense of flatness about the room in 31, Cumberland-mansions, W. It is a relief to hear the doorbell and the announcement of a newcomer. A small, tidy figure enters, looking unsure of what she has stumbled upon. Without hesitation Rose rises from her seat by the fire and walks towards Mary with her hand outstretched. "Rose Miller. Delighted to meet you."

Mary tentatively offers her gloved hand in return and both ladies smile. Mary removes her long-armed gloves, finger by finger, places them inside her hat and offers them to the maid who then disappears back into the hallway.

Rose and Mary sit and talk in hushed tones, of the love triangle in which one is caught, and the blinded soldier husband and expected child of the other. The remaining guests in the room talk amongst themselves, leaving the young women to acquaint themselves. The moments slip by and pass into hours. Luncheon is served. The clock ticks. Tea is served. The light fades early. Dinner is served. Conversation diminishes to a hush.

Late in the evening the friends depart. Thoughtful. Calmed. Refreshed.

Thursday 14th January 1915

Mrs Frances Moresby

Frances grabbed her hat and coat, pulled on her gloves, and set off on the two-mile hike to Hastings Military Hospital. With Edward away more and more, and God knows what he was doing, Frances had decided to grab life with both hands and mould something for herself for a change. Goodness knows everyone else was doing just that, so why not her? Freda had announced her latest crack-brained scheme to administer to wounded soldiers from the far-flung corners of the Empire, and what with her in Brighton and Edward in London during the week, the only thing left for Frances was to strike out on her own.

She arrived at the hospital, cold and windswept, but determined. That charming young man called Hampstead (where did they get these names?) would be looking forward to the next chapter of Mrs Dowdall's new book 'Joking Apart' and, to be honest, Frances was looking forward to it too. As she approached his bed she stopped at the sight of a young woman sitting by his side, holding his hand and dabbing his brow with a damp flannel. This must be Mary of whom Hampstead spoke, his young wife who was expecting his child. Frances had thought this was delirium on his part, but clearly here was Mary herself.

Mary turned her head at the click of Frances' shoes, released Hampstead's hand and rose to greet the nice lady who had been reading to her poor, troubled husband. Frances smiled in greeting and extended her hand.

"Good morning. You must be Mary. I've heard so much about you, I was almost wondering if you were a figment of this man's fine imagination. But here you are! Delighted!"

"How nice to meet you Mrs Moresby. My husband and I are so grateful to you for the time you've taken to read to him. It's such a comfort to me knowing you're filling in the gaps when I cannot be at his bedside." Mary lowered her eyes in deference, and both ladies sat down. Frances felt somewhat unnecessary, superfluous. After some uncomfortable moments she took her leave, pretending she had pressing concerns elsewhere on the ward.

In the corridor outside Frances allowed a tear to roll down her cheek in memory of Teddy, her only son, before she set off in search of other troubled souls to whom she could administer some solace.

Thursday 4th February 1915

Mr Tobias Butler

It was a bitterly cold morning and Tobias Butler was very glad of the new heating system that had been installed in his digs. It was worth paying that little bit more for a better class of accommodation. As he shaved his delicate chin with the hot running water his thoughts turned to the invitation from Judge Moresby to meet some of his new friends in London. His role as secretary to the judge was beginning to pay dividends.

Thursday 11th February 1915

Secrets

Frances Moresby readied herself to brave the February cold. As she opened the door to the mist and fog that surrounded her Hastings home, her thoughts drifted to the hazy memory of late November and her last 'at home'. Since then much water had passed beneath Frances' bridge, and even her resolve was beginning to wane.

Freda had gone off to Brighton, swanning around with other

young girls, telling her mother she was working as a nurse. Nurse indeed! And with those Indian Sherpas at the Pavilion! Had she taken leave of her senses? This wretched war was turning her world on its head. The most trying part of it all was dear Edward, working all hours of the day and night, pursuing one worthy cause after another. Frances hardly saw her husband; the closest she came was the rustling of his overcoat and the clunk of his shoes on his dressing room floor. She often toyed with the idea of knocking on his bedroom door (and Frances was not a woman in the habit of toying) but propriety always won out, which was a comfort to Frances, indicating that all had not been lost in these difficult times.

As Frances pulled the door to, and gingerly felt her way down the five stone steps before her, she noticed a tall, angular silhouette moving along the street, shrouded in the mist. The reason that this shape appeared familiar soon became apparent for she found herself confronted by the outstretched hand of Tobias Butler, her husband's secretary. Frances reached out and offered her limp hand to Tobias' long-fingered shake.

"You are looking very well, Mrs Moresby. I trust the judge is well?"

"My husband? Edward. I expect so. Yes. Surely you do not need to ask me, Mr Butler, you are after all my husband's right hand man."

"I see so little of him lately what with his war commitments. Wonderful job he's doing with those unfortunate people in London. Wonderful."

"In London? Unfortunate people?"

"The house. Cumberland Mansions. Enjoyed my visit. Inspiring. Comforting almost."

Inspiring? Comforting? Cumberland Mansions? What was this man talking about? What on earth was Edward up to now? Of course it wouldn't do for Mr Butler to see that she didn't know of her husband's activities. Maybe she could glean some more information.

"Ah, Edward is always putting the needs of others before himself. It's his role as District Judge. I am glad to hear that these unfortunate people benefit from my husband's efforts."

"Oh yes! It is a refuge for all kinds of people. The one thing they have in common is the war. They certainly look forward to the start of the week. Mondays are the day they work towards. It keeps them going. Very nice to see you Mrs Moresby. "

And with that he was off into the mist. Oh dear. No time today, must go to the soldiers' canteen at the railway station as planned. Teas to serve. Good spirits to dispense. Later. At last now she could discover Edward's secret. But not today. Priorities.

Monday 15th February 1915

Mr Isa Harburg

At 31, Cumberland-mansions, W., tea is being served. The sharp morning sun beams a ribbon of light onto the embroidered tablecloth on Mrs Dennis' round table. The gilt edges of the teacups glint as the guests ease their way into the morning. Today's newcomer is Isa Harburg whose thoughts are focused on a distant hospital filled with the wounded and the dying. All the patients are young and strong and virile and finished. Isa visualises Blanch, tending to the sick and dying, his beloved daughter, about the age her mother was when Blanch's life triumphed over her own.

Everything in Isa's life had led up to that day when his treasured wife had given birth to their first and only child; everything, yet nothing. Escaping Petrograd five years earlier; walking bare-foot, mile upon mile to reach freedom and safety; scrimping and scraping as a junior assistant in a tailor's on Saville Row; finding a place for himself and his wife to start a new life. Then the day arrived when they were to become a family, and Blanch was taken from him, for want of money to secure a safe birth. When Blanch had died Isa had thought he wouldn't be able to continue breathing. But he did. In and out, in and out, day in, day out. Relentlessly. Gradually the new life from Blanch gave him reason to continue, and so he called her Blanch in memory of the childhood companion who had braved the New World with him and had dreamed of new beginnings. And here he sat, longing for the return of his daughter from the Front, struggling with the fear of losing her forever.

When Isa paid for the advertisement in the Personal Column of the Telegraph, he hoped it would bring his daughter back to him. Instead it has brought him to this calm and comforting room where people sit and talk and reflect and dream. He looks around him and wonders at them all. He feels drawn to the striking, tall, dark-featured man of early middle years who speaks of patients and teeth and patriotic duty. It appears he is a fellow Jew.

"Dr Goldberg" says the dentist, offering an outstretched hand.

"Isa Harburg. Pleased to make your acquaintance. I can't help wondering if you have found yourself in London as an exile, as I have myself."

Dr Goldberg is immediately defensive. "I'm not a German; I have no affiliation to the German race despite the stories people are maliciously spreading."

"Dr Goldberg, I do apologise. I meant your name - like mine - just wondered; but of course, you are too young. Perhaps your parents migrated. I myself am from Petrograd."

"Mr Harburg. My place of birth is the United States of America. It is my research that brought me to London. Now I am proudly serving King and Country with my Patriotic Patients."

Isa is rescued from this difficult encounter by the offer of tea from Mrs Dennis. Dr Goldberg retreats to the window seat where Mary is partaking of refreshment, anxious and alone. He is able to bring some comfort and hope to her, most unexpected for this deeply conflicted man.

"Hospitals for the blind" Mary sits to attention, hanging on Dr Goldberg's every word.

"I read it in the paper only last week, requests for help in setting them up. Lots of chaps blinded, long lives ahead of them, nothing to do. The reader who placed the advertisement was very keen to hear from people with loved ones wounded in this way."

Mary makes a note to visit the Telegraph offices and to contact this man who may offer Hampstead a way out of his darkness.

Suddenly a black, furry object lands on Isa's neatly pressed trousers and he is too taken aback to move. "I'm so sorry Mr Harburg. What must you think of us? Wuffy. Get down at once." But the little black spaniel stays rooted to the newcomer's lap, and Isa feels towards his pocket for his clothes brush. Yes. It is there. Before he leaves to return to the outside world he will give his trousers a good brush, and he will walk proud as the tailor of Saville Row. He finds an unfamiliar comfort in the warmth of the little dog, and he sits gazing at the ball of fur for some minutes.

"Mrs Dennis. Look here at this dreadful situation." Edward points to the newspaper article he is reading. "Children standing in line, waiting for bread in the dark hours before dawn. Parents can't afford the real thing; queueing for scraps."

"Edward, you must mention this at your next council meeting and see what can be done. There is that wonderful society that may help. Now, what is it called?"

"The National Society for the Prevention of Cruelty to Children. Is that the one you mean, Mrs Dennis?"

"Oh yes, that's it." Such a clever man.

The morning turns to lunch time, and lunch time to tea, and tea to evening. Shadows lengthen over the rugs and drapes of Mrs Dennis' tranquil room. The talk continues, and with each passing hour the burdens upon the shoulders of the group lighten. Time seems to hang in the balance, awaiting the next journey. Biding itself.

The evening wears on.

Suddenly, a knock at the door and an announcement.

"Mr Tobias Butler, Madam"

"Good evening Judge Moresby – I thought I might find you here."

Monday 1st March 1915

Mrs W. R. Peppiatt

It has been a difficult fortnight. Tobias' visit to inform Edward that his wife, Frances, knows of his activities but does not know where they are taking place has unsettled both Edward and Mrs Dennis. Besides this, there is so much in the paper this week that the personals have been overtaken by the obituaries, which leads Edward and Mrs Dennis to allow their personal grief to colour their decision. Thus the newest visitor to 31, Cumberland-mansions, W. is Mrs W. R. Peppiatt, widowed and now bereft of her eldest son William who has been killed in action on the 5th inst..

Mrs Peppiatt eases gently into the cushioned sofa provided by Mrs Dennis and mulls over thoughts of the memorial service that took place last week at Woodford Parish Church.

"There was no burial," she says, to no one in particular.

"We had no body to bury. Nothing. Just a telegram telling us my dear boy was gone. My other sons tell me I must take comfort in his Glorious End, and of course I do, but nothing to bury ......"

Emily pauses and the room is silent.

"A hero's death! Surely a hero is given a burial? A proper goodbye... Oh, forgive me! Mrs Dennis! You have been so kind to invite me, a stranger, into your home. How very disrespectful of me. Can you forgive me?"

Mrs Dennis refreshes Emily Peppiatt's tea cup and pats her knee.

"Don't worry Mrs Peppiatt; this is why you are here - why we are all here. To share our troubles."

Emily tells Mrs Dennis she feels in limbo, neither mother nor widowed mother. What do they call a mother who has lost a child?

"If you lose your husband you have a place in society, you have a title. People can understand; you can explain where you are in the Order of Things. But a mother without her eldest son? And no body? What then?"

A silence follows while Emily gathers her thoughts.

"I have been greatly troubled, Mrs Dennis, by this letter from William's school friend, Bunny Underhill." and Emily pulls a neatly folded paper from her clutch bag and immerses herself, for the umpteenth time, in its lines:

"We had been brought up on histories of the Boer War and patriotism and heroics and everything and we thought the war was going to be over before we could get there. Well in about half a minute I wondered what the devil I had got myself into because it was nothing but mud and filth. All the chaps that were already there were like tramps all plastered in filth and dirt - unshaven..."

Emily can bring herself to read no more. Instead, she runs around in her mind the words, long memorised, of William's commanding officer Major Burnell. "I personally feel very much his loss; he was one of those always willing to help and always cheerful even when things were at their worst."

A movement of the door and a tapping of feet in the hall announce the arrival of Mr Neville Thursby, a man whose countenance and demeanour speak of Certainty and Dignity and Trust. Edward greets him, taking him aside to explain the reason he is here and nodding in the direction of Mrs Peppiatt. After some moments Neville moves towards the fireplace where Mrs Peppiatt is sitting. Emily's tired eyes are able to focus on the smart morning suit and clipped moustache, but she realises immediately that something is amiss. Mr Neville Thursby extends his hand and the customary greeting between strangers of a certain social class takes place, just as if nothing has happened at all to shake the equilibrium. As he sits down, however, and relaxes into his position in the setting provided by 31, Cumberland-mansions, W., all the cares of the last two weeks flow out through his eyes and plant themselves squarely on the shoulders of Emily, Mrs W.R. Peppiatt.

"Mrs Peppiatt. Forgive me if I seem abrupt. I hope I may be of some comfort to you. My son, too, has disappeared from our lives in a similar fashion."

Neville pauses, apparently lost in thought.

"Mrs Thursby was thirty-five years old when our twins were born; long-awaited gifts we called them. Brought such comfort to Zoe, my wife. Very proud of him; very proud. Good lad! Honor, his twin sister, very proud too. Very proud."

His voice tails off. Emily and Neville Thursby sit in companionable silence.

"A little odd to have 'no remains' but this is war. All his belongings gone too. Nothing. Odd that, what?"

He pours all this out to Emily, not because he is in the habit of spilling his heart but because she seems to be before him expressly for this purpose. She then tells him the desperate story of William, whose untimely demise was nine days prior to that of Mr Thursby's own son, Audley (always called him Arthur; not sure why; Mother liked it.)

28

Edward Moresby is anxious to share the obituary in the paper this week for Kenneth Powell, famous tennis player and general athlete. "A fine obituary for a fine life," announces Edward, and passes the paper around for all to digest. The first to begin reading is Isa Harburg. As he reads the details of Kenneth Powell's athletic career he is stopped in his tracks by the inclusion of a fragment of a letter written by Kenneth to his mother on 13th December last. He doesn't know why but he feels compelled to read it aloud to his friends and confidants in this room of comfort and consolation.

" 'On the ninth, at night, the fifty fittest men in our company were required to go to the support trenches. Of our section only four were taken. Our trench was a line of underground dugouts by a hedge about half a mile behind our nearest first-line trenches, where others of our battalion were stationed. M and I shared for three days a hole eight feet long, four feet deep, two feet six inches wide with six inches of mud at the bottom, and a straw cover which let in the rain. We had to sit facing each other, and I had the outside seat on a damp board, with a mackintosh sheet between me and the elements. You can imagine the discomfort to two large men, especially to their legs. We soon got covered in mud all over. As soon as I could I went out to get dry straw for the bottom, and was successful, though there were some bullets about. M. miraculously made a fire in a brazier from time to time with boxwood as fuel, and this helped us to keep warm, with soup tablets and tea. We both got choked with the smoke. Once a day, at dusk, I got relief by going to get water from a neighbouring farm; but the farm has been shelled to pieces now, which is disgusting. My way to it led by a dead cow and the remains of a French soldier, and was all under the fire of German bullets which came over our first line of trenches, and are described as 'strays' as they were not aimed at anyone, though they hurt just the same.' "

A silence falls over the room. Mary shifts uncomfortably in her chair; poor Hampstead may be blind but at least he is out of it. She still has the father of her child, and he still has a life to live. Thoughts of a flooded grave race in front of Mary's line of vision which settles itself on Rose Muller's downcast face.

"Mary, I've seen an advertisement and wonder if I should tell Tom about it."

She shows Mary the advertisement in the paper for a house steward and wife for the Ulster Club in Belfast.

"This could be the answer to our problems. We could take the girls with us..."

"But you're married to Toby, and he's fighting for our safety!" Mary speaks in hushed tones so the others do not hear.

If Toby is to survive the war, thinks Rose, and this seems unlikely, he will not return as the man who had left. Surely she and Tom would be justified in moving away and starting afresh. The only problem is the children. There must be a way. It was proving so difficult to meet up with Tom these days; crossed wires, aborted rendezvous, mistakes, fears, distress. She must find a way out of it all.

Wuffy wriggles in Isa Harburg's lap, rubs his nose and snuggles deep into the comfort of his friend whose visits he enjoys as much as his dinner and his walks in Regents Park. Isa, for his part, pats the little dog who means more to him than he would care to admit; Wuffy had gravitated to Isa from the moment he entered the house and Isa's is the only lap Wuffy frequents. Isa feels, habitually, for the clothes brush that is secure in his trouser pocket. He pats the prostrated head and mutters, "My boy."

The third newcomer for today enters the room with a swish of his morning coat and a tip of his top hat. Colonel Thomas Sewell brings with him an air of briskness and determination. Everyone feels they should stand to attention but they stop short because it seems so alien in this room of camaraderie and relaxed friendship. Colonel Sewell had been rather taken aback when Judge Moresby had contacted him via the Telegraph, but he is willing to give this man some leeway as he describes himself as a District Judge so must know what he is doing. Strange idea though, what? Now here he is, to find out what it's all about. He feels in his inside coat pocket for the letter, unopened, he has received this morning from France.

Tea is served and pleasantries imparted. Introductions are made and seats allocated, according to personal preference. Colonel Sewell chooses to stand, hands behind his back, warming them on the fire from the open grate. Thus the three newcomers are in close proximity. The clink of china and the crackles from the fire fill the room with their familiarity. Anything familiar is welcomed in this new world of confusion and questions. Over the course of the morning, and on through lunch, and into the early afternoon, shadows lengthening with the day, the visitors exchange stories.

"My son, Major Sidney Davies Sewell, has heroically given his life for King and Country. Damn fine man. Not sure exact date. No details. Just doing his duty. Damn fine man. Died leading the 3rd London Field Company you know..."

Colonel Sewell is an old man, in his mid-seventies, but he is not to be beaten by this; military training has prepared him well for such an eventuality. Just as well he was contacted by Judge Moresby; these people, sitting about, chit-chatting, doing nothing. They need a good talking to. How are we going to win the war with this attitude? As these thoughts run through Colonel Thomas Sewell's mind he feels the paper in his inside pocket. Pulling out the envelope he decides that now is the time to open it and to see what news it will bring him of his fine son, father of four, husband, military man. He had lived a full and useful life. He had died in the glory of his country's cause for freedom. Why, the boy had even been born in Belgium, in the years before the terrible atrocities the Germans had wrought there. Yes. Indeed. A fine and useful life, ended in a fitting and glorious fashion.

Colonel Sewell pulls out the letter from the envelope in his hand. It is signed at the bottom by a member of his son's company. The text of the letter reads as follows:

'We stumbled up the cellar steps, added the body to a long row of others who had finished their soldiering, and made our silent way back to our billets feeling numbed and shocked at the suddenness and absence of glory in this incident which had taken from us the dominant personality who so far had directed and led the company.'

Colonel Thomas Sewell folds the letter gingerly and with trembling fingers he replaces it, with some difficulty, in the envelope in which it came. He then replaces the envelope in his inside coat pocket. In ordinary times he would have clasped his hands behind his back and warmed his back on the fire. But these are not ordinary times. He looks around him at the people in this room, men and women of differing ages and walks of life. An air of calm lies over them and a glow of tranquility fills the spaces between them. Thomas sees an armchair to his left by the fireside and, for the first time in his life, he sits down to contemplate his thoughts without any intention of doing anything about them. His life of action over seventy-five years has served its purpose. Today he will think, but he will not act. Today he will see things because he wants to see them, not because his position requires him to do so.

Monday 8th March 1915

Miss Maud Burt-Marshall

It wouldn't have been quite so distressing if the War Office had kept their eye on the ball in the first place and reported him KIA. But this hadn't been the case. In November a telegram had arrived stating 'missing, believed taken Prisoner of War'. The last three months had been trying in the extreme, and only her devotion to her big brother Will had kept her at it. Every corner she turned, Maud found another obstacle. Nothing had taken her to a resolution. Her brother had just disappeared off the face of the earth. Then, in February, she was informed he 'fell in the German trenches in Ploegstreet Wood' and subsequently died in a German field hospital in France. In November, for goodness sake. How was she possibly to believe this? There was no body, no grave, no burial, nothing tangible. It was just not possible. No. She would continue her search.

Placing a notice in the personals of the Telegraph had been recommended by her friend Freda who was working at the Pavilion in Brighton. Maud had visited the Pavilion hoping to help out in any way she could, taking a train down from Victoria one morning, feeling the search for her darling Will could somehow be enhanced by an actual journey to the coast. Of course she had been right; physical movement towards a planned destination had given her a sense of well-being that Maud had not felt since those distant days of November when Will had disappeared from their lives in such an inconclusive manner. Arriving at the Pavilion she had been introduced to some of the nursing staff and there she had met Freda, so purposeful and fulfilled in her role at the hospital for Soldiers of the Empire. Maud had made regular trips to Brighton ever since, once or twice a week. Her family had thought her mad, but so preoccupied with their own troubles were they that they had ceased to care. So Maud was left to her own devices much more so than would have been possible before the war. A sense of freedom had eased her troubles to some extent, and this was how she had survived the last three months.

She had placed the notice at the Telegraph offices in an attempt to do something to relieve the despair she was feeling at the latest news from the War Office. How could they possibly know? Had the Germans sent them a list of dead and wounded? She doubted this. Even if they had, how could she believe the Hun who were shooting at our brave British lads? Relentlessly. In the event, Maud only had to wait two days for a response to her advert, but it was not the response she had hoped for or expected. From a Judge Moresby (strange he should have the same surname as Freda) and a Mrs Dennis, inviting her to an 'at home' for tea and cakes! This was not what she, Maud Burt-Marshall, required. Tea and cakes indeed! She was searching for her darling brother, the one who had always been there for her when no one else in the family was taking her seriously. Will was always standing up for her schemes and plans, telling Mater and Pater that Maud needed things to do outside the home because she was an intelligent woman. Of course Mater was bright too, but times were changing, and Maud wanted to move with the times in which she was living. It had all been very slow and infuriating, although Maud always got her way in the end. But without Will? Maud wasn't sure it would have been the same. Tea and cakes were hardly going to mend the bridges that had been burnt since November, nor fill the Awful Silence, the name Maud had given to this terrible period of her life.

Maud had not told Freda of the response she had received because she hadn't been down to Brighton in the last few days. She would have liked to talk it over with Freda and get her opinion on this strange invitation, but the tea and cakes were planned for today, Monday, and so she had to decide whether to attend or not. Train rides and the application of bandages had enabled Maud to get through the last three months with a fairly strong mind, and with nothing planned on this Monday morning she decided that action was preferable to inaction and so she climbed the steps of 31, Cumberland-mansions, W., resigned to a morning of pleasantries and idle chit chat.

Before Maud has time to find the bell-pull the door opens and Mrs Dennis welcomes her into the hall. A little black spaniel races around excitedly, wagging his tail; on sight of Maud the dog stops short, tail moving less energetically, and looks up at Mrs Dennis.

"Mr Harburg will be here presently, Wuffy. Have patience little man!"

With that, Maud is relieved of her coat and muffler, and shown into the large, sunny, golden glow of Mrs Dennis' morning room. The angle of the windows is just right, allowing every trace of late winter light to settle in the room without glare or harshness. A gentleness pervades the room and a figure from the far corner rises up from the easy chair in which he is sitting and Judge Moresby introduces himself with outstretched hand. Maud feels a sense of having met this man before, but she cannot quite explain the familiarity she feels. Judge Moresby shows her to a comfortable seat by the open fire, and Maud braces herself for small talk and explanations and social niceties. Instead of this, she finds herself sitting in a comfortable arm chair, looking around her at the disparate people in the room, and being left completely to her own thoughts. It is not that she is left out on a limb because tea is poured and cakes offered and warm smiles given. She feels a comfort and ease as if this is a place she has frequented all her life, and which belongs to no one and nowhere. Observing the men and women around the room she surmises that they all feel the same, for there are no pleasantries or small talk in evidence; just people; living.

Mrs Emily Peppiatt sits nearby, telling her story, to no one in particular, but Maud is struck by its similarity to her own. Her son is called William; he too has gone missing. He is dead but with no body, no burial, no funeral, no grave. It is all so depressingly familiar. Emily tells Maud of Mr Neville Thursby, over on the window seat looking out at the day; his son, too, has been pronounced dead with 'no remains'. Nobody is able to make sense of it.

A loud yapping at the door announces the arrival of Mr Isa Harburg, Wuffy's companion. Mr Harburg removes his overcoat and bowler hat, and sits in his customary position on the sofa, with Wuffy snuggled happily in his lap. Maud observes the ease with which people enter the room, find their seat, and carry on in the most independent way without infringing on others' space. This is all quite alien to Maud who has been brought up to observe the endless rules and courtesies of pleasant society.

"Mrs Peppiatt..."

"Call me Emily, dear"

"...my brother cannot be dead because I would have been informed months since. November they now tell me; but that is four months; it isn't possible. No, it's all a mistake. My brother is in a German prison. We must all be patient; he will be returned to us when this wretched war is over. It can't be long now. Mother is beside herself with worry. If only Father were here to help; but no, we must be strong. All will be well when Will is returned to us."

Emily listens, and nods, and Maud speaks less and less. The

morning wears on, and the cares that Maud has brought to the house seem to have slipped from her shoulders and to reside elsewhere.

Just as luncheon is served another guest arrives, tall with fine features, dark hair, moustache, morning suit. He introduces himself to Maud as Dr Goldberg.

"I am a dental surgeon Miss Burt-Marshall. I have been treating soldiers who cannot afford my services, completely free of charge. The government pays. Now the authorities are setting up hospitals for the treatment of men's teeth. I'm working with the government to do this, and I'm very proud to serve this good country in any way I can. One day my fellow Americans will come to the aid of this great nation."

"Goodness! I certainly hope not! It will all be over long before that is necessary."

"I would not be so sure Miss Burt-Marshall. The opportunities opening up on account of this war are endless. Why, there are even opportunities for working with horses' teeth. So many slaughtered animals, we are adapting their teeth for human dentures. No. I think we're in it for the long game. Don't you agree Miss Burt-Marshall?"

Over lunch he tells her of his plans to send as many good young men to the Front as he can by fixing their teeth for them. Maud listens, transfixed by the virility and passion of this man before her, who is sending men off to their deaths at the Front, and even using animals' teeth. How horrid! He seems to be driven by more than just wanting to help, in his patriotic fervour; the problem of his origins rears its head in his conversation; the quest for money and betterment play a bit-part; ego floats in the wings. Maud keeps these thoughts to herself, storing them up for another time, aware that there will be another time and another place with this man who has walked, unaccountably, into this room as she sits here. In the normal course of events Maud would not be in a situation where she would meet a Harley Street dentist other than by sitting in his chair and opening her mouth for inspection. This day is causing a shift in things.

Up to this point Dr Goldberg has seemed earnest and preoccupied, explaining his plans but weighed down by the urgency of them. Suddenly, without warning, he asks a question of Maud and, in so doing, looks directly at her and smiles. In this instant everything changes. She feels she could go anywhere in the world with him after this smile. Their destiny begins with this smile.

Tuesday 9th March 1915

The Move

Frances was fond of Hampstead. She had spent many hours sitting at his bedside reading to him, penetrating the darkness. In some ways it had eased the pain of her losing Teddy; she wondered why she had not done this when Teddy was a child, rather than entrusting this duty to the governess. Frances was starting to wonder why she hadn't questioned these things before. Duty had always seemed natural to her. Like breathing. Now the whole Natural Order seemed to be turned on its head, what with all these young men lying helplessly in beds on the wards at Hastings Military Hospital, and Teddy never to be seen again, not to mention Chestnut, Teddy's horse. It often played on Frances' mind that nothing had been reported of Chestnut, whose mane she had brushed and whose coat she had taken so much time over so that it shone in the morning sun. How she had loved that horse, and how handsome Teddy had looked on Chestnut as they'd trotted up the gangplank of the troop ship on their way to do their bit. Now that Frances was left to clean up the mess, she wasn't sure where it all would end. The certainties of her fifty years prior to the war now seemed fragile and vacuous.

Hampstead was a little older than Teddy, but still young enough to be Frances' son. Mary, too, was a delight and the three had sat for whole afternoons discussing the stories Frances read. They had never talked about day to day life, least of all what the future held for Hampstead. So when Mary announced her plan to move Hampstead to St Dunstan's, a new hospital for blinded soldiers in Regent's Park, London, Frances was taken aback. She was, however, able to convince both Mary and Hampstead that she should come with them to help with the transfer.

Today was the day of the move, Tuesday 9th March, and Frances arrived at the hospital with a half an hour to spare. As she approached the ward she heard Mary's gentle voice: "...and we will be so much nearer the house. You will meet Edward and Mrs Dennis..."

Frances' interest was heightened by the mention of an Edward, but she dismissed her thoughts as fanciful. She made a mental note to see that secretary of her husband's, Tobias, to get some more information on this meeting place in London. She braced herself and stepped smartly onto the ward, making sure her heels announced her arrival so the companions were not taken by surprise. Mary stood up to greet Frances with a warm clasp of the hand and a peck on the cheek.

"Hello Mrs Moresby, so good of you to come."

Orderlies were tiptoeing around Hampstead's bed, planning the move onto a stretcher and into the private ambulance that Mary had arranged for him. Frances thought of Freda, now in Brighton with her ambulance and her soldiers from the Empire. She came back to the present moment when she realised how unlike Frances Moresby it was to be so fanciful; for goodness sake, what was this war doing to her? Pull yourself together old girl!

As the orderlies and nurses prepared Hampstead for the long journey to London Frances took a walk around the ward to see if she could be of assistance elsewhere. Down the corridor, from a distant ward, wafted the sound of singing, a gentle female voice she recognised as that of the singer down at the Pier whom she had heard on occasion on a Sunday afternoon:

> *Dear face that holds so sweet a smile for me,*
> *Were you not mine, how dark the world would be!*
> *I know no light above that could replace*
> *Love's radiant sunshine in your dear, dear face.*

> *Give me your smile, the love-light in your eyes,*
> *Life could not hold a fairer Paradise!*
> *Give me the right to love you all the while,*
> *My world forever, the sunshine of your smile!*

> *Shadows may fall upon the land and sea,*
> *Sunshine from all the world may hidden be;*
> *But I shall see no cloud across the sun;*
> *Your smile shall light my life, till life is done!*

> *Give me your smile, the love-light in your eyes,*
> *Life could not hold a fairer Paradise!*
> *Give me the right to love you all the while,*
> *My world forever, the sunshine of your smile!*

Frances watched the faces around her, listening, straining to hear, blocking out the explosions inside their heads, reaching for the gently lilting voice. For the second time in under an hour she felt disconnected from the world she had known.

Once in the ambulance the journey was slow and long, but apart from the bumps and jolts it was much the same as sitting by Hampstead's bed at Hastings. They arrived at St Dunstan's as the sun was setting on a damp, grey late winter day. A sense of foreboding settled itself on Frances as she walked alongside the stretcher being wheeled into the grand entrance of the big white house.

Monday 15th March 1915

Emily and Neville

Neville and Emily sit together on the chaise longue at 31, Cumberland-mansions, W.. As a rule, neither Mrs Peppiatt nor Mr Thursby are in the habit of sitting on a chaise longue, but 31, Cumberland-mansions, W. is not concerned with one's habits.

"William was such a talented athlete you know, he won the Mile Open in his last year at Bancroft's. Then he worked with his father in the Euston offices of the London North Western Railway Company. His father had been the general manager before his untimely death. Then there were the concert parties and entertainments at our church in Woodford where William accompanied on the piano."

A silence surrounds the chaise longue. Emily recalls the clumsy fingers banging away on the keys when William was small. As he grew older and the fingers became long and lean the playing became more delicate and beautiful. The sound of her son's playing fills the space around her; the melodies float away and she is left wondering what became of those hands, so delicate and beautiful. The thought is too painful to bear and Emily is relieved when Mr Thursby offers to pour her a cup of tea.

Pouring tea is quite a new occupation for Neville Thursby who has, during his sixty-seven years, only observed this activity while having tea poured for him. It is with a trembling hand that he adds a cube of sugar hanging from the end of the sugar tongs (damned idiotic contraption), passes the cup and saucer to Emily, and sits back down to listen more to this dear lady who is as bewildered by events as he is himself.

"William's successes in marathon walking with his battalion, winning the London to Brighton walk in record time, made me so proud. Of course this was all before the war. William joined the 5th Battalion London Rifle Brigade in 1912 you know; we knew there would be a war sooner or later, and he more than did his bit. He was a seasoned soldier even before the war began. His father was so proud. Even when he went to the Front we still thought him safe. Imagine!"

She tells Mr Thursby of a letter that her friend, Mrs Gray, had received from her son John who was an old school friend and fighting in the same battalion as William. The letter arrived last month and detailed Christmas Day in the trenches. It all seemed so hopeful then. Emily rummages in her bag to see if she can find the letter - it is one of a few that she usually carries with her, for comfort.

"Ah, here it is, I thought I had it." Emily reads the letter aloud to Neville Thursby:

" 'We managed to get something approaching a Christmas dinner, of course we were in the trenches both Christmas and Boxing Day, but we and our opponents cheerfully forbore to pot each other, and swopped greetings and cigars instead. It seems our particular pals opposite are Saxons, and so by no means so nasty as the Prussian proper, or improper - where the English are concerned.' "

The effort demanded of Emily in reading this to Neville Thursby is almost too much, and she slumps back into the chaise with a sigh she is unable to conceal. It had all seemed so friendly: greetings, cigars, Saxons. Emily's thoughts come to a standstill and she is rooted in the mud of a trench, severed hands strewn about, still-smoking cigarettes littering the ground. She has to shake her head to rid her mind of these thoughts. "I am, of course, fortunate that my son died for a worthy cause for which my two remaining sons, Leslie and Kenneth, are still fighting."

Neville Thursby ruminates on the young life that has been snubbed out, leaving the bereaved woman beside him. Thoughts turn to his own son, Arthur, in his young days at Eton. Suddenly, there is a crashing of china as Edward Moresby's cup and saucer drop to the hard floor at his feet. Neville Thursby looks up to see Edward standing stock still as the young Mary clears up around him.

"You look unwell, Judge Moresby."

"Overdoing things a bit lately Mary, nothing to worry about. I will sit for a while. Please will you pour me some more tea?" Edward feels for the chair behind him. So Frances has been visiting Mary's blind husband during her mornings helping out at Hastings Military Hospital! And now she is at St Dunstan's, just across the road, settling him in! It isn't that Edward wants to keep secrets from Frances, good lord no, but he does so enjoy his Mondays with Mrs Dennis and their unlikely companions. It is his world, their world; Frances simply wouldn't understand. Why, she hadn't even shed a tear for Teddy. In fact Edward seemed to recall tears over Chestnut, Teddy's horse, but none over poor old Teddy boy. The equilibrium of the room is displaced and Edward struggles for breath. Mrs Dennis, long used to the travails of a soldier's wife, brings tea and comfort to her friend. Soon these feelings subside and Edward breathes with less effort.

Across the room, by the fireplace, Colonel Sewell sits in his now customary chair. He is visibly older than when he first appeared at the house, upright and head held high. His seventy-five years have caught up with him and the events of the last months have taken their toll. He doesn't know when his life-long belief in the glory of battle left him, but leave him it certainly has. Perhaps it was when he read that ghastly letter, by this very fireplace last week. Yes, perhaps it was then. Whenever it had been it was a damned nuisance! Certainty had turned to Uncertainty, Hope to Despair, all in one instant. Unfamiliar thoughts flit across his mind. Flit. Never has Colonel Sewell flitted, but there it is. He stares into the fire's glow and absorbs what strength he can from the heat of the coals. A glass of sherry appears by his side, offered by the charming Rose Muller; tall, courteous, sophisticated Rose. She too has her troubles but is able to smile in such a charming way as she hands him the glass. As Colonel Sewell accepts this gift of friendship and consolation he smiles too.

Rose sits in the chair at the opposite side of the fire and tells Colonel Sewell of her troubled week. "Darling Toby has written from the Front, putting on a brave show of it but really I am not at all sure that he is as well as all that. Dreadful stories other people tell me, the casualty lists in the paper, I really do wonder Colonel Sewell."

Rose doesn't mention the added complication of Tom but she ponders on this problem nonetheless. The Colonel listens with rapt attention, glorying in the youth and vitality of this woman before him whose zest for life and love overpowers all other feelings in the space around the hearth. Yes, indeed, all is not lost. And with each sip of his sherry Colonel Sewell feels renewed vigour to face the week ahead.

Monday 22nd March 1915

St Luke's, Nutford Place

Frances Moresby alighted from the omnibus at Seymour Place, turned right at Harrowby Street and left into Brown Street. Within only a few minutes she found herself at the steps of 31, Cumberland-mansions, W., poised and ready to make her entrance into the world of her husband's Monday circle. At the foot of the steps leading to the front door, Frances hesitated. On impulse she turned to her left and headed on further down Brown Street. At the corner of Cumberland Mansions she came within sight of a modern church which was on the other side of Nutford Place, quite tall without being imposing; it had a warm look about it, inviting. Frances Moresby was not a believer. Of course she always attended church on a Sunday morning, and she observed all the Lenten services leading up to Easter. She helped, from time to time, with sales of bric-a-brac and organising of outings for the Sunday school (why, her own daughter Freda had been Sunday school teacher at home in Hastings before she took off with that silly group to Brighton). Frances did all these things from a Sense of Duty; these small efforts were required of a woman in her position, wife of the District Judge, a Lady of Society. It had not occurred to Frances to look any deeper into her role. Faith should be left to the vicar's wife (such a dear) and was not part of Frances' role at all. This was what Frances valued most in her life: the wonderful Order of Things. This is what made life what it was; and this is what made the current circumstances due to this wretched war so difficult to navigate.

As Frances gazed up at the window above the five arches on street level which made up the structure of St Luke's church, her resolve to enter into Edward's other world began to wane. She seemed to gravitate towards the arches that welcomed her into the heart of the building, and she uncharacteristically followed this impulse. She didn't stop to consider what might be drawing her in and consequently pulling her away from her intended task. With her back to the windows of Mrs Dennis' room in the mansions Frances crossed the road at Nutford Place and entered in through the doorway of St Luke's. A sign on the wall to the right of the entrance read 'Built in 1849 in thanksgiving for the deliverance of the people of Marylebone during the cholera epidemic.' Eighteen forty-nine. Only thirteen years older than Frances herself, and yet there was a feeling of timelessness within its walls, a sense of order and calm which Frances had known all her life until last summer when everything had been turned on its head. To experience this familiar aura was a tonic to her and so she sat in a rear pew to the left side of the nave of the church and breathed in the stillness and tranquility around her.

Apart from her, the only other signs of life in the church building came from the altar where a parishioner was arranging spring flowers for the Easter services, and a bowed head, reverently covered with a silken scarf, belonging to an elderly lady praying in the front pew. Palms were still in evidence all around the church, Palm Sunday having been only yesterday, but with this landmark in the Lenten calendar over it was time to herald the coming celebrations. Daylight flooded in through the stained glass windows around the altar; the gold cross above the altar twinkled and glinted in the sunlight; the wooden framed stations of the cross lined the walls in the chronological pattern of Jesus' life; the kneeler in the front pew creaked at the movement of the old lady's knees, transferring weight from one to another in the absorption of prayer. Frances observed it all with the eye of a novice; she had seen it all before during the fifty years of her church-going, and yet she had seen none of it in the way she was seeing it now. All thoughts of Cumberland Mansions dropped from her shoulders. The church grew gradually darker and the air around her sharper and colder. Time stood still for Frances yet the day marched on in its accustomed manner. Her thoughts became absorbed with her young days before she had met Edward when she was adored by all around her, men and ladies alike, all eager to have the company of Frances Frobisher, elegant, tall, poised and charming. It had all started with such promise and indeed had continued in that vein right up until September 1914.

When Teddy had been reported killed in action, there had been a shift in the order of things. Frances had continued as she always had done, fulfilling her duties in every way. But her daughter and husband had changed altogether. Freda was tending to soldiers from the colonies as if she were a working nurse for goodness sake, not at all what Frances had brought her up to be, and Edward had taken leave of his senses entirely, firstly going off with that showgirl from the pier and then absenting himself in the direction of London every Monday morning, arriving home at all hours, often not until Tuesday or Wednesday! Frances' trip today had been taken with Edward in mind, but somehow she had found herself reflecting on her life in a church instead. Although none of this was lost on the capable and efficient woman Frances nonetheless continued to be absorbed in the life of the church: the flowers, the palms, the bowed head, the colourful windows, the stations; and it was only when she was no longer able to make out the detail of the stained glass images for lack of daylight that she eased herself up from the pew where she had sat for the entire afternoon, and made her way to the street outside.

Immediately opposite the entrance to the church were the bay windows of 31, Cumberland-mansions, W., but Frances was too absorbed in thought to notice as she made her way back to Seymour Place and the tram stop to take her back to Charing Cross for her train home.

———

From the window of 31, Cumberland-mansions, W., Maud Burt-Marshall observes the figure making its way from the church across the road to the corner of Brown Street, and she watches as the figure disappears around the corner of the building. There is something familiar in the figure that Maud is unable to explain. As she turns to accept a fine china cup and saucer from Edward's outstretched hand, she feels the same wave of familiarity sweep over her.

"Do you know, Edward, I feel I have known you before. It is a queer feeling. I feel I belong here, as if I am among family, and yet I have been here only once before."

Ever since she first arrived at the house she has felt this sense of belonging. Maud cannot understand it and she wonders at it for a second time. As Edward helps her to two lumps of sugar (expert with the sugar tongs as he is) Maud hears the sound of Dr Goldberg's voice in the hall and her heart stands still. During all this time she has not given a thought to her brother, Will, still missing but reported dead.

Dr Goldberg makes straight for the window seat where Maud sips her tea, and gracefully bows before taking his seat beside her. Graceful. That's what he is, not a usual description she would use for a man, but graceful he certainly is. Dr Goldberg launches into his update on teeth.

"You would not credit how busy I have been, my dear! Shipments of teeth from France - men's teeth, horses' teeth, you name it - the dentures we are making! The scope for developing new methods! The money to be made..." He trails off, suddenly thoughtful. "Of course, terrible business all of it. But life goes on, and we are making good use of what is left behind."

He trails off again, looking into the distance and then to the floor at his feet.

Maud struggles to reconcile the unsophisticated nature of the conversation and thoughts of this sophisticated and graceful man. She wonders if her brother Will's teeth are up for grabs, but shakes the thought away with a turn of her head so that she is facing away from Dr Goldberg and towards the fireplace. Dr Goldberg immediately senses her discomfort and apologises for his thoughtless talk.

"Have you heard news of your brother?"

Noticing Maud's lack of response Dr Goldberg reassures her:

"Chin up! They'll find him, just you see. Keep at it. We're all praying for his safe return."

Maud turns back in the direction of the dentist and loses herself in the gaze of his dark brown eyes. They sip tea and talk of childhood and dreams and simnel cake. Maud tells Dr Goldberg she has seen a recipe for hot cross buns and is tempted to try her hand at cooking, if only she knew where to find something called mace.

"I can find mace for you. I will bring some next Monday."

He collects his thoughts.

"Of course that will be Easter Monday and it will be too late to make your buns. Perhaps we could meet later this week, say Thursday, and then the buns could be ready for Good Friday. I don't celebrate Easter myself but I'm happy to lend a hand."

Maud is not at all sure what the reaction of the servants will be if she comes down to the kitchen to actually bake, but she is sure her mother wouldn't notice at all, so distracted by grief is she on account of her missing son. They continue their conversation and Maud is concerned with her embarrassment at not knowing Dr Goldberg's nugget of information: that nutmeg and mace are essential ingredients in her native dish of haggis. How much this man knows, and how much there is still to learn.

In the usual course of events Maud would have spent Easter with her parents and her brother in the family home at Luncarty in Perthshire. Such a nuisance that the railways have been taken over by the production of munitions and to the transportation of troops to and from the Front, returning the wounded and replacing them with new, fresh young men. Of course this is the way it has to be, but Maud cannot help feeling the melancholy of this lost Easter. Suddenly she is listening to Dr Goldberg suggesting they motor down to Brighton for the day on Thursday; he could book two rooms at the Old Ship Hotel, they could find some mace for the hot cross buns - on and on he talks, gushing with enthusiasm which makes her fondness for him grow. So it is settled. To Brighton on Thursday. He will meet her at Victoria station, by the soldier's canteen, and they will have a grand time. Maud wonders if it is quite appropriate to go alone with Dr Goldberg; perhaps she should bring her old governess who stayed on at the house as a ladies' maid once Maud had grown out of the school room. No matter. She will think about it later.

Dinner is served by Mrs Dennis' maid. The food at the mansions is always perfectly prepared and beautifully served. Tonight the steak tartare with asparagus ("sent from South Africa in tins - better than fresh") is served with potato dauphinoise.

"The new season's fruits are plentiful, and Lillie has tried a new recipe using rhubarb; Edward found it in the newspaper, so clever, we do hope you all enjoy our Rhubarb and Banana Amber."

The friends sit together, enjoying the food and the company. In the far corner of the table Isa Harburg surreptitiously feeds tidbits to Wuffy who accepts the gifts from his friend in a quiet and grateful manner, seemingly understanding the need for secrecy in this exchange. Mrs Dennis, at the next table place, pretends not to notice, and Edward next to her regales the company with stories he has heard about the changes in Folkestone, just along the coast from his home in Hastings. There is a marvellous cafe at the harbour where the troops stop before embarking on the sea journey. They sign a book as a record that they have passed through. The teas and cakes are made by local women and served by local women, his wife among them, providing an au revoir from home to our brave boys. He doesn't know if there is a book to sign for returning soldiers. At this thought there is a natural hush around the table, and Edward feels no need to fill it with sound.

Colonel Thomas Sewell pours from a bottle of table water and listens to his friend Neville Thursby. The two men are only a decade apart in age, and they both had sons who have been killed in action. However, there is one fundamental difference between the two: Thomas Sewell has a body to arrange collection of. "Having the devil of a time arranging transport from France. Minefield! So many hurdles. Poor communications. Willing to pay, money's no problem. Just isn't the capacity. More bodies than trains."

Colonel Sewell slumps back in his chair with a sense of despondency. He had not accounted for this.

"It will be worth all your efforts Colonel. You'll be able to say a proper goodbye, do the right thing by him." Neville wanders off into a safer place, where the pain of his son's complete disappearance is less keenly felt.

"Damn good dessert this. Rhubarb and banana you say, Mrs Dennis?"

After dessert the two men retire to the armchairs by the fireplace, now festooned with spring flowers, the scent of which brings a sense of calm to the old man. Neville and Colonel Sewell discuss at length the problem of transporting a body against the problem of having no body to bring home for a full soldier's burial; Neville Thursby has no remains. They look at it from every angle, analyse as intelligent men will, and find they have arrived at no conclusion. This is unfamiliar territory to these two men whose lives have followed tried and tested formulae. Here is something new, something for which they have not been prepared, for which they have not thought to prepare. The loss of a son, in Neville's case his only son, a lifeless body, 'no remains'; emptiness either way. Neville Thursby takes some comfort in realising that either result is hideous. He could order a coffin, book a service, buy a burial plot, perform the whole ceremony with an empty box. It makes no difference. His son is gone. Thomas' son is gone. It is all the same. The most pressing and urgent concern of the two men, in the twilight of their own years, is what they are to do with their own continued existence. Neither man has any idea. But speaking their concerns seems to bring a sense of calm that neither of them has felt since the telegrams announcing the loss of their sons. A sense of calm that enables them to breathe again, to function for another day. This they have been given in this house of friendship and consolation, and although they do not discuss this particular aspect of the thing, they feel it keenly.

Further along the table Emily Peppiatt listens while Rose enunciates the problems with her children. How is she to explain her move to Belfast? How is she to explain that they cannot come but must stay with their grandparents?

"And now Toby has written announcing he has leave for the

Easter weekend arriving on Friday! Friday!! Only four days away. What am I to do?"

"But how wonderful! Your children will see their father."

"Oh I know, Emily, why am I being so selfish? He sounds weary in his letter, but terribly excited about seeing the girls and me."

Rose pauses, sips her tea and sighs.

"He is even looking forward to seeing Tom, Lord help me!"

Emily contemplates the confusion of it all. Although Rose has only spoken of her involvement with Tom to Mary, Emily senses that all is not as it should be.

"They are best friends you say Rose?"

This simple question hangs in the air.

Emily listens with a mixture of concern and amusement. This young woman next to her at table is struggling with the minutiae of life, anxious, exasperated, in love, tormented: all the things that speak of Life and Living and Being. All the things her William has lost. She hears the young woman's angst but she feels she must tell her she is lucky: she has Life, a Future, Hope. But Emily keeps these thoughts to herself and listens with care and understanding. Perhaps Rose's predicament does not need soothing words and balm; it is all a part of life, and life is to be lived, as only the living can do. Nothing seems to have the same level of trauma that it used to have. Emily sees the big picture, the beginning, middle and end. It is all part of the process, and one day Rose will see this too. But not today. And not tomorrow. One day.

At the head of the table Edward Moresby is deep in conversation with Mary.

"I don't know how we could have undertaken the move without the assistance of Mrs Moresby. I have this moment noticed she has the same surname as yourself Edward - how coincidental. She reads to Hampstead; such beautiful reading; I enjoy listening as much as Hampstead does. To hear her bringing such meaning and interest to every phrase is an inspiration to me."

"Nothing more than you deserve Mary; it wouldn't be right for you to shoulder your burdens alone."

Edward rolls thoughts around in his ever active mind: Frances has never read aloud in his presence; he doesn't remember her reading to the children when they were young; how many hidden talents did we keep from our nearest and dearest? Life just took over and set the pace. If Edward is honest with himself, he has withheld untold parts of himself from his wife and his children. Perhaps this is why he is enjoying the war so much: it has given him so much scope, so many more contacts outside of the small coastal town that has occupied his fifty-six years to now. These thoughts Edward holds inside himself to be revisited another time. For now he will listen to this delightful child beside him, and bask in the Intimacy of Silence.

Mary is troubled by what happened at St Dunstan's just yesterday. Hampstead was being taken for a lesson in reading braille. It was a marvellous opportunity to open his horizons, feeling his way back into the world of literature which he loved so much. Mary braces herself and then turns to Edward.

"The doctors told him how fortunate he is. A man in the next ward has lost his sight, and both his hands were blown off too. 'Blown off'. That's what they said. I cannot credit it."

Some time elapses.

"I've been unable to think of anything else for even one moment."

Edward nods and sighs, all the while thinking how little the usual things matter. If Frances chooses to read to blind soldiers where is the harm? If he chooses to spend the start of each week in the company of these people without his wife's knowledge, what does it really matter? They can all see. They have hands to hold, fingers to touch, comforts to offer. Edward and Mary sit in quiet contemplation and do not notice Wuffy jump onto Isa's lap and snuggle down on the perfectly tailored trousers of his friend.

As the evening draws to a close and the time comes for the guests to make their way into the night, and back to their unconnected lives, Mrs Dennis asks to be permitted to read a small article she has seen in the paper today. "A Glasgow firm of engineers has accepted the services of a well-known Glasgow minister, the Rev. Stuart Robertson, and on Monday he will assist in making shells for the government. The reverend gentleman will travel by the workmen's early morning train and work the ordinary hours. When questioned yesterday, Mr Robertson said that if he made shells during the week to fire at the Prussians and shells on Sunday to fire at the devil, that would be a fair division."

Mrs Dennis is not about to question the clergy, but she feels nonetheless uncomfortable with the article. They all agree that the clergyman must know best. The discomfort that Mrs Dennis feels embeds itself, however, in the consciousness of her guests as they get up, one by one, to return to their lives.

Monday 5th April 1915

Easter Monday

Mrs Dennis' preparations for the Monday soiree are in full swing. She is grateful to Maud for supplying not only a recipe for hot cross buns but also the mace she has procured from the Lanes in Brighton. Mrs Dennis is somewhat surprised that Maud has taken a trip to Brighton with Dr Goldberg and no chaperone, but times are changing and one must change with them. The buns had been such a success on Good Friday with Mrs Dennis' friends that she has asked her maid, Lillie, who also serves as cook of the house, to make some more for her friends today. Mrs Dennis has treated the household to some new stainless steel cutlery; it comes recommended by a friend, otherwise Mrs Dennis would not have considered such a purchase, sceptical of such a claim as "never again need knives be cleaned". Indeed! Mrs Dennis has spent many an hour cleaning her silverware, her Goddard's powder always to hand; tarnished cutlery has indeed been a constant bane in Mrs Dennis' domestic life as she has never been in a position to have enough servants to do this cleaning for her. So it is with anticipation that she sets out the cutlery today with as open a mind as she can muster.

Her first guest is of course Edward, always in attendance for the arrival of 'their' guests. There is a feeling of Order in this arrangement that they both appreciate. As Lillie relieves Edward of his coat he is bursting with indignation at a piece he has read in the Telegraph on his train journey up from Hastings.

"This benighted Herr-von-something, blaming us for the war! Us! The Germans are taking over countries not their own, I ask you. This dreadful man claiming we dragged Belgium into the war; listen to this Mrs Dennis" and here Edward reads directly from the newspaper in his hand:

"'Germany being desirous of keeping Belgium out of the war and guaranteeing her integrity and independence.' Mrs Dennis, the dreadful atrocities at the hands of the Hun! The refugees we have housed in Hastings! The horror of it all. And he blames us!"

Edward is so affected by this reprehensible outpouring of lies that he needs a sherry to calm him down, and an understanding ear to listen. Both these needs are satisfied by Mrs Dennis without any trouble at all and Edward soon returns to his controlled and pleasing demeanour, much to Mrs Dennis' relief.

A knock on the door rouses Wuffy from his position by the fire, tail wagging, paw pads tapping, nose uplifted as he makes for the front door in time for Lillie to open it and reveal his friend Isa Harburg. Before Isa is even through the door he is patting Wuffy's head and talking in low and reassuring tones to the small creature who has filled such a large gap in his life. Once he has entered the room and seated himself by the fire, Wuffy snuggled in his lap, Isa speaks to Edward of his worries in the tailoring world.

"'Completed suits!' My beautiful suits reduced to this."

He reads from the advertisement in the newspaper that has caused this consternation. Edward listens with concern.

"'Whether you require a smart Lounge Suit, a Sporting outrig, a Morning or a Dress Suit, allow Burberrys an opportunity to demonstrate how the Completed Suit idea saves time, obviates disappointment, and enables you to obtain better and more perfectly-fitting suits.'   Saves time!   Obviates disappointment! What is time?   Only time can produce a beautiful garment. Without time there is no care, without care there is no quality.   Mr Moresby, where is our world heading?"

Edward reassures him with tales of friends who would not consider such mass produced clothing, and he recommends that Isa seek a more select clientele; indeed, Edward will speak to his friends and colleagues, and they in turn will undoubtedly pass on the word.   Isa feels relieved and placated by this kind offer from the dignified man sitting opposite him by the fire. The warmth from the coals and from Wuffy's little body and from Judge Moresby's words fills the gaps between Isa's doubts and worries, and soon spills over to cover all his concerns. The golden glow in the room from the early morning sun soothes and calms; the clock ticks with a reassuring regularity.

Next to arrive is Emily on this Easter Monday morning. Mrs Dennis is touched that both she and Isa have come on a holiday, but as Emily Peppiatt points out, Easter is somewhat curtailed because of the war: lack of excursion trains, provisions in short supply, boys away at the Front, even daughters nursing in London hospitals and taking ambulances to France. Yes, an unusual holiday.

"What beautiful spring flowers, Mrs Dennis.   A feast for the senses."

On every table and mantle, yellow, white, orange - the room is filled with colour and scent which is such a contrast to the cold, blustery day that Emily has left at the front door to 31, Cumberland-mansions, W..   She settles in the third armchair by the fire and listens while Isa regales her with tales of his tailoring troubles and how the kind Judge Moresby has calmed his fears and relieved him of all worry.

"Ah, Mr Harburg, you are just the man I need for a project I'm planning. I'm answering the call to make sandbags for our boys at the Front. Could you possibly provide me with some canvas or coarse linen - I will pay you, of course. Not having made sandbags before you will wonder at my keenness. I feel once you read the explanation in the paper you will see why I feel confident; it is so clear and simple Mr Harburg."

Isa assures her he will find some material at the best prices and they agree to meet at Isa's shop on Saville Row later in the week

The morning takes on its own character as the scent of flowers combines with that of the freshly baked buns and the Earl Grey tea. Rose Muller arrives just as the buns are being served and she takes a seat at an occasional table looking stiff and tired and troubled. Isa gently tips Wuffy from his lap and makes his way over to where Rose is sipping her tea.

"Mr Harburg. How lovely to see you again. You have forsaken the dog in favour of little old me: how sweet. I am glad to have someone to talk to; such a tense few days! Toby's leave is over now and I am more in turmoil than I was before I saw him."

Rose does not elaborate on her turmoil, and Isa ponders why Rose is quite so distraught. He has an inkling that it may have something to do with Tom, Rose's husband's best friend. Settling himself at the table Isa watches the tea pouring from the spout, glinting in the sun. He remembers the two women in his life. It is certainly possible to love a wife and a daughter at one and the same time; perhaps love for different people is a different kind of love with each one. Isa and Rose settle into the morning with these thoughts in their minds.

The sounds of the morning fill the room: tea cup clinks, fire crackles, branches brushing against a window, footsteps and horses' hooves on the street, church bells. Rose and Isa talk of the Passover they both celebrated in very different ways last Monday evening after they had left 31, Cumberland-mansions, W.. They speak of its ritual and diligence and sense of history that is so important to impart to the young. Isa remarks on the absence of his daughter and being alone for the Passover; although invited by neighbours he preferred to be alone. Rose was with Toby, himself not Jewish but nonetheless he attended, with her family and the children.

"He's not the same somehow. Toby. I asked him about life at the Front, the trenches, what he does all day. He gave me very little response, Mr Harburg. He said it is as you would expect, but I don't know what I expect. 'It's war,' he said. But what is war, Mr Harburg? It's different for us here, I told him, and we want to know. But nothing."

Rose stares into the middle distance. She could see things weren't right. A twitch in the eye, a vacant look, a slight tremble of the hand. These were not characteristic of Toby with whom she had lived and with whom she had brought up two little girls until last September when he had announced he was enlisting. Rose was not able to explain, to herself or anyone else, what it was about Toby that had changed, but something had changed, and it was not for the better. Perhaps Tom had understood; she had not seen him since the Passover meal that they had all shared so she had not been able to talk with him and to make sense of Toby's transformation. Rose holds these thoughts.

"I'm seeing Tom tomorrow. He'll make sense of things. I always feel better when I have spoken with Tom. He knows how to make a girl feel on top."

Isa ponders on Tom's role in all this, but he keeps his own counsel.

Dr Goldberg arrives and catches the tail end of the conversation regarding the Passover. He sits himself next to Rose and Isa, and regales them with stories of his large family gathering, the unleavened bread with bitter herbs dipped in salt-water. A bond develops between them as they converse in Hebrew, and Dr Goldberg is startled to see Maud enter the room in her Easter bonnet, radiant and young and alive. Where has this woman been all these years? He is thirty-eight years old, eligible and sought after by every young Jewish girl in Golders Green. Dr Goldberg has never been interested in any of them, silly girls, empty-headed, looking for security and marriage and money. He has kept himself aloof but polite, which has made him all the more attractive to these would-be brides. Now here, in this house, he has found the woman he has been waiting for in the person of Maud Burt-Marshall. What if she is a gentile? He will find a way around this. After all, he is a man used to having his way.

Maud sees Dr Goldberg and catches her breath. She hopes her hat with its shallow veil will have concealed this most embarrassing emission, and she is relieved to see that it has done so: Dr Goldberg holds her gaze and she feels herself laid bare in a way that feels natural and correct. They gravitate together toward the window seat overlooking St Luke's in Nutford Place.

"Dr Goldberg, I have heard that people are sending hampers to the Prisoners of War, and I have obtained an address to which I can send these. Do you think it would be completely crackpot to send one, say once a week, just in case Will receives it? If he doesn't then some other poor prisoner will. What do you think? I could fill each hamper with his favourite things. Do say you approve!"

The genuine seeking of approval from this beautiful young lady melts Dr Goldberg's heart further.

"An excellent idea. How thoughtful. I am sure, in time, a hamper will find itself with your brother."

Dr Goldberg is not sure of this at all. He is, in fact, unsure whether Will Burt-Marshall is even alive, but he doesn't convey this to Maud. She feels it is something positive she can do until she is able to find Will and bring him home. This is enough for Dr Goldberg. They do not discuss their trip to Brighton, nor the Lanes, the mace and the Old Ship Hotel. Maud blushes at the thought! A trip to Brighton, no chaperone! Her mother is too preoccupied with searching for Will to be attending to her daughter's movements, and her father died when Maud was only eight years old, she hardly remembers him. So Maud has total freedom to do what she pleases with her days.

"I was quite taken with your friend Freda. Seemed quite familiar, wasn't sure if I'd met her before."

They sit in contemplation of their trip and of their friendship and these thoughts remain unspoken; each one wonders if the other feels the same but neither is brave enough to broach the subject. Instead, they sit in the warm glow that surrounds them, unaware of the five other people in the room with them. They do not notice, either, the entrance of Mary who makes straight for the seat Dr Goldberg has previously vacated next to Rose.

"Rose, dear, what fun it was shopping last week. Your dress looks so handsome." The two women examine the dress each is wearing with approval and satisfaction.

"You look radiant in anything you wear darling. Such a natural beauty."

Rose wonders why Mary chose such a plain looking dress with all that was on offer, but to Mary she smiles in genuine friendship and fondness. It occurs to Rose that Mary possesses something she does not, but she shakes this thought from her mind and sips her tea. The two women discuss, in an excited manner, their trip to the West End and their purchases of an Easter frock each.

Isa listens, quietly wondering at the possibilities of branching out in these difficult times to ladies tailoring. He observes the frocks that Rose and Mary are wearing, bought from a large department store, and is struck by the clumsy fussiness of the designs: he is sure he can create something more comfortable yet feminine for these beautiful creatures before him. The clean lines of a man's suit are so much more elegant than these voluminous offerings simply designed to cover the shape of the woman's figure. Yes, indeed, there is scope here. Isa ponders on this as Wuffy rubs against his left leg and yaps at him to be accommodated.

The day passes in quiet contemplation with veiled looks and unspoken understandings. The only guests who do not arrive are Neville Thursby and Colonel Sewell. It is assumed that they have family celebrations to attend, which of course Edward has as well. He hopes his wife will be her usual understanding self. With Teddy dead and Freda in Brighton there seems little point in being at home in Hastings; Frances announced just yesterday she would be visiting her blind soldiers today, so Edward relaxes into his afternoon, confident of his place at Mrs Dennis' table. Simnel cake is served, covered with marzipan eggs and accompanied by sweet sherry and Orange Pekoe. Conversation flows naturally. Silences are comfortable. More cake is served. A fine Madeira is added to the liquid accompaniments. Edward is content. No, he is happy.

⁓

Across the road at St Luke's, Neville Thursby and Colonel Sewell make their way down the nave of the church and, upon reaching the main altar, turn left to the side altar and kneel at the communion rail. Each man holds his own thoughts, aware of the other beside him. Colonel Sewell prays for the strength to accept the loss of his son in all its physical form. Neville Thursby prays that the news he has received today will have a happier outcome than he expects; he also prays for his wife Zoe and daughter Honor who, having faced the loss of their son and twin brother, have another hill to climb in the coming months.

The two men light a candle each, in memory of their sons and in reverence to the Lord from whom all good things flow. With the weariness of age, they slowly climb to their feet, turn away from the altar and make their way, with halting gait, to the back of the church. Colonel Sewell steps aside to allow Neville through the door to the street, and he follows close behind. As they return to the world in the twilight of the evening, their backs straighten and their feet move to the rhythm of the young men they once were, ready to face the world and whatever it has in store for them. With briskness and mutual respect they shake hands as Colonel Sewell turns left down Nutford Place and Neville Thursby turns right towards Brown Street to hail a hansom cab which will take him home.

Monday 12th April 1915

Hampstead

Anew visitor has arrived at the mansions this morning and is sitting somewhat uncomfortably in a straight-backed chair toward the back of the room, facing the windows that look out onto St Luke's. He is unaware of the position of the windows as he is unaware of every detail in the room. The perfect symmetry of the light in the room is wasted on him, although the scent of the flowers in various positions all around him is intensified in his senses. Mary was unsure of this visit, but Frances Moresby had been anxious that Hampstead be given an opportunity to socialise in some way outside the walls of St Dunstan's.

Frances herself is not in attendance, having made a decision to leave Cumberland Mansions to those whose refuge it has become; but she is keen to help in any way she can in the recovery of Hampstead who has become like a son to her. She comes up on the train each Monday, and often stays until Tuesday or Wednesday, according to Edward's movements. They have come to an understanding on the length of Edward's stay each week, although he is not aware of Frances' visits which are undertaken completely separately from his. This is where she has the upper hand; not that she looks upon it this way, but it is certain to come in handy on some future occasion.

Hampstead is deeply uneasy in this unfamiliar setting. Every movement creates a booming sound in his tired head, and each word spoken fills him with a sense of unease. He does not convey this to anyone, least of all Mary, as this is all part of the process in the New Life he is learning to live. The constant strain is just a continuance of what began in the trenches last September, and it simply has to be borne. However, the thing that really troubles Hampstead is that he cannot, for the life of him, recall Mary's face. He cannot recall what anything in domestic life looks like; he can't even remember colours. Living with this is one thing, but to lose the memory of Mary's face is too much to bear. But bear it he does. Alone.

What Hampstead does remember, however, in flat grey, is the sights in the trenches: the mud, the filthy water, the cloud-filled skies, the tears that roll down the faces of men braver than he; but most of all he remembers the rats. Bulbous, hideous, cat-sized, blood oozing from their greedy mouths, flesh- eating monsters gorging on the remains of his friends. This sight he remembers and cannot erase. They follow him through the day and into the night. He often awakes in a sweat, frantic, alone; and yet after falling asleep he again awakens to another day. Was there no limit to human endurance? Did there not come a time when enough was enough?

The only relief Hampstead has found is when being read to by the eternally patient Mrs Moresby. The stories she finds for him, all newly published novels, create a world that he can imagine, that he can see. The hours she spends by his bedside are the only hours that give relief from the rats and the mud and the bodies. Even Mary is unable to reach this part of him that Mrs Moresby has awakened. And now there is the added strain of keeping these things from Mary.

Hampstead is introduced to Mrs Dennis, "How lovely to have you with us Hampstead," and to Judge Moresby, "Call me Edward old boy." Strange. That name again. Perhaps there is some meaning in the name. Hampstead makes a mental note to find out. "Always welcome at our Monday gatherings." Edward himself stores the knowledge of Frances and her reading to Hampstead in his own silent space. It is not always the spoken things that are important; often the things unsaid count for more.

After these introductions Hampstead is left very much to himself which is an unexpected relief. He is able to feel a part of the proceedings without having to answer difficult questions or to call on his stiff upper lip. He can absorb the scents and sounds around him. Suddenly he feels a warm touch on his lower trouser leg, a rubbing motion and a sniff. This continues in a very gentle fashion until Hampstead decides to investigate by putting his hand out to where the movement is. He feels a soft, fluffy coat, floppy ears, a wet nose. All these things Hampstead sees in clarity and colour, the first 'vision' since his waking, blinded in the clearing station in France. His mind leaps back to his early childhood, before being sent away to school, and his beloved dog Bonzo, his first playmate and friend. He sees every detail of Bonzo's face, the brown eyes, the wet black nose, the white whiskers: he sees it all. Wuffy climbs carefully and tenderly onto Hampstead's lap and a light appears in Hampstead's mind that might just see him through the years ahead.

All this goes unnoticed by everyone around as they gather for the morning's tea. At the arrival of Isa Harburg, however, the presence of Hampstead is noticed immediately for Wuffy is no longer charging up to his friend in anticipation of companionship. At first Isa is taken aback, then slightly put out, but he quickly assesses the situation when he is introduced to Hampstead by the tender and delightful Mary, and Isa employs great restraint in accepting the situation. He even sits to chat with Hampstead.

"Welcome to our home. You will find it heymish. We are all fond of Mary, beautiful lady, bluming." No mention is made of the child she is carrying, for these things form part of the necessarily unspoken area of life, but both Isa and Hampstead know what is inferred. Isa then moves to his customary seat and allows the day to take its course.

Dr Goldberg is deep in conversation with Maud, knees almost touching, fingers outstretched.

"The demands on me are becoming greater. The Military Powers need more and more teeth as the need for conscripts increases. It seems I am becoming a victim of my own success Maudy. My work in America has put me in the spotlight and my services are in great demand. So thankful am I for this sanctuary" - he looks around him - "and for you, Maudy."

He takes her hand in his and kisses her finger tenderly. With 31, Cumberland-mansions, W. and with Maud it is different: no demands are made of him here. So for this one day a week he can revitalise and remain human, not a machine. Even more so with Maud. They have agreed to meet once during each week between the Monday gatherings, and to stay together in Dr Goldberg's apartment. Maud tells her mother she is in Brighton. Nobody knows and there is no harm done. Moreover, their love-making makes no demands on him; it is an end in itself, complete.

Maud, for her part, feels all her needs are met by this fine man who shares a part of himself with her that he has shared with no one else. For two days of every week Maud is able to find some relief from the otherwise relentless search for her brother.

"Dr Goldberg, what can I add to my hampers to make them even more attractive to the prisoners?"

She still refers to him as Dr Goldberg and sees no reason to address him otherwise. He, himself, never refers to it.

"I can supply toothbrushes and powder, at no cost to yourself of course." After a slight pause he continues. "Why not attach a note to each one in case it is the one that reaches your brother."

Although Maud feels a growing conviction that Will is, indeed, finished, she is not ready to broach the possibility with anyone else, not even Dr Goldberg. Both she and Dr Goldberg are delighted at the thought of Will receiving his parcel with the note that Maud agrees to attach to each one. 'For William Burt-Marshall and all fellow prisoners: awaiting your return at the end of hostilities. Maud.'

At the table, twiddling with a spoon and tea cup, Rose anxiously relates to Edward the latest development in her relationship with Tom. "If only he would stop placing messages in the Personal Column of the newspaper Mr Moresby. It simply torments me! Is there no way out of this?"

Edward reassures her with a fatherly pat on the knee and a top up of her tea. It seems to Edward that the war will resolve these issues for her anyway, in time. Not necessarily in the time Rose would like, but in the scheme of things. He does not share these thoughts with Rose.

Meanwhile, Colonel Sewell and Neville Thursby have returned to the fold after their absence on Easter Monday. It is only Emily Peppiatt who notices the change in Neville, so slight and imperceptible it is. She hears the laboured breathing where others do not, and observes the anxious depths of his faded blue eyes. She reads to him the record of Private Hyslop of the Gordons, of his medal for gallantry reported in the Telegraph today.

"'There is Private Hyslop, for example, of the Gordons, who succeeded in getting through with 'a most urgent message' after six of his comrades had been killed in the attempt. Yet even that was not enough heroism for a single day, for at dusk he acted as guide to 'an officer's position, a place of danger, situated only fifty yards from the enemy's trench.' Those few lines of print means that the medal which Private Hyslop will wear shines bright with the gallantry of the six nameless dead as well as with his own.' "

Emily and Neville discuss the gallantry and bravery of their own sons, now dead, and for whom these medals must also be meant: 'The gallantry of the six nameless dead'. Nameless dead. Six. Six hundred. Six thousand. Six million. They both know the numbers in the casualty lists go far beyond the reach of medals for every gallant soldier. Besides, their gallant soldiers are mere boys, hardly out of short trousers. Where will it all end? And will they both be there to see the end?

Emily moves across the room to speak with Isa Harburg, pulling out her first attempt at a sandbag. "The rough linen you supplied for my sandbags is simply perfect Mr Harburg, far easier to work with than canvas, and just as strong and hard-wearing. What do you think of my stitching Mr Harburg? Your professional opinion: will it hold?"

"Toygn," he says, "perfection my dear," a twinkle in his old, dimming eyes. "The small opening for the filling of the sand, and the string to tie it - inspired! Bravo."

He explains he can ask one of his seamstresses to set aside time to help her with the production of these, and thereby contribute to the war effort himself. Just as this has been agreed they hear a commotion at the back of the room where Hampstead is being helped to his feet by Mary and Edward, ready to return to St Dunstan's; the driver is waiting in the street. With a determined patter, Wuffy makes his way to Isa, jumps up, and settles in the familiar lap. Isa is disinclined (and frankly unable) to hide his delight and Emily leaves the two of them to return to her friend Neville.

Discussion of possible banning of all alcohol sales for the

duration of the war takes place. Claret is poured, Madeira, ginger wine; thoughts become mellow and tempered. Of course any temperance is directed at the working men in the shipyards and coal mines of the north and is not intended for soirees at 31, Cumberland-mansions, W.

Monday 19th April 1915

Lillie

Maud is speaking to Neville Thursby in anxious and hushed tones.

"It's only because Will is so young that his last will and testament leaves everything to me. In the natural course, without this horrible war, Mother would have passed long before Will. Now all this death duty to pay because I am his sister, not his child. Something about 'lineal descendant'. What makes it worse, Mr Thursby, is that Will is not dead at all, and all his affairs being broadcast publicly! The shame of it! How is Mother to cope? All the money mine, not her's. Of course, I will see she is looked after, but how much will be left after all this duty to pay? And when he returns - what then?"

Neville listens intently, allowing Maud to relieve her thoughts without interruption, with the understanding manner of a man who has seen more of life than has been good for him. He reassures Maud that all will be sorted in her favour; the laws are being discussed in Parliament and she must not worry; there are even men who have inherited from a lost brother and are now dead themselves, killed in action, their inheritance being passed on again in only a matter of months; these are all things to be ironed out and resolved.

"Leave it to the politicians. They know what they are doing. It will all be well, you mustn't worry. There are many others in your predicament."

Neville suspects there may be hundreds, even thousands, in this predicament, looking at the latest casualty lists.

"How are your hampers for the prisoners taking shape?"

A sound of giggling and a swishing of skirts announce the entrance of Rose and Mary, bubbling with the excitement from their trip to the Strand Corner House, a new establishment serving light refreshments.

"Such beautiful music, a string quartet, delicious food - not quite up to yours of course Mrs Dennis - so many soldiers on leave with their girls. If it wasn't for the soldiers' uniforms, we would have quite forgotten there was a war on."

Mary moves to the fireplace, no longer lit. The fine spring morning, and its warmth, enters between the drapes of the large windows of this comforting room. Colonel Sewell stands with his back to the fireplace, feeling much more himself than two weeks ago when his world turned around. Strange how quickly one grew accustomed to things. Never occurred to him before; life had seemed to follow a well understood pattern before the shift. Still, they are all here, another Monday, life continues.

Mary takes her place in the armchair nearest to Colonel Sewell. "I have had a meeting, Colonel, with a very important man called Sir Arthur Pearson. Imagine me talking to a Sir." The Colonel smiles to himself. "He is the wonderful sight specialist who is responsible for founding St Dunstan's. Are you familiar with St Dunstan's, Colonel?"

"St Dunstan-In-The-West on Fleet Street? Used to attend there when I was working in the City. Damn fine building that."

"Oh no Colonel, not a church. It's a hospital recently opened in Regent's Park - actually in the park itself. Such a restful setting. It's sad that the patients can't see the beauty all around them; but they do enjoy walks among the trees, and now the spring flowers. Hampstead loves to smell the roses."

Mary drifts off into a reverie. A story she has read is troubling her. Sir Arthur has told her of a man in the 2nd London General Hospital who has had his face blown up by a dummy sentry in a German trench. The poor man was sent over to the German side to check if the trench was empty, saw the dummy, nudged it, and it was full of explosives and blew him into the air. His face was so badly damaged they had to remove both his eyes! Sir Arthur is arranging for him to be brought to St Dunstan's. Mary turns to Colonel Sewell, also deep in thought:

"Sir Arthur is planning to provide work for all these men. They're making great strides in this area. Hampstead is learning to read braille. There is real hope."

Mary slumps back in her chair, weighed down with the thought of all the effort Hampstead will have to put into his daily life. She rests her hand gently but firmly on her rounded stomach and wonders at the task ahead.

Colonel Sewell looks back on his military life. In the wars and battles he had been engaged in, men certainly were wounded, and many were killed. He struggles to remember men losing their sight; and in such numbers. Perhaps it is the new artillery, the weapons of war that have transformed so quickly the whole theatre, as he and his men had referred to it. Machine guns, shells, airplanes, bombs, and now even tanks! It was certainly a different world. The dice were loaded; survival of any kind seemed a miracle.

Mrs Dennis helps Lillie to serve tea to all her guests. Wuffy demands the attention of Edward as Isa Harburg has not yet arrived. Edward gently strokes the head of the little black spaniel and allows his thoughts to subside; a sense of relief surrounds him as Wuffy nuzzles into the palm of his left hand and Edward partakes of his tea with his free hand. Mrs Dennis returns to her chair by her friend and looks fondly at Wuffy.

"Seven shillings and sixpence for a dog licence! Do you know, Edward, with so many soldiers having to leave their dogs behind when they go to the Front, hundreds are being slaughtered - there is simply no one to look after them let alone pay the licence. I think of poor Wuffy and imagine him left all alone. I simply have to do something. I may contact the National Canine Defence League to see how I can help. What do you think, Edward?"

"A fine idea, Mrs Dennis, fine idea." So many worthy causes, thinks Edward, how many more can everyone take on? Mrs Dennis ponders on the problem before her: dogs left to roam the streets untended; family dogs where seven shillings and sixpence means the difference between eating that week or not; dogs no longer wanted with the man of the house away; work dogs with no work.

"Mrs Dennis, why don't you and Lillie bake some of your delicious cakes and invite the ladies of the neighbourhood to attend an afternoon tea for which they can make a donation to the fund."

"Charge people for my hospitality?" Mrs Dennis is not at all sure of such an idea. But times are changing. No. She will talk to the vicar over the road at St Luke's and ask his advice. He isn't particularly approachable but maybe he will agree to announce from the pulpit this urgent need for dog licences. Good grief. What is it all coming to? Asking the vicar for help with licences for dogs with no owners. Dear, dear, dear.

Mrs Dennis looks across the room to where Mary is sitting with Colonel Sewell. Now that is an idea. She asks Edward to excuse her for one moment and she makes her way to the fireplace, seating herself in the armchair next to Mary.

"How are you today, my dear? And that fine husband of yours - how is Hampstead coming along? Did he enjoy his visit here last week?"

"He certainly did, Mrs Dennis. We are so grateful. He hasn't stopped talking about Wuffy since he jumped onto his lap and befriended him. You see, he had a dog as a small boy, and he's never forgotten him. Stroking Wuffy and feeling his breath on his hand has enabled Hampstead to see the dog in his mind's eye. It's years since he thought of Bonzo; my husband thought he had long forgotten him. It seems to have done him the world of good because he's been brighter ever since his visit."

This is exactly what Mrs Dennis wants to hear, and she tells Mary of her plan to find a dog for Hampstead. "A dog could be a friend and a guide to him. There are so many dogs left untended when their masters go off to fight. All it would cost is the licence fee of seven shillings and sixpence. What say you Mary?"

Mary is filled with emotion at such a kind thought, and she is quite unable to speak. It occurs to her that there may be a conflict of ownership if the dog's master returned from the Front, but no matter, a kindly thought and one she will certainly suggest to her husband.

Lillie enters the room near where Edward is sitting with Wuffy. She has on a tray an upside down pineapple cake which she has made using tinned pineapple "all the way from America," she tells Judge Moresby. Lillie is not sure where, or what, America is but she knows the pineapple is delicious, "I tasted some while I was baking! No one'll know, and there is still plenty of pineapple in the cake!" Despite her words Lillie feels a pang of guilt when she thinks of the delicious ring of pineapple, the soft moistness of it as it slid down her throat. Edward is delighted that she has shared her guilty secret with him, and he winks at her in acknowledgement that he will not spill the beans.

"Delicious, Lillie. Another triumph. How do you do it?" Such a kind, gentle man. Lillie wishes her father had been more like the Judge. As she wends her way back to the basement kitchen, Lillie takes a mental note of her chores for the day. When the guests leave she must make sure and clean up with the new Daisy that Mrs Dennis has kindly bought for her; of course, without Judge Moresby to work the bellows she doesn't know how she would use the contraption - it required the strength of a man. Yes, such a kind man. Fancy them making a machine for cleaning that needed a man's strength! What were they thinking? And tomorrow she would have to start on the cleaning of the paintwork; what with the spring cleaning and all, she really had her work cut out. The door bell rings and Lillie climbs wearily up the steps from the kitchen to the front door. Facing her is Dr Goldberg. Of course, thinks Lillie, Dr Goldberg is from America! Pineapple in tins, Dr Goldberg; Lillie builds a picture in her mind of this unknown place and wonders at the strangeness of things.

As Dr Goldberg enters the room, Maud looks up and her cheeks flush so slightly that only she and Dr Goldberg are aware of it, although Neville Thursby wonders at the innocence of youth that they would assume such exclusivity. Neville makes his excuses, and rises slowly from his chair by Maud's side, allowing room for Dr Goldberg to settle with his Assam tea and listen while Maud brings him up to date with her second life in Brighton. She and Freda are becoming bosom pals, and Maud is finding her role as visitor to the soldiers whom Freda is nursing very rewarding.

"I met such an inspiring lady, Dr Goldberg. She was visiting the soldiers at the Pavilion and we fell into conversation. Not someone I would usually meet. Her name is Mrs Waters. She sells wine in her husband's shop. Imagine me befriending such a woman, but the war is making unusual friendships possible."

Maud averts her eyes from the gaze of this handsome, intelligent man whom she would have had no chance of meeting prior to the war. Both Maud and Dr Goldberg acknowledge internally the irony of Maud's observation.

"Mrs Waters has six children, and she also has to work and she has no servants to help!"

Maud has never encountered a woman who works for a living; she knows they exist, but has never come across them in her social circle, so this is all new and rather exhilarating. She wonders what the war will bring to her next. Dr Goldberg listens with tenderness and delight as this woman, whom he loves, shares the wonder of her ever increasing world.

"She is beside herself with worry, Dr Goldberg. If Lloyd George has his way with the new laws regarding alcohol sales Mrs Waters' children will surely starve. I have been lying awake thinking about it."

Maud also lays awake thinking about Dr Goldberg, but this she omits from the conversation. Dr Goldberg assures Maud that compensation will be made if prohibition is passed, and she is not to worry about Mrs Waters. After some time, during which Maud resolves to help Mrs Waters in any way she can, Dr Goldberg shows Maud an advertisement he has seen in the newspaper for an auction.

"Did you say your friend Freda was looking for an ambulance to take to France? Here's just the thing: an auction on Wednesday, the day after tomorrow. Look. An ambulance with four stretchers. What do you think?"

Maud is delighted. "I'll tell Freda, I'll write this very evening.

We could attend the auction together on Wednesday. Freda is anxious to get out to France to help in the Field Hospitals. Really, I don't know where she finds her stamina; she has me withering just listening to her."

"Then this ambulance would be just what she needs: four stretchers, and such a good cause, raising money for a field kitchen."

How kind of this man to be so concerned for her friend. Maud is too young and inexperienced to understand the role that motive plays in human action, and so she has the luxury of basking in the magnanimity of her friend and lover. She is unaware that Dr Goldberg indulges her with this plan because it does not interfere with his own.

After another quiet period, during which tea is sipped and glances exchanged, Dr Goldberg asks if Maud would like to meet earlier than usual on Thursday and take a trip to Madam Tussaud's to see some German trophies from the trenches. There are swords and rifles, and even a sword bayonet that Dr Goldberg is very keen to view. Not for the first time, Maud wonders at the base nature of this talk from a man who is otherwise sophisticated, educated and gentle. She thinks of her kind, protective brother, held captive by these very men whose weapons are on display as in a freak show. Yet Will, too, carries a rifle and... she will not think about these terrible things! Nothing good can come of it. She turns her head away, which has the desired effect of causing Dr Goldberg to change the subject.

Edward looks on, absorbing all he hears and sees, storing it all for a future occasion. Freda going to France in an ambulance indeed. Using his money to pay for the thing, no doubt. He would see about that. Edward moves from his thoughts back into the room at 31, Cumberland-mansions, W., and assesses the situation. Maud doesn't need to be told that Freda is his daughter. Neither does Mary need to know that Frances is his wife. The Moresby name is there for all to see; if people chose not to ask questions then they would not receive answers. Remaining silent, for his part, is not dishonest, although there is a small part of him that feels it to be so. As Edward weighs up the rights and wrongs of his position Colonel Sewell walks over from the far end of the room to sit with the Judge. He is full of what he has read about the Independent Labour Party conference that took place in Norwich last Tuesday.

"Wondering what they're fighting for eh? Hmm. Even intimated the end to German militarism was not a good enough reason to continue the war. Well, I'll be blowed. If that isn't good enough reason, I don't know what is. And as for leaving a spirit of revenge, what are they thinking? We will fight 'em to the end, and there'll be nothing left with which to take revenge. Simple! Blasted Lefties, what?"

Edward listens, half-amused, half in agreement. A year ago there would have been no question, but now there are questions at every turn. But not for Colonel Sewell. How quickly he has recovered from that dreadful letter, and how quickly he has returned to form.

Thoughts of fire steps, a stretcher, a clearing station, deflated comrades, silence; all these things trouble Colonel Sewell. But most of all he is haunted by the Silence. This is the thing he cannot shake. Silence is nothing. It is empty. It has no substance. This is proving to be the most tangible thing of all, and he cannot remove it from his thoughts.

Rose takes a seat at the window, overlooking St Luke's. She hasn't told her new friends in the house that Toby is German. He is fighting for the English, under the name Miller. But really he is a Muller. His parents were German immigrants, but he grew up in England. Why, he is more English than Rose herself, yet still she cannot bring herself to share this secret. She wonders about the

English women who married German men before the war; moved to Germany; had German children. Now their husbands have died at the German Front and they are returning home. Home! Where was home? Questions, questions. And still the confusions with Tom.

Monday 26th April 1915

Reverend Alford

Reverend Alford pulled on his cassock and prepared to brave the world of Mrs Dennis' 'at home'. In all his thirty-eight years as vicar of St Luke's, Nutford Place, the Reverend had never attended an 'at home'. In fact, he had avoided such invitations with a wave of the hand and a chuckle. "My Dear Lady, if I had the time to sit drinking tea and gossiping nothing would get done in the parish." However, this invitation had been difficult to ignore, coming from such a pillar of the community as a Colonel.

It was for some weeks now that Colonel Sewell had been visiting St Luke's, always on a Monday, often with his friend, with whom Reverend Alford was not acquainted, and only for short periods of silent repose. At first the Reverend had watched from behind a pillar, fascinated that anyone should come and pray at his very quiet church; why, even at Sunday services the place was practically empty. Of course Reverend Alford had done his best over the years to encourage attendance, but he didn't stand a chance against the Chapels. With the population of the area being largely Irish Roman Catholics, a significant section of the parish was immediately removed from his remit, and when he took into account the Chapels with their friendly services and free soup, it wasn't a level playing field. But the Reverend was quite at terms with the situation; not for him the preaching of a strong, emotional gospel: this would only attract the sentimental; and if he were to give away soup tickets he would only be attracting the fickle. No. Reverend Alford chose to exercise a more civilising influence. It was not all to do with church services and incense; he and his staff were a body of people visiting in the district. No matter that it went unnoticed by some; to the people that mattered, he and his workers were appreciated; he and the Lord knew what he was about. Reverend Alford conducted his church services for the rich in the parish: the money gathered at collection time was invaluable for the work he was doing. He viewed his visit to Mrs Dennis at 31, Cumberland-mansions, W., as an extension of this and nothing more.

With an almost imperceptible grin, Reverend Alford opened the large, wooden door to his sacristy, pulled it to behind him, and stepped out onto the street. Just across the road he could see the windows of the house where this dreary coffee morning was to take place. He would be as polite as possible, stress the needs of the poor in the parish, and thereby fund another week of work among the Deserving. Not being one for small talk, the Reverend prepared himself for the trying morning ahead

Climbing the steps of 31, Cumberland-mansions, W., the Reverend pulled on the doorbell. The door was opened almost instantly, and he was welcomed into the hallway and on into the morning room of the house.

⁓

As he enters, daylight floods the centre of the room between the luxurious window drapes; a fire glows at the far wall, surrounded by easy chairs; a chaise longue is positioned near a window seat; nearer to the doorway where the Reverend stands surveying the scene is a dining table and chairs, the table laden with flowers and fruit and teacups. A sense of calm and tranquility lies in the air. It occurs to Reverend Alford that this is how a church should feel:

friendly, cosy, comforting, warm and tranquil. This is far from the feeling in his own church which is much more in the line of austere and cold and dark. The Reverend has never entertained a thought of this kind before; it comes to him in a flash and embeds itself in his mind.

"Welcome, Reverend Alford. So nice of you to join us. Colonel Sewell has told us to expect you. We are deeply touched."

Deeply touched? What does Mrs Dennis mean? Deeply touched? No one has spoken to him in such a manner in all the time he has been a vicar. This morning is starting to get interesting. Being a man who takes great pleasure in being candid, he asks Mrs Dennis if all her guests touch her quite so deeply. Not knowing how to respond, Mrs Dennis is saved from a difficult moment by Judge Moresby, who insists on being addressed as Edward (what sort of people are they?) and who offers the Reverend a seat by the fire, "Your friend Colonel Sewell always sits here, so when he arrives you will be comfortable together".

"Judge Moresby, I assure you I am not friends with your Colonel Sewell. He comes to my church to pray. He invited me to this little gathering. I came so I could arrange a little redistribution of wealth around the parish. That is all. Besides, I do enjoy a decent cup of tea."

Edward is taken aback by this response and is at a loss for words. Something about the Vicar has brought an unsettled atmosphere to the room. Just then, Dr Goldberg arrives and makes for the fireside, introducing himself to the vicar as he does so. The assurance of the tall, handsome, cultured man before him causes Reverend Alford to withdraw into himself. He listens as Dr Goldberg tells him of the valuable work he and his colleagues are doing for the war effort. It has not occurred to the Reverend that teeth could be a problem for a soldier; why, ninety per cent of his parishioners have rotten teeth and often no teeth at all, so the idea of providing false teeth for so many men seems quite incredible. This gives him food for thought that only moments ago would have seemed ridiculous. Something in the way Dr Goldberg speaks of his work fascinates the Reverend and brings him to a place that is unfamiliar.

As he ponders, another guest arrives and takes her place on the chaise longue near the window seat. Reverend Alford is well placed to hear everything she says from a distance but far enough to go unnoticed by Rose. She tells Mrs Dennis that Mary will not be attending today as she is at St Dunstan's for an important concert. Queen Alexandra will be in attendance and many other royal personages. Mary is terribly excited. Rose is certain she will tell everyone about it next Monday.

St Dunstan's. Mmm. Reverend Alford has heard about this new hospital within his parish boundary at Regent's Park. He has not, however, met anyone who has visited. He is most intrigued to hear of this Mary and her husband Hampstead (is this not the name of an area just north of here?). The Reverend is somewhat disgruntled that the young woman, Mary, knows more about his parish than he, himself, does. Perhaps he should extend his visit this morning; he may hear more that is of interest.

The day wears on with little else being said that is of interest to Reverend Alford, but he finds himself more intrigued by this dearth of information than he would have thought possible. The atmosphere is rich and full in a way that is unfamiliar to him, engendering a satisfying feeling he has not experienced before. He is unsure what to make of it.

As he bids the company farewell, now late into the evening, all thought of anything in particular has long since gone from the Reverend's mind.

Monday 3rd May 1915

Twelve and the Vicar

F rances Moresby was engaged on her weekly visit to St
Dunstan's. Although she visited many blinded soldiers on
her days at the hospital, it was always her visit to Hampstead
to which she looked forward the most. On the train journey
from Hastings she browsed the books she had brought with her.
Such a shame that the most interesting of all, 'Wonders of Wild
Nature', would be lost on Hampstead as it was in the magnificent
photographs that the interest was held. However, 'The Story
Behind the Verdict' would be just the thing for her intelligent
Hampstead. Of course, since the arrival of the dog, visits had
been even more enjoyable. The ever creative Mary had decided
to buy a dog for Hampstead after she had seen the joy in his face
when the black spaniel at that wretched house had jumped on his
lap. Mary had told Frances all about Wuffy (ridiculous name!)
and how Hampstead had come to life, remembering Bonzo from
his childhood days. Mary had found a darling Westie which
Hampstead had named Sidelights. A very odd name in Frances'
opinion, but Hampstead told her it was inspired by one of the dogs
that Ernest Shackleton (whoever he was) had taken on his expedition
to the Antarctic (quite what he was doing in the Antarctic Frances
could not imagine), and Hampstead had thought it an appropriate
name as Sidelights would be providing illumination for him into
the world of the sighted. Frances allowed for these eccentricities in
all her soldiers because they had so much to bear, and they bore it

so bravely, but on this occasion she felt it necessary to draw a line, and she thought long and hard about how to change Hampstead's mind. That wretched house where Edward spent so much of his time gnawed at her thoughts, and finally the name came to her in this unexpected way: Cumberland. Both Mary and Hampstead thought this was perfect, and so the renaming was done.

As Frances approached Hampstead's bedside today she noticed that, although early in the morning, he was already up and out of the ward. She made her way to the garden and looked in every corner but to no avail. Finally she asked one of the nursing staff, only to be told that Hampstead had gone out for the day with Mary to visit friends in Marylebone. So that was it, that darned house again. Oh well. She would just have to visit her other soldiers and hope that Hampstead returned before visiting time ended.

～

At the steps of 31, Cumberland-mansions, W., Mary linked arms with her husband while Cumberland followed on from the end of his lead. Mary wondered whether it had been sensible to bring the dog with them on this, Hampstead's second visit to the house. She negotiated the steps slowly and patiently as Hampstead felt the way beneath his feet. The door was opened before the bell had been pulled, and Lillie welcomed them in.

～

As the day is cool with rain clouds threatening above, Mrs Dennis' plan to be in the garden is thwarted and Lillie shows them into the morning room. There is a scurrying of paws and a yelping from Wuffy who is most put out at the prospect of a rival. Cumberland cowers behind Hampstead's leg, and Mary almost loses her resolve. With a swift motion, Isa Harburg gathers Wuffy under his arm and reassures him that all is well. After some soothing words Wuffy is placated and placed back on the floor. He eyes the little terrier with suspicion, and slopes off into the corner by the fire, chin on paw, watching nervously every move this scruffy creature makes.

Hampstead and Mary sit in the armchairs around the window seat where Edward is talking with Neville Thursby. Edward is most concerned about the articles in the paper regarding nerve gas being used by the Hun.

"Jolly bad show. Paying no heed to the conventions of warfare, whatever will they do next? Our poor fellows unable to breathe, blinded..." his voice trails off as he becomes aware of Hampstead close by. Cumberland relieves the tensions around them, eager to be stroked by as many hands as possible in as short a time as can be achieved. The white, hairy creature procures smiles all round, and even Neville, who up until now has seemed out of sorts, regains a twinkle in his tired eyes.

Mary notices the change in Neville more than anyone else in the room and she is most concerned. Neville's breathing is more laboured than it was last week, and his hand shakes as he holds his cup to his lips. She doesn't say anything, but both she and Neville know that she has noticed. They keep this knowledge to themselves, storing it for another time. Neville is strengthened by the reserve of this kind, young woman who bears all her own troubles in this quiet manner.

Hampstead is keen for Edward to continue the conversation regarding the gassing. He has heard some mumbles of this in the hospital, but without the resource of the newspapers he is at the mercy of others for his information. He is most concerned that their host continue his discussion and so Edward relates the news from the Front as he has had it related to him in the Telegraph. It is dirty tactics on the part of the Hun, and Edward cannot surmise where it will all end. The details are presented and mulled over, looked at from every angle, with understanding thoughts from Mary, all but defeated thoughts from Neville Thursby, anxious thoughts from Hampstead who is eager to know all he can of his fellow soldiers, and soothing balm from Mrs Dennis who pours refreshing lime cordial for her guests.

"Such a delightful concert at St Dunstan's, don't you agree Hampstead?"

"The music fairly overwhelmed me, filled my senses," replies Hampstead but the frightened air he creates around him does not go unnoticed. He doesn't let Mary know that the music sent him back to a place of crashes and bangs, flashes of light he can still see, terror.

"The patients themselves provided the jolliest part of the entertainment, singing along at the end with Keep the Homes Fires Burning" says Mary. "It's their unbroken determination to realise a better world ahead that I so admire."

As they sip their cordial, a strength of spirit takes hold and the friends lift their heads, reset their shoulders and continue the struggle.

At the other end of the morning room, in an armchair by the fireplace, Emily Peppiatt carefully cuts out a piece from the newspaper appealing for respirators, complete with instructions for sewing these, for the soldiers who are facing gassing in the trenches. Isa Harburg sits close by in the adjacent armchair by the fire with his friend Wuffy, who is still sulking and eyeing up the newcomer at the other side of the room. He relates to Rose, who is sitting on a straight-backed dining chair by his side, the terrible ordeal his beloved daughter is facing in Boulogne with English ambulance trains arriving from the battlefields at Ypres, bringing endless wounded men.

"Her most recent letter describes the terrible state the poor men are in. Really Rose, my dear, I could not tell you what she has written. It breaks an old man's heart to hear his very own daughter utter such details. How can my little Blanch see all these cruel sights? It is not right. Even so, much of her letter is crossed out by the commanding officer, but what is left is cruel beyond words."

"Your Blanch sounds strong and capable, Mr Harburg. You have reason to be very proud of her. We women are stronger than you think. Blanch will surprise you, I wouldn't wonder."

"I don't want to be proud of my daughter. I want to protect my child. She doesn't think of herself nearly enough. When she was young, with no mother, she was always looking out for me, protecting me. Now all she writes about is these poor men - what will become of them, crippled and blinded, what will they do after the war is over - always about them, never herself." He pauses to collect his thoughts. "Many of them have missing limbs you know, young men, in the prime of their lives." He leans towards Rose and tells her, in little more than a whisper, "Some are in such a state of shock they cannot even walk in a straight line."

Rose pats Isa's knee with an overwhelming feeling of compassion. Visions of Toby stumbling and staggering in an attempt to reach her along an unending, straight road fill her mind to bursting.

"Oy, gevalt! Vos vet zayn der sof?" Isa mutters quietly to himself, but he stirs himself as Rose asks him how business is going. The effort this demands from Rose doesn't go unnoticed by Emily, carefully folding her newspaper cutting into her handbag.

"Of course the latest fashions are hideous," he tells her. "Everything so big and puffy and fussy. If only I could tailor some ladies fashions, with waists and darts and a beautiful cut; the master tailors know how to make an ugly woman beautiful, a lumpy woman svelte. These items produced in big factories, all cut to the same shape for women of many different shapes. Tut, tut, tut, vos vet zayn der sof indeed!"

As Rose listens she has an idea.

"Mr Harburg, please excuse my interruption, but perhaps you could make a beautiful set of clothes for me, and if they work well you could gain some ideas for a line in Ladies Wear."

Isa chuckles to himself, flattered that this beautiful 'isha' should take an interest in his livelihood. He looks at Rose, her erect, slim stature, her poise, her womanhood. Yes, he thinks to himself, this would give some purpose back to his life.

"Beseder. This is what we shall do." And they arrange a time for Rose to visit Isa's shop and to be fitted for this innovation in Ladies Wear.

There are two new arrivals at the house who take their place at the dining table just as food is about to be served. Dr Goldberg and Maud have taken to arriving at the house together, and it occurs to no one to question this. Dr Goldberg is a very busy dentist, sought after in every circle of society, war work demanding of him at every turn, yet he finds time to indulge and tend to the needs of Maud. And Maud is a young woman of pressing needs.

"Do you think I would be able to go to the Prisoner of War camp in Austria-Hungary to see if I can find my brother? Freda tells me that an outbreak of typhus has killed thousands in the camps; it is impossible to keep clean, there isn't enough food, there are lice everywhere. It's all too much to keep in one's mind; it's driving me to distraction Dr Goldberg."

"I have some contacts Maudy. Leave it to me. I'll see if I cannot contact the International Prisoners of War Agency in Geneva and find out where your brother is being held. In the meantime, you can contact the Red Cross and make sure your parcels are getting through to the correct camp."

Maud is reassured and almost purrs with satisfaction; this perfect man is making everything alright again. Dr Goldberg, however, ponders on how long he will be able to keep up this pretence with the woman he loves. Her brother is never coming home. He died, as the War Office has already told her, in Ploegsteert Wood last November. He fully understands why she cannot accept this; the report took so long in coming; the initial information telling her he was 'suspected taken prisoner' just added to the confusion. But he, Dr Goldberg, knows there is no hope. His problem is how to convey this to Maud. He takes her hand in his, unable to make eye contact, longing for it all to be over and life to revert to normal. But nothing would ever be normal again. It is all changed, all gone, finished. He hides these thoughts, holds them close, reveals them to no one, and reassures Maud with the stroking of her hand.

Emily Peppiatt observes all this from the corner of her eye, taking things in, pondering, organising her thoughts into a system that makes them bearable. The loss of her son, William, is all the more poignant when she hears Maud talking of her brother Will, a shared name and a shared grief. She feels a close bond to Maud, not just for the namesake, but because her son will never be buried in the usual way, just as Maud's brother will never be returned to her. This she knows. This Dr Goldberg knows. The fact that Maud does not yet know this makes it all the more poignant to Emily. Dr Goldberg smiles towards Emily without changing anything in his facial expression. She acknowledges this with a hardly noticeable nod, then turns to face Lillie who is offering a glass of cordial on a silver tray. Emily looks into the glowing, green liquid with the green basil leaf floating on its surface, and clutches at the peace and calm it offers.

The party of five around the window seat move towards the dining table: Edward and Neville followed closely by Mary, Hampstead and Cumberland. They join Mrs Dennis at her table festooned with spring flowers and tropical fruits, pansies from the garden, and cut glass decanters.

"I so wish we could have sat in the garden. Maybe next week," says Mrs Dennis as Edward pours red wine for each guest. Isa, Rose and Emily make their way from the fireplace to the dining table with Wuffy at Isa's heels. Now that Wuffy is within sniffing distance of Cumberland he decides to brave the new world and edges up to the hairy white creature. Cumberland wags an excited tail and bounds up to Wuffy which causes the black dog to retreat to Isa's feet. The two dogs stay close to their respective masters' feet with a tacit understanding between them.

Just as the friends are about to eat there is a ring on the doorbell and, after some time, Lillie announces the arrival of Colonel Sewell and, to the surprise of everyone present, Reverend Alford, making the company complete.

"Lighting a candle for the old boy. A tad delayed. Brought the Reverend along. Hope you don't mind." And with that Colonel Sewell takes his seat at the table with Reverend Alford hesitantly taking his place by the Colonel's side.

The twelve friends sit around the table while Reverend Alford adjusts himself to the setting in which he finds himself. The dark chill of his church seems light years away, and yet it is just across the road. The sombreness of both himself and his parishioners seem to have no place here; moreover, they seem to have no place at all. What has he been thinking all these years? Is this why his fellow man has remained such a mystery to him? As the dinner is served, Reverend Alford wonders if he will be able to digest what has been placed before him.

Monday 10th May 1915

The Lusitania

Mrs Dennis is disappointed again at the unreliability of the weather, an inch of rain yesterday and only forty-eight degrees. The garden will have to wait. Colonel Thomas Sewell sits by the fire somewhat stiff of limb and heavy of heart. The unseasonal May weather is playing havoc with these damned legs. At seventy-five years of age he has seen a long and interesting life, and today's news brings a sluggishness to his mental state that is quite alien to the Colonel. This is not war. This is sabotage. Murder. He thinks of his friend, Frank, who is due in London from the Lusitania. He has not heard from him, but then he would not expect to; their arranged meeting is for next week, but he is anxious all the same. Jolly poor show. Women and children! Frank was on board with his wife and four children, all under five years old. Colonel Sewell wonders what will have become of them all. Another tragedy. Another thing to have to face. That is it. He will speak to Reverend Alford; the Vicar will know what to do, how to react, how to face this latest ordeal.

～

Reverend Alford ruminated on the latest request from Mrs Dennis. A service especially for her group of visitors! As they only met on a Monday she had requested that it be at the beginning of next week. A service on a Monday. The Reverend had heard of many strange happenings in his forty years at St Luke's - they had survived the cholera epidemic and untold misery and deprivation during the four decades of his residency - but never had he heard of a service on a Monday. What was the Dear Lady thinking? He turned over in his mind the vital work he must undertake on Monday, tending to the poor and needy of his parish, and he calculated that this left a solitary gap between two after noon and three after noon for the service to take place. Of course he would make it plain to Mrs Dennis that his services came at a cost, and the services, moreover, of his rector and his flower ladies would need to be factored in. He assessed the cost to equate to precisely two shillings which he would then redistribute where the need was most urgent within the parish. He decided to tell Mrs Dennis that five shillings would be an adequate sum to meet the requirements of her and her cronies.

Reverend Alford was formulating this in his mind when he heard a knock on the door of the presbytery. He stirred himself and made for the door to find Mrs Dennis on his step anxious to have him walk over the road with her to 31, Cumberland-mansions, W.

"I am so sorry to trouble you Reverend Alford, but the Colonel is very agitated. You see there has been some terrible news in this morning's paper about the sinking of a ship, on Friday I believe. The poor Colonel has a friend who was on the ship with his wife and four children. There is no news of his friend, but the Colonel fears the worst." Mrs Dennis paused for breath. "I know he would welcome some soothing words from yourself, Reverend Alford. I wonder would you come across and help us at this difficult time."

Soothing words?

"I was planning on a visit later today to discuss your proposed service, so I may as well kill two birds." And with that the two hurried across the road to 31, Cumberland-mansions, W.

In the time it took to cross the road and enter the Mansions, Reverend Alford's sharp mind was able to evaluate the situation:

people expecting him to provide answers where there were none, parishioners looking for comfort and consolation when he could find none himself, the toffs failing when things got tough, needing reassurance where they should have been providing it. Here he was again, dispensing calm and consolation when he himself was feeling despair.

~

As Mrs Dennis returns to the house with Reverend Alford in tow, she is greeted by the sound of anxious voices and a hubbub quite alien to the morning room at 31, Cumberland-mansions, W. All her regular guests have arrived and the talk is of the Lusitania and nothing else. Reverend Alford braces himself. Mrs Dennis asks Lillie if she will make haste and serve some tea to the Reverend. With the exception of Colonel Sewell, the entire room is filled with people standing, pacing, swaying, all in the throes of animated conversation. Colonel Sewell sits at the far end of the room staring into the middle distance. Reverend Alford, for no reason other than his desire to extricate himself from the crowd, makes a beeline for the chair adjacent to the Colonel's, and sits down with the intention of drinking tea. No sooner is he seated, than Colonel Sewell begins his story.

"Frank. Great pal. Did some business together. Moved to America you know. Did very well for himself. Kept in touch."

The Colonel disappears into the middle distance again, giving time for the Reverend to slurp some tea. "Delightful wife, fine children."

He looks towards Reverend Alford. "No news. What do you think? Damn business."

Reverend Alford doesn't know what he thinks. The Colonel continues.

"Damned Germans! A passenger ship! Jolly poor show. Not playing the game at all."

Again he drifts off, and the Reverend takes the opportunity to rest before the inevitable onslaught of the next grieving guest seeking his soothing balm. Strangely the room has become calm and peaceful, as it has been on the Reverend's previous visits. Conversation has died down and in its place is a quiet and serene stillness.

Reverend Alford is prepared for most eventualities, but the quietness he encounters when he visits this room leaves him at a loss. Some of the visitors have their eyes closed, some stare blankly at the rug on the floor, others gaze out of the window to the street outside. After some moments he realises this silence is likely to last some time, and so he rests back upon his own thoughts and prepares to sit it out with them. After some minutes of this the Reverend realises that his role as Purveyor of the Word of God may not hold so much water in this room; for the first time in his role as Vicar of St Luke's he feels a sense of redundancy, and for the first time he questions his role in the Theatre of Life. If these people do not require his knowledge and wisdom, indeed appear to view him no differently from themselves, then where does that leave him? What position can he claim in society if he is no longer sought for his superior understanding of things? These thoughts flit across his mind only in fleeting moments, but the essence of them lingers. Even when he retreats from them by sheer effort of will, he is still not approached by any of the guests, and everyone remains silent and alone in their thoughts.

Quite what Mrs Dennis expects from a service at St Luke's eludes him, but the prospect of money for his work is too much to resist. He offers a hand to Colonel Sewell.

"Glad I could be of some assistance to you, Colonel". Even he realises the irony of these words and swiftly moves towards Mrs Dennis.

"Mrs Dennis. We must meet to discuss your service at a later date." He stumbles from the room in a more agitated state than any of Mrs Dennis' guests, who have now found a sense of calm and contemplation. Mrs Dennis thanks him for his visit and remarks that he has helped the Colonel at a great time of need. With this, she sees him to the door. Reverend Alford feels certain he has been of no assistance whatsoever, and is keen to return to his needy parishioners whose poverty and destitution are far easier to understand.

Back in the morning room, Rose Muller is striking up a conversation with Dr Goldberg and it is all the latter can do to refrain from pouring out his own worries and exasperation at what life is throwing at him. He listens as patiently as he is able to Rose's very real concerns.

"My husband, Dr Goldberg, is fighting in France under the name of Miller. His actual name is Muller. He is not ashamed of his ancestry Dr Goldberg, but people were asking awkward questions and insinuating things. Now my children are being taunted at school because of this name."

For pity's sake, did the woman not realise he had heard this story time and again when Rose had told practically everyone else in the room, one by one, on and on. Aloud he says:

"What a worry this must be for you."

Dr Goldberg is aware of the inadequacy of his response, but really! The woman should be told!

"And such a forward-thinking school - Henrietta Barnett's - do you know it?"

Of course Dr Goldberg does not, and is struggling with himself to remain polite and seemingly interested in a topic so alien to his world.

"She caters for every class of child; so helpful with people like us who are financially affected by the war."

Good Lord! The woman was now telling him her financial standing. And still she wittered on. Dr Goldberg nodded and shook his head at just the right moments, appropriately punctuating Rose's outpourings.

"Toby was with the railways, you know, the London North-Eastern. He was very happy there prior to the war, under Mr Ree, but after he left it was never the same again under Mr Turnbull. Still, I've no complaints about Mr Turnbull myself; he's arranged for the men still working on the railway to contribute a little each week, so I still get something for myself and the children. And dear Henrietta, refusing to take any school fees while things are difficult."

At this Dr Goldberg begins to pay more attention. Working men contributing to a fund for families of soldiers? A headmistress dispensing of fees at her own expense? He had no idea these things were happening around him. Rose notices her listener's renewed interest and feels encouraged.

"Of course I feel terribly ungrateful for feeling anxious, but this name really is proving a problem."

"Perhaps you should change it to Miller as well, then you would all have the same name as your husband."

The oddness of this statement does not escape Dr Goldberg.

"That is just what I have been thinking Dr Goldberg. And with this news of the sinking ship..."

"The Lusitania"

"Yes, that's it. Now the anger towards Germans is greater than ever."

Dr Goldberg sits back in his chair with a heavy sigh. He can sympathise with Rose completely, but his own concerns are more pressing. For the second time since the outbreak of war he has been pushed to the edge: a second notice has been put in the Personal Column on his behalf by his solicitor, stating again that he is not German and does not have any affiliation to any Germans; moreover, a monetary reward is offered for any information supplied as to the propagators of these lies. The lack of dignity in his position is what troubles Dr Goldberg the most. His hard-earned position as eminent dental surgeon is put into question, all because of a name. He is consoled slightly at the thought that it diverts from the Jewish problem for once, but the consolation is small. He glances at Rose, deep in thought, and takes comfort from their shared troubles. Two people with nothing in common except a shared social stigma brought about by two very different names. He averts his eyes as Rose looks up, and he takes in the room around him and the familiar faces, all of whom have troubles and vexations caused by this blasted war. The common threads appear before his vision: war, separation, loss, anxiety, even this room; all these things bind them together with ties that can never be broken. A sense of belonging fills Dr Goldberg until he feels he will overflow. Nothing in his life before this has given him such a sense of self and purpose. People outside this room could accuse him of whatever they liked, could hurl insults and stand in his path; but none of them could touch the deep places reached in this room with these people and at this time. He lights his pipe, sits back, breathes deeply of the atmosphere around him, and for the first time in a week feels the strength to forge on into his future.

Isa Harburg quietly and humbly approaches Rose with a brown paper parcel tied with string. He has completed the jacket suit that

Rose had been fitted for last Thursday, carefully stitching each seam himself, enjoying the touch of the beautiful fabric they had chosen together from his vast supply that had been in his shop since before the outbreak of war last August. So difficult to find these now, the rich colours, the soft touch. Everything now was muted and coarse and of military style. Yes, Isa is delighted with his stock and with the use he has made of it for his friend whose cares are etched on her face on this sombre morning. He presents the package to Rose in gingerly fashion, careful not to intrude on the thoughts that are so clearly pressing down on her. The sight of the package causes Rose's face to soften and her demeanour to lighten in an instant.

"How wonderful! Just the tonic I needed today. Thank you Mr Harburg." She graciously receives the gift and Mrs Dennis, always aware of the significant moments in her home, suggests she go upstairs and change into the outfit so that all her friends can enjoy the moment with her. This kind invitation causes Rose to swallow back a tear, and she makes her way to the hallway and climbs the stairs to Mrs Dennis' dressing room.

Mary and Hampstead sit by the window, Cumberland happily snuggled in his master's lap. Mary lays a hand upon her growing stomach. With only two months to go until three become four Mary is filled with the joy of new life, new beginnings. Even the events of the week with the dastardly sinking of the passenger ship cannot quite blot out the delight Mary feels from this life inside her. As she moves her hand from her stomach to her husband's knee, the door of the room suddenly opens and standing in the doorway is Rose in her new outfit. Everyone in the room looks up, except for Hampstead who is unaware of the vision before him. There is a slight intake of breath from Maud and Emily, sitting close by on the window seat. The line of the skirt, the lilac glow of the dress, the stunning detail of the buttons and the shape of the tunic! Rose's hat is a perfect match; her shoes even compliment the whole look.

Isa beams with pride. Dr Goldberg holds Maud's gaze. Mary describes it all in fine detail to Hampstead: the curve of the bodice, the high neck-line, the purple flowers on a lilac background. Mrs Dennis tells Rose and Isa how delighted she is for them both: the Creator and the Model. Edward, Neville Thursby and Colonel Sewell sit transfixed by the beauty before them, made more poignant by the horror of the days just passed.

Monday 17th May 1915

The Memorial Service

Mrs Dennis' original plan when she asked Reverend Alford to perform a service in St Luke's was to gather with her friends to ask for God's strength over the coming months. After the sinking of the Lusitania and the effect it has on them all, she decides it makes sense to call it a Memorial Service. This covers everyone's requirements: it will be especially for the victims of the disaster but would also be in memory of those loved ones that have been lost to the group personally.

She has found the friends to be unanimous in their agreement that the service go ahead and she is keen to ensure it is well planned in advance.

"As we are all aware, Reverend Alford is a man of whom many demands are made from those less fortunate than ourselves within the Parish, and I am sure we will all understand when I tell you he has only one free hour available for us."

There is a general murmur of surprise which Mrs Dennis is quick to stifle.

"With this in mind, the Reverend and I have arranged for us all to attend St Luke's between two o'clock and three o'clock this very afternoon. I'm most anxious that any one who has a contribution to make must be given the opportunity to be heard."

Discussions begin with the choosing of the hymns.

"It must be borne in mind that there will be no organist so we must choose hymns we are all familiar with and confident to sing unaccompanied."

"Onward Christian Soldiers!"

The room is silent in thought at the Colonel's suggestion, the stirring element and reference to war foremost in the friends' minds, and there seems to be an unspoken consensus to move on. Mary recommends 'Lead Kindly Light', which causes the entire company to glance briefly at Hampstead. "Perfect," says Emily, and all are in agreement that this is a powerful yet consoling hymn with the added advantage that it has only three verses. Emily offers to write down the words so everyone can spend some time familiarising themselves, particularly with the third.

"And with the morn, those angel faces smile, which I have loved long since, and lost awhile!"

Emily relaxes against the back of her armchair, remembering the beautiful fingers of her now dead son on the piano, the lilt of this haunting melody floating in the room around her, chased by delicate hands and tear-soaked eyes. It is some minutes before she is able to bring herself back into the present and to resume preparations.

With the unseasonal weather, wet and cold and grey, it is difficult to pick flowers from Mrs Dennis' colourful garden, but Lillie nonetheless enters with some damp daffodils and Mrs Dennis is comforted to see these followed by a stunning display of primroses, violets and bluebells. "How clever you are, Lillie, to create something so spring-like on such a day as this. Thank you so much."

"I like flowers madam, they are so pretty."

All present are heartened by the display. Mrs Dennis herself

106

suggests 'My Faith Looks Up To Thee', and this is agreed unanimously, not least because all the friends are so fond of Mrs Dennis and ever aware that these Monday meetings would not have taken place at all without her.

"Perhaps we could just sing the third and fourth verses as the words are pertinent, do you agree?" Mrs Dennis asks the group as a whole.

> *'While life's dark maze I tread,*
> *And griefs around me spread,*
> *Be Thou my guide;*
> *Bid darkness turn to day,*
> *Wipe sorrow's tears away,*
> *Nor let me ever stray*
> *From Thee aside.*
>
> *When ends life's transient dream,*
> *When death's cold, sullen stream*
> *Shall o'er me roll;*
> *Blest Saviour, then in love,*
> *Fear and distrust remove;*
> *Oh, bear me safe above,*
> *A ransomed soul!'*

"For the closing of the service may I suggest 'There is a Blessed Home'. I would like the first two verses, as three and four are less calming and beautiful I feel."

Maud's suggestion is questioned by no one as most do not know the words, being an American hymn, but they are all agreed that, owing to the great loss the United States has suffered "at the hands of the Hun" on the Lusitania, it is appropriate to include this. Maud sits with Emily to recite the words to her while she reminds

107

everyone of the melody. Fortunately the melody is more familiar to the assembled group and it is agreed that this be the closing piece.

"Mrs Dennis, I wonder if you would do me the honour of allowing a Hebrew prayer in the service?"

"Why, Mr Harburg, I'm not sure what Reverend Alford would think of that. It is, after all, his Church. I'm not sure what to say."

"The service is to be in a Christian Church, and we are, after all, mostly Christians here, so I think it only right and proper that we confine ourselves to Christian prayers," says the Colonel.

"I think Mr Harburg has every right to have a prayer of his own. After all, God is the God of all," says Rose.

"I have to say, I think the Colonel has a point. This is, of course, a Christian country, and it is for the survival of Christianity that our boys are fighting," says Neville, not at all sure he believes any more in what he is saying.

"We are all friends here, and we must allow everyone their point of view," says Emily, lowering her eyes as they meet Neville's, uncomfortable to be in disagreement with him for the first time.

"And who is to lead these prayers?" asks Dr Goldberg, somewhat conflicted in his thoughts on the matter.

"It is customary for the men to lead the prayers in a Christian church," says the Colonel.

"I would like to lead one of the prayers, and I don't see why I shouldn't just because I am a woman," says Rose, indignant at the Colonel's dismissal of all the women in the room.

This is exactly the opposite of what Mrs Dennis had in mind. She is on the verge of cancelling the service when Isa makes a suggestion. "Perhaps we could write our own prayers, Mrs Dennis." A hush falls over the room and thoughts turn inwards.

After some minutes the silence is broken with the unexpected voice of Hampstead.

"Guide us, dear Lord, by the light of thine understanding, and lead us through the troubled waters to thine Eternal Calm."

Mary clasps her husband's hand and rests her other hand on her growing child; how apt, how perfect. She glows with pride and contentment. Even Colonel Sewell and Neville Thursby are taken aback with this contribution given so simply and so boldly.

The room takes on the familiar Quiet and Stillness. When someone does speak it is in an unhurried manner without a sense of urgency. During the course of the next hour or so it is agreed upon that the service will be rich enough with the three hymns and Hampstead's prayer which will be spoken by them all. Maud suggests they say the prayer before and after each hymn which seems a little trite and unnecessary to Colonel Sewell but the idea is embraced by the room as a whole. And so the preparations are made.

The flowers will be taken over by Lillie prior to the two o'clock service, and she will ask the lady helpers at the church to place them in the centre where everyone can see them. " This will act as a centrepiece, a symbol of stability and strength in adversity," says Mrs Dennis.

Again Colonel Sewell raises his eyes but in a subtle manner: he would not like anyone to see. Neville Thursby takes note of this. Although he has some sympathy with the Colonel's attitude he feels sorry for him that he is unable to let his guard down sufficiently, today of all days. No matter. He is confident no one else has seen.

Hampstead is aware of a feeling in the room, only just discernible, pointing to someone being out of kilter with the rest; he is learning to live with his heightened senses, and is slowly allowing this to compensate in some part for the loss of his most significant sense. He wonders from whom this feeling is coming. There is a snarling somewhere close to his feet, and Hampstead leans towards it, playfully pulling the playmates apart, seeing clearly the face of Bonzo as he pats Cumberland.

—

At St Luke's it was approaching the O'clock and Reverend Alford wondered where the flowers had appeared from. The church was usually festooned with flowers on a Sunday, but it had been his habit to redistribute them around the select few of his parish: the middle class, not-so-well-off-but-so-very-deserving minority who lacked the money and the gentility of the Rich, but were devoid of the coarseness and feckless nature of the Poor. These were his soul mates, at least as close as Reverend Alford could get to soul mates. In the homes of the Middle Classes he understood the rules and the social niceties yet did not feel inadequate. Conversely, with the Poor there was just no order or structure, and this left the Reverend feeling unsettled each time he left a home in the slums. He felt a sense of shame, deep down, but that was how it was. Nothing to be done about it. Again, with the Wealthy, like that crowd from over the road, he felt at a loss: a service on a Monday, then flowers appearing from nowhere. He prepared himself for a short and simple service in which he would preach about the love of God and the importance of Duty and National Pride in these difficult times. He would touch on the dastardly nature of the Hun, but this would not be dwelt upon too much, just enough to make the point. He would explain to Mrs Dennis that, on account of no organist, there would be no hymns.

Reverend Alford watched as the twelve friends walked down the central aisle of his church to take their places in the front two pews. He noticed with interest that Lillie the maid was among them. How odd. Most unexpected. Then, the older woman about Mrs

Dennis' age bustled up to him waving a paper in her hand which she placed on the pulpit. He glanced down to see, in neat and elegant writing, the words of no less than three hymns, the first and the last with two verses, the second with four! The Reverend made his way to Mrs Dennis.

"My Dear Lady, we have no organist, hymns are out of the question. Did I not make myself clear at our last meeting?"

Mrs Dennis assured him that her friends were aware of this and had come with every confidence in their acapella singing abilities.

"It doesn't matter which language you will be singing in, my dear, but without an organ I can assure you it is quite impossible. I have been vicar of this parish for forty plus years, and never has a congregation sung organless."

Mrs Dennis replied that there was always a first time for everything and with that she turned and walked back to her place in the front pew.

The Reverend was quite taken aback and it was all he could do to muster the wherewithal to take his place behind the pulpit. No sooner had he settled himself in his familiar position, preparing for the welcome and the homily he generally used for memorials, open-mouthed and ready to speak, than the blind soldier spoke.

"Guide us, dear Lord, by the light of thine understanding, and lead us through the troubled waters to thine Eternal Calm."

Without a moment's hesitation the entire group of twelve, including the maid, burst into song! No sooner had this ended than the blind soldier piped up again.

"Guide us, dear Lord, by the light of thine understanding, and lead us through the troubled waters to thine Eternal Calm."

Then another song (four verses!), followed by the whole group joining in,

"Guide us, dear Lord, by the light of thine understanding, and lead us through the troubled waters to thine Eternal Calm."

At this point the Reverend decided to reclaim his church for his own and so the homily began.

Although the church was silent but for the voice of Reverend Alford this was not because the Reverend's sermon was captivating in any way. The group were simply ruminating on their own thoughts and allowed this lone voice to create a backdrop, along with the altar and the arches and the flowers, to the fundamentals of their lives. Colonel Sewell found himself repeating the words he had so scorned earlier that morning as he thought of his friend Frank.

"Guide us, dear Lord, by the light of thine understanding, and lead us through the troubled waters to thine Eternal Calm."

Frank and his wife Amy had survived, along with young Master Stuart and the baby Audrey. But the loss of young Amy and Susan - mere babies themselves - was almost too much for Colonel Sewell to grasp. Frank had been an invaluable business partner to the Colonel's son Sidney. The Colonel had met the family on their visits to England, but Sidney had lived almost as one of the family until he had joined the Colours last August. Colonel Sewell thought of that dreadful letter again as he felt its curled corners in his overcoat pocket. Those wretched 'cellar steps', the 'absence of glory', the 'dominant personality'. Not dominant now. And two dead babies.

"Guide us, dear Lord, by the light of thine understanding, and lead us through the troubled waters to thine Eternal Calm."

Maud Burt-Marshall sat next to her tall, strong lover Dr

112

Goldberg and wondered how long they would be free to continue in this half-life of love and romance. One day they would come and get him, of that she was sure. Only a matter of time.

Emily Peppiatt was heavy with thoughts of the useless gas masks she had been making and sending to the Front. New regulations my foot! First they tell you one thing, then another. She had made them with all care and attention to detail, just as described in the War Office instructions, but still she could not rid herself of the fear that she had caused a poor boy, or maybe many poor lads, to die a slow and agonising death due to her faulty offerings.

While these thoughts and events circulated in the air of St Luke's, the Reverend continued his homily, unaware. When, finally, there was a silence, the group, without so much as a hint of hesitation, prayed:

"Guide us, dear Lord, by the light of thine understanding, and lead us through the troubled waters to thine Eternal Calm."

Reverend Alford, uncharacteristically, was at a loss for words. Then, to add insult, the happy band burst forth into song once more. After two verses of this hymn, a favourite with the Reverend, they ceased singing and once again prayed,

"Guide us, dear Lord, by the light of thine understanding, and lead us through the troubled waters to thine Eternal Calm."

But the last two verses are the good ones! They spoke of the Lord and his sacrifice, the nitty gritty of the Faith, of wounds and hands and feet, lambs to the slaughter, toil and woe. That was the stuff of his work. Not for the first time Reverend Alford felt redundant and superfluous to requirements. He would be pleased to see the back of them. But not before he claimed his five shilling fee.

O joy all joys beyond,
To see the Lamb Who died,
And count each sacred wound
In hands, and feet, and side;
To give to Him the praise
Of every triumph won,
And sing through endless days
The great things He hath done.

Look up, ye saints of God,
Nor fear to tread below
The path your Saviour trod
Of daily toil and woe;
Wait but a little while
In uncomplaining love,
His own most gracious smile
Shall welcome you above.

James Dennis, Mrs Dennis' late husband.

James Dennis was born on 13th August 1838. He joined the 5th Dragoon Guards at the age of 23, and worked his way up from adjutant to Captain and then Major. He was finally promoted to Lieutenant-Colonel in the 6th Dragoon Guards (Carabiniers) in 1887. He retired in 1891 after thirty years service in the cavalry. The son of James and Mrs Dennis, John Owen Cunninghame Dennis, was born three years before his father's retirement in 1888. It is imagined that Mrs Dennis was some years younger than her husband. An image of John, their son, has yet to be located.

reproduced with kind permission of The Old Bancroftians' Association

William Henry Peppiatt, Emily's son.

William Henry Peppiatt was the second eldest son of W.R.Peppiatt and Emily E. Peppiatt of Beaconsfield, Bucks. He attended Bancrofts School until 1907 when he began a career working in the offices of the London North Western Railway company. He was active in the local church in Woodford providing the piano accompaniment for various entertainments. He enlisted with the 5th Battalion the London Rifle Brigade in 1912 and, being a keen distance runner, was part of the winning marathon team for his battalion. He was Killed in Action on 5th February 1915 in Ploegsteert Wood. On the anniversary of his death in 1918 Emily and her daughter placed the following tribute in the Times:

'In constant and ever-loving memory of our dear boy William Henry Peppiatt who was killed in action at Ploegstreet 5th Feb 1915. Mother and Jessica. "Sorrow is then a part of love and love does not seek to throw it off" but "Greater love hath no man than this, that a man lay down his life for his friends."

© IWM used under licence number HU120869

William Burt-Marshall, Maud's brother.

William was born in Luncarty, Perthshire in 1887. Educated at Rugby and Sandhurst, he was an all-round athlete as was common among his contemporaries. He died on November 8th 1914 in Ploegsteert Wood. Captain Clark of the Argyll & Sutherland Highlanders described his final night as follows: "He was at the head of his men, and led the charge. He ran right up to the German barbed wire, was hit, and fell, but rose again, and dashed on to the parapet of the trench, where he fell again. No one could get up to him, and those who were able crawled back to re-form with the remnant of the companies." On the 8th February 1915 the War Office reported confirmation of his death. Shortly after this date, a notice was placed in the Telegraph by a "Miss Burt-Marshall" which initiated the creation of Maud who was searching for her brother, disbelieving the information she had received from the War Office.

© IWM used under licence number HU119113

Audley Delves Thursby, Neville's son.

Neville's only son, Audley was educated at Eton and trained at Sandhurst. From 1908 he served in the King's Royal Rifle Corps in Crete, Malta and India. By 1914 he had reached the rank of Captain. He was a formidable jockey, and an all-round athlete, representing his battalion in polo, cricket, football and gymnastics. He was eleventh in the Malta Garrison marathon out of 700 competitors in 1909. His mother was called Zoe and he had a twin sister called Honor. Audley was killed on 15th February 1915 while acting as a guide in a night attack to retake trenches at St Eloi.

reproduced with kind permission of Tonbridge School

Major Sidney Davies Sewell, Colonel Sewell's Son.

Sidney Davies Sewell was the elder son of Colonel T. Davies Sewell. Born in 1874 he attended Tonbridge School from 1888 to 1892. On leaving school he joined the 1st Middlesex Regiment and was promoted to Major in 1910 and placed in command of the 3rd Field Company of the 2nd London Royal Engineers. He took them to France on January 19th 1915, and after being engaged in hut building for a time they were employed in digging trenches in the neighbourhood of Ypres. On the night of 18th February they succeeded in digging a trench under heavy fire within 25 yards of the German trenches. On that night Major Sewell and three other officers of the company were killed. He was buried in the Menin Gate Cemetery at Ypres. *See also p189*

V

Sir (Cyril) Arthur Pearson, 1866-1921.

Arthur Pearson founded the Daily Express in 1900, a halfpenny rival to the Daily Mail, and in 1904 purchased the Standard. In 1910 he retired from the newspaper industry due to failing sight caused by glaucoma, and spent his time and personal fortune in the research and treatment of the blind. In 1915 he established at his house, St. Dunstan's, in Regent's Park, London, a hospital for blinded soldiers where Hampstead finds solace. He became chairman of the Blinded Soldiers and Sailors Care Committee. He also became president of the National Institution for the Blind. He was keen to encourage blinded soldiers who did not have the benefit of wealth and servants, so he made it his practice to have his bath unaided. Tragically, on December 9th 1921 he accidentally slipped, striking his head on the tap and suffocating in his own bath.

Dame Henrietta Barnett, 1851-1936.

Henrietta and her husband, Samuel, were socialists and philanthropists who undertook many projects including an experiment to send slum children for country holidays which grew into the Children's Country Holiday Fund established in 1877. They bought up hundreds of acres of land around Hampstead Heath in 1904, protecting part of the heath from development and establishing Hampstead Garden Suburb, a model garden city. It included St Jude's Church, as well as a clubhouse and a tea house (for non-alcoholic social gatherings), a Quaker meeting house, children's homes, a nursery school, and housing for old people. In 1909 they established a school for girls, the Henrietta Barnett School, which Rose's daughters attend.

had fallen side by side, over each other, in a wild, general mix-up. Few men were shot or killed in the trenches, almost every one of them between the lines. Almost every dead soldier, both Belgian and German, fell with his rifle beside him. With many of them the doctor had to use force in breaking open their stiff fingers around the barrel.

The doctors and their helpers were busy all night. All night long we saw them move about the battlefield, some with camp lanterns, others with small electric torches. And the "aumoniers," the Belgian priests, do they ever sleep? When dawn broke, one of them was sitting quite close to our trench, almost stiff with the cold, but with a wounded soldier's head in his lap, till the doctor came and told the priest that his man was not sleeping, but dead.

wheels practically dry. The body was riddled with bullet holes, and many spokes in both the rear wheels were torn out. Yet he went on all right after plugging the holes with canvas. His escape was a miracle, for he swerved quite a foot on the pontoon when the shell burst, and the pontoon lay right over. I thought he had been shot, and quite expected him to drop in. He came through, and, smart chap that he was, went out with a couple of engineers to stop the holes in the pontoon through which the water was sinking the whole bridge. The number of wounded that we carried that night was staggering. Hospital after hospital reported itself unable to take any more, and this when ambulance trains were carrying trainloads southwards at the rate of one every hour or so. Whatever will become of these broken men after the war? There must be hundreds of thousands of men whose injuries will affect their constitutions throughout the rest of their lives. Reading in one's newspaper of so many wounded fails to convey the effect of the carnage.

Two poignant articles taken from the Telegraph of 1914.

VIII

Monday 24th May 1915

The Garden

Frances Moresby was tiring of her visits to St Dunstan's. It was all so well organised, quite unlike the hospital in Hastings. There were activities set up for the blind soldiers and she felt like an extra limb. She would just pop in to see Hampstead this morning, knowing that Mary was otherwise engaged in Marylebone. As she approached the ward she was greeted by the yapping of the tiny Cumberland who was as excited as ever to see her; but he was excited to see every visitor, and this thought caused a flattening of spirits to the already flagging Frances. Really, you must pull yourself together old girl; self-pity will never do. Just get on. Frances presented her latest offering to Hampstead; a book entitled 'The Irish Nuns At Ypres'. This was another reason for concern; Hampstead was interested in factual books, books about the war, hearing it in all its depressing detail. No. Frances would leave them to it. Plenty of young debutantes eager to read at the bedside of the blind. Not to mention the extra money the War Office had put aside for this very hospital. Frances would move on to some other worthy war effort. As Hampstead sipped his tea, unaided, Frances glanced at the cutting from the paper she had taken from her purse.

The main problem Frances could foresee with this new venture was the distance; the closest area would be Somerset - but such a trek! Of course there would be the problem of accommodation.

She toyed with the idea of Suffolk. The chauffeur could deliver her and she could find a sympathetic hostess; she would enquire of Edward his contacts in that part of the world.

—

Meanwhile, at 31, Cumberland-mansions, W., Mrs Dennis is showing Edward her tulips that have bloomed just this week. The garden is full of colour and verve, the Bank Holiday sunshine giving a boost to the whole scene. How she loves her London garden, a secret treasure tucked away which makes it all the more special. Her guests have never ventured out here, only Edward, and she believes they aren't even aware of its existence. She has waited for this day, the weather is kind, and now the tulips have risen to the occasion. Mrs Dennis is delighted, and she anticipates the arrival of her guests on this Monday more eagerly than she has done on any previous week.

Edward is deep in thought, sitting on a tip-up garden chair, cross-legged, pipe in hand. The colours are most certainly arresting, a feast for the eyes. He settles on the bluebell patch and concerns himself with the women in his life. Frances seems forever active, fit to drop; Freda is just a distant postmark delivered once daily (got to give it to her for the consistency and loyalty of such regular letter writing); and Mrs Dennis, the rock of the whole scenario, keeping him on solid ground when all around seems chaotic. The sun climbs into the sky even this early on a Monday morning and the day promises warmth and contentment. As Lillie places a glass of lime cordial on the cloth-covered wicker table before him, Edward looks across to Mrs Dennis as she arranges the tulips she has picked for the table display; her attention to detail makes Edward feel cocooned and comforted. His life in these turbulent times feels insecure, but here at the mansions all is well, and the future holds nothing to fear.

Mrs Dennis takes a seat in the wicker chair adjacent to Edward's and the pair sit and talk of the Big Picture.

"Look here, Mrs Dennis, new conditions of enlistment, age limit now forty. Nineteen to forty! The Powers That Be must be desperate for new volunteers. It won't be long before compulsory conscription, mark my words Mrs Dennis."

"Do you know I was reading about a man called Mr Charles Stewart who is apparently the Public Trustee. I'm not sure what that is, Edward. However, that is by the by. The point is that he and his wife have lost both their sons and also a son-in-law. Not a single son left."

A silence falls between them.

"I see the workers are striking in Tyneside, Mrs Dennis. Only a matter of time before it spreads southwards. Rather unpatriotic I say, in these difficult times."

"I prefer to read about spring flowers, Edward. Our May tulips are flowering now, and what a feast for the eyes. What do you say, Edward?" And with this Mrs Dennis walks towards the summer house, picks up her watering can and sprinkles the red and pink and orange flowers in the beds around her garden.

"Mrs Dennis," Edward calls across the garden, reading from his newspaper: "'A Reserve Battalion of the New Army likely to remain in its present quarters for some time requires shrubs and plants to make its surroundings more pleasant, attractive and homely.' There we are, Mrs Dennis. Just the job. It can be our little bit for the war effort."

"But Edward, how long are they expecting the war to continue if they're planting shrubs?"

This had not occurred to Edward and the idea causes him to ponder. The only sounds in the garden are the tweeting of birds and Mrs Dennis' watering can. Edward wonders how permanent a state of affairs this could possibly be. Will he even see an end to it in his lifetime?

The anxiety they both feel floats up into the air and is carried on the breeze, so that when the first visitors make their entrance Edward and Mrs Dennis are prepared.

The first to arrive today are Dr Goldberg and Maud preoccupied with their plans to stay at the new hotel in town, while resolved it must be their secret.

"The opening night is Wednesday, but we will keep to our accustomed rendezvous on Thursday" whispers Dr Goldberg as they approach their host.

Edward and Mrs Dennis greet their friends and pull up two chairs. Despite the excitement of their shared adventure there is a dullness behind Dr Goldberg's eyes. He sits beside Edward and, over a period of time during which drinks are served and savouries consumed, Dr Goldberg reveals the latest ignominy of the wretched domiciled Germans.

"A councillor in the district of Paddington, a Mr Meyer, is stepping down for the duration of the war, despite forty-three years living in England, thirty-eight of which he has been a naturalised citizen. The scandal of it."

Even though Dr Goldberg is not German he feels the horror of it because of his Jewish blood and his understanding of having to explain himself, justify his existence, plead his position when others believe him to be German also. Edward listens from a different angle, a fellow pillar of the community; every aspect of society affected. The morning breeze passes across the partly shaded garden and rests upon the spaces between the two men, the same breeze that has passed across the men at the Front, fighting for the very existence of this garden.

Maud tells Mrs Dennis, between sips of her cordial, that she has been to see Freda in Brighton and changes are imminent.

"Freda has seen too much blood and missing limbs, heard too many groans and moans of pain, even the gramophones can't obliterate the sound any more. She needs a break and a change of scene, to spend time out of doors. I've found just the thing: hay-making in Suffolk. Freda and I could go together and find lodgings when we arrive, and it would be like a holiday for us both, while still helping in the war effort. Hundreds are needed; it could be just the thing."

Mrs Dennis wonders how Maud will broach the subject with Dr Goldberg. She wonders at the opportunities opening up for these young women, but at what cost! Will there be any men left at the end of it all for them to marry and produce children? However, she encourages Maud in her plans; at least it will keep her mind off the Prisoner of War camp and her brother Will. Maud tosses over in her mind the fact of Will and his death last November in Ploegsteert Wood; one day she will have to break the news to the others that he has died and isn't a prisoner, but the right time never seems to present itself, and so she awaits another day.

There is a rustling in the bushes at the side of the lawn and a wagging tail can be seen pointing skyward. Wuffy is delighted to be out in the spring sunshine and does not even try to hold back his enthusiasm; the four friends watch with delight as he nuzzles at the shrubs then twirls around and chases a butterfly. His excitement at every moving object appears to know no bounds, and when Lillie announces the arrival of Isa and Rose the little creature looks as if he will burst at the wonder of it all. He races up to Isa who gathers his friend in his arms and carries him to the nearest garden chair to carry out his greetings in full. Rose, meanwhile, wanders around the lawn smelling flowers and feeling the leaves, breathing in all that the garden has to offer. She, too, has plans. She walks around with Isa and Wuffy, eager to tell someone her news.

"Mr Harburg, there are opportunities to act in moving pictures! Imagine! One is paid while being taught the ropes. This is such an opportunity, as I was wondering how I would continue to pay the maid's salary, and keep the children well dressed and provide all their school equipment. It could be just what I have been waiting for."

Amid all the devastation this war is bringing there is some light. Her friend Isa is keen to find out more about this as it is advertised for all ages. The fact that one must be of the right social class passes unmentioned but is mutually understood.

All six guests sit around the table and breathe in the spring air, carefully placing their chairs in the shaded areas on the lawn, spring blouses and hats giving shade to the ladies. Dr Goldberg and Edward decide to remove their jackets and to sit in shirt sleeves, but Isa prefers to brave the heat in his perfectly tailored suit; some things remain more important than comfort.

As Lillie serves cold meats and pickle, and more refreshing drinks, Emily Peppiatt arrives and announces she can only stay for lunch because she is meeting her husband for a trip to the zoo.

"It's only a hansom cab ride away so we have planned it for the Bank Holiday; I seldom spend time with my husband these days, he is always so busy."

The friends talk of the animals they have seen at the zoo over the years, how wonderful it is to have the chance to see animals from all around the Empire in one spot in Regent's Park. Emily is especially keen to see the leopards who are housed with the lions; such a thrill to see an animal from a different world living within our own parkland. Everyone agrees it is a marvellous spectacle and all are eager to hear Emily's tales when she returns next week. It is only Isa, gently stroking Wuffy's soft fur, who wonders at the lot of these animals, locked in cages when they should be roaming the plains. But there was more to trouble his mind at the thought of Blanch, worn and wretched, heading home for a break, longing to see her father. Isa is delighted at the prospect of their reunion. Quite how he is to broach the subject of acting in films Isa is unsure, but Rose is so keen and makes it all sound sensible and rejuvenating at the same time, Isa cannot help but be carried along. He puts these thoughts aside for another day, and wanders around the edges of the lawn, Wuffy sniffing and acrobating at his feet.

"Emily, you could visit Hampstead today, as he's very close to the zoo in the park, and Mary is with him for the Bank Holiday."

Emily acknowledges this suggestion from Rose with a nod of the head. First there is her friend Neville Thursby to tend to. He arrives, a little weaker of limb, still upright and dignified, but as he draws on his pipe he emits an involuntary cough, and Emily casts her eyes down to the grass, where the sun is throwing a beam of light, to avoid the indignity that is written so clearly on her friend's face. His breathing is more difficult to filter, so laboured and pathetic are the sounds he emits.

"Neville, dear, feast your eyes on the tulips, just in bloom." The reds, oranges and yellows fill the garden with colour and promise. Neville remarks on the bluebells, how his children loved to play in the woods full of these nymph-like blue carpets, and how he loved to watch them at play. Both Neville and Emily enjoy the memory of their respective sons, now dead in mud and decimated fields, their lives thrown on the wind, the same wind that passes through the garden of 31, Cumberland-mansions, W., today. No matter that there is a shortness of breath, a wracking cough: these signify Pain and Life, Sorrow and Hope. Their boys have none of these luxuries. Neville will take every breath, bear every cough, in remembrance of his brave son; Emily will endure the sound of these laboured breaths in memory of her son for whom there could be no burial, and whose hands will never again produce sound to waft on the breeze and lighten one's soul. They are the lucky ones, the older generation, the ones who have had their lives, and still draw more from the Well when it has run dry for their own children.

~

After her luncheon at the mansions and after her visit to the zoo with her busy and elusive husband, Emily suggested they drop in on her friends Mary and Hampstead at St Dunstan's. As they made their way up the steps to the main entrance they passed a lady, in late mid-life, hurrying down the steps away from the hospital. She dropped her clutch bag and Mr Peppiatt immediately stooped to retrieve it and return it to its owner. Frances Moresby was most grateful and apologised for her carelessness: she was hurrying off to Whitehall on an urgent appointment with a Major Smith regarding hay-making. Of all the things, thought Mr Peppiatt - a lady enquiring regarding hay-making. Whatever would be happening next in this dreadful war? Emily remarked to her husband that friends of hers had been speaking of this very thing only that morning. What a coincidence! As they entered the building they were greeted by a terrier, welcoming them.

"Cumberland. How wonderful!"

Emily's husband was at a loss for words. He didn't try to make connections any further: just let the thing roll, everyone else seemed to understand what it was all about. By keeping quiet he could feign understanding too.

~

Back at 31, Cumberland-mansions, W., the shadows are lengthening and Maud removes herself to the summer house. How is she to tell

Dr Goldberg that she is planning to go away? Only to Suffolk, but far enough to be unable to continue their Thursday rendezvous and these Monday gatherings. Added to this, she cannot decide when to reveal to him that her brother Will actually died November last. Problems. Problems. She watches as Dr Goldberg pulls on his pipe and laughs with his friends, quite at ease in this garden where no judgements are made nor questions asked. This Place of Escape, a world within a world, where only the important things matter: friendship, acceptance, understanding. Maud wonders where else she will find these strengths. She is young with her life ahead of her. Will she look back in later years and remember this place for these very things? Is Cumberland Mansions to be found elsewhere or is it unique, a Place in Time?

As Maud ponders in the summer house, Mrs Dennis drinks in the energy from all around her in this, her Garden of Life. To think it all began with the man sitting at her table who took the time to seek her out, from a newspaper clipping, to bring condolences and understanding. It was, indeed, the little things that counted.

DAILY WEATHER REPORT.   Tuesday 25th May,   1915.

NOTES ON YESTERDAY'S WEATHER.

The thermometer rose to 70° and upwards in several parts of the United Kingdom, and reached 75° at Bournemouth. On the north-east coast of England, where fog and mist prevailed, it did not reach 60°. The amount of bright sunshine was again very large in nearly all districts

The Daily Weather Report is sent free by post to any address in the United Kingdom on payment of £1 per annum, for postage and wrappers. Single copies 1d. at M.O. and at the bookstalls at certain Railway Termini in London.

Monday 31st May 1915

Gas Masks

"Not to worry old girl, our boys will not have suffered through your endeavours. At the very worst your labours were wasted. Chin up! Every effort put into the war is offered in good faith. That's what counts when the chips are down."

Edward is not able to reassure Emily who is haunted by visions of a young man, often her son William, gasping for air, pulling on his mask to avoid suffocation and consequently inhaling gas.

"Horror! Horror! Horror!" Emily rocks back and forth in her chair.

"If you ask me, it's the War Office laying it on a bit thick," says the Colonel. "New-fangled equipment indeed! Your gas masks will have enabled our brave boys to carry on the fight. Calm down madam, don't take on so."

"But where will it all end, Colonel Sewell, and how much can we endure? The Germans seem so far ahead with their inventions, with their knowledge of scientific things."

Colonel Sewell is deeply affected by her remarks. This line of thought is not what built the Empire. He searches in his memory for words that will rally the flagging spirits of this kind and well-meaning lady. Of course, the added dangers to themselves in the form of airships and all the problems this brings weigh heavy on even the Colonel, military man though he is.

Neville Thursby, sitting nearby in an easy chair, concerns himself with thoughts of fighting for breath inside a wretched contraption like the ones Emily has made and despatched to the Front, breathing being a trial to him at the best of times these days. After some moments the words of a poem he learnt some years ago, so taken with it was he at the time, come back to his mind. He recites them as accurately as he can, captivating both Emily and Edward as they sit around the fire that Lillie has found necessary to light, with the drop in temperature today.

"If you think you are beaten, you are
If you think you dare not, you don't
If you like to win, but you think you can't
It is almost certain you won't.
If you think you'll lose, you've lost
For out of the world we find
Success begins with a fellow's will
It's all in the state of the mind.
If you think you are outclassed, you are
You've got to think high to rise,
You've got to be sure of yourself before
You can ever win a prize.
Life's battles don't always go
To the stronger or faster man
But sooner or later the man who wins
Is the man who thinks he can!" [1]

Emily is delighted with this. She is also taken aback that Neville should even have read a poem, let alone memorised one and recited it to her on this otherwise dull and despondent morning in May.

She, herself, is deeply fond of poetry and has dabbled a bit in the past with her own, but since the death of her son, William, hasn't felt inspired to write; strange really - she thought such deep sorrow would unleash untold emotions that could be spilled out through the pen. But no. Nothing. A Strange Paralysis. And still those beautiful hands, wandering up and down the keys then flying off in all directions. Emily shudders at the vision. She reaches for her bag, placed neatly under her chair, opens it and pulls out a brand new copy of a book of poems by Ella Wheeler Wilcox. She opens the book where she has previously placed a bookmark. Now seems a perfect opportunity to share something she would otherwise have kept to herself. Quite unexpected that Neville should evoke such a situation. Nothing ever is as we expect, thinks Emily. She takes a deep breath.

> *There are ghosts in the room.*
> *As I sit here alone, from the dark corners there*
> *They come out of the gloom,*
> *And they stand at my side and they lean on my chair.*
>
> *There's the ghost of a Hope*
> *That lighted my days with a fanciful glow.*
> *In her hand is the rope*
> *That strangled her life out. Hope was slain long ago.*
>
> *But her ghost comes to-night,*
> *With its skeleton face and expressionless eyes,*
> *And it stands in the light,*
> *And mocks me, and jeers me with sobs and with sighs.*
>
> *There's the ghost of a Joy,*
> *A frail, fragile thing, and I prized it too much,*
> *And the hands that destroy*
> *Clasped it close, and it died at the withering touch.*

There's the ghost of a Love,
Born with joy, reared with hope, died in pain and unrest,
But he towers above
All the others... this ghost: yet a ghost at the best.

I am weary, and fain
Would forget all these dead: but the gibbering host
Make my struggle in vain,
In each shadowy corner there lurketh a ghost.

The three friends huddle together, not physically but at a deep, psychological level.

"This poem was written six and forty years since, in 1869, and yet you would think it was written for the four of us" says Emily, now contemplating its meaning. Colonel Sewell has never read any poetry; he has been brought up to consider poems very much part of a woman's world. He has been busy 'doing' in his life. It is only now, in the luxury of this room, that he sees the rich world of thinking.

The doorbell rings and Lillie leads Hampstead, Mary and Cumberland into the room, guiding Hampstead to his usual place by the window seat. Mary and Cumberland settle into the cushioned window seat itself, taking what they can from the sun's rays that are mostly obscured by gathering storm clouds. Hampstead enjoys the warmth of the sun on his face and Mary, noticing his ease and contentment in this position, picks up Cumberland, places him on Hampstead's lap and moves to where Mrs Dennis is pouring tea at the dining table.

"Mrs Dennis, I feel compelled to share with you a distressing story I read this morning. It is from a newspaper left at St Dunstan's by one of the visitors."

She hands the Halifax Evening Mail dated 11th May to Mrs

Dennis who sits and digests the information from the article Mary has circled with cartridge pen, making a quavering circle that bleeds into the paper.

"Alfred Clarke, 55, owns A. R. Clarke and Co. of Toronto, Ontario, Canada, which makes leather linings, vests, and moccasins. He is a British subject, married, and has a son and daughter. On the last voyage of the *Lusitania*, his ticket was 13105 and he stayed in cabin D-3. On the day of the disaster, Clarke 'was on the top deck about 2 o'clock on Friday afternoon when [he] suddenly heard a crash and splinters flew around.' He tried to get down to his D deck cabin, but couldn't at the time because of all the people coming up the stairs. He watched the crew ready the lifeboats and decided to try again for his lifejacket in his cabin. Clarke finally made it and he found it 'utterly dark'. When he closed the door, it was stuck due to the angle of the ship. He finally escaped and made it back on deck. He had failed to get a belt until a man gave him one on deck. Clarke encountered a tablemate from the dining saloon and encouraged him to get into one of the last lifeboats. The man refused and Clarke jumped into one of the boats. No sooner did he do that, the ship went down and he found himself in the water. He was picked up by a collapsible that was helmed by Charles Lauriat which came to pick up the thirty-three on the raft."

Mrs Dennis does not pass comment. The two ladies absorb the horror of it. They do not attempt to converse; they sit, and they wait until the moment is right again for discourse.

Seeing Hampstead by the window as he enters the room, Dr Goldberg ventures over to talk pleasantries. He has not yet conversed one to one with the blind soldier, and has always felt ill at ease in his presence. Today, however, he is preoccupied with thoughts of the now absent Maud and he is glad of the chance to sit by someone who cannot read his every thought in his facial expressions. It is becoming harder for Dr Goldberg to conceal his thoughts, and he gambles that Hampstead is a pretty sure bet today. No sooner has he sat down and offered his greetings than Hampstead asks him what is troubling him today! Dr Goldberg is taken aback, almost affronted. He calculates, however, that the best line to take is one of complete openness; if an unsighted man can gather one's mood simply by a 'hello' then there is no point in hiding anything. So Dr Goldberg opens the canals of his heart bit by bit over the course of an hour, getting closer to the centre of the problem than he himself has ever done previously. Much as he loves Maud, and she him, there are too many obstacles, two worlds too far apart. Here at the Mansions it works well; but in public places there are people in every corner and crevice whom Dr Goldberg knows as friends, acquaintances or patients, and people are starting to talk.

"I must marry a good Jewish girl. There is no other option for me. Maud knows this. I know this. So where are we to go from here?" Dr Goldberg pauses.

"My work places such demands on my energy and time I have little left for Maudy; only our time here on Mondays." He does not mention Thursdays at the Regents Palace.

Hampstead listens as Dr Goldberg explains that Maud is now in Suffolk with her friend Freda. They have joined the Foraging Corps recently set up by the Military in a desperate attempt to harvest the hay needed for the troops and the horses at the Front.

"I have no idea how delicate women can be of any use in the fields - making tea for the agricultural labourers I expect."

Hampstead nods and visualises the scene in Suffolk. Ironically the vision in Hampstead's head is very much clearer than the one in Dr Goldberg's; the latter cannot see anything clearly with so much clattering about in his tired mind. Hampstead, on the other hand, sees only too clearly the young women breathing in the fresh air, enjoying the hard physical labour that their bodies will never have experienced before, freeing their minds from all the cares of the past ten months. He thinks back to his short time in the trenches, before the fatal shell that ended it all for him. He recollects the feeling in his taut muscles after hours of marching, the strength in his body after training when he was fit and healthy and full of youth's vigour. Before the water and the mud, the soggy socks in cold boots, the waiting, the cramp in his legs as he remained for hours in one unnatural position, waiting for the order to advance, waiting to go Over the Top. Before all this he felt invigorated, alive. He sees the girls cutting the grasses, forcing their muscles to make one more effort, flopping down at the end of the day, exhausted, spent, content. He sees it all in sharp focus, the liberation of lives that have been confined until now in folds of fabric and tight leather shoes, hair now flying in the wind that was once pinned and tamed, fingernails black with dirt that were once polished and useless. The blind Hampstead sees what the sighted Hampstead would never have glimpsed; darkness allows him access to a clearer light than ever before. He sees it with a clarity of vision that is not available to Dr Goldberg. He understands Restriction and Freedom, Inactivity and Physical Fitness, Life and Death.

"I feel certain the ladies will be invaluable in providing refreshment for the men." he assures Dr Goldberg.

~

After leaving the Mansions, Neville Thursby and Colonel Sewell made their way across Nutford Place to St Luke's. The two men felt a shared desire to round off the day with a prayer and a lighting of candles for their dead sons. They entered the church through the left side door and walked slowly and deliberately down the side aisle toward the votives. Several half-burnt candles flickered and glowed in the twilight of the side altar. The two friends fumbled for matches in their waistcoat pockets, struck these simultaneously and lighted their respective wicks. As they did so a stirring was heard at the other side altar, behind the pillar adjacent to the pulpit. Both men looked in the direction of the movement, but there was nothing and no one to be seen. As they averted their eyes to the lighted candles, a shadow passed across the main altar as Reverend Alford tiptoed into the sacristy to the right of the church. He lingered in the doorway of the sacristy just long enough to observe whether the two elderly gentlemen, from the house across the road, dropped their pennies into the collection box in payment for their candles. The two friends made their payment and Reverend Alford noticed that the dropping of their coins fell lightly. With a sense of satisfaction he closed the sacristy door with a gentle push, making a mental note to change the sign reading 'one penny' for one with a higher currency. Redistribution. Robin Hood. Reverend Alford.

—

The shadows lengthened into evening. The hay-makers crowded around the woman lying prostrate at the foot of the pile. Freda felt for a pulse and was relieved when Maud opened her eyes, winked and then winced at the pain in her ankle. What an infernal fool she must look! Fancy losing her footing like that! It was all due to the long hours they had been enduring for a whole week now. Freda was used to it, having worked for three months as a nurse at the Pavilion. Long hours and heavy work were things to which Freda was now accustomed.

"You'll have to go home, old girl" said Freda soothingly. "I'll go with you. Don't worry. You won't be alone."

Frances watched, tea tray in hand, with a mixture of horror and disappointment. At least it was just a damaged ankle. But how was she to discover what her husband was doing at the home of the mysterious Mrs Dennis now that Freda's friend was leaving?

So far she had gathered that it was a meeting place for a collection of people who had nothing in common but this wretched war (and who doesn't have that?) and the Daily Telegraph! Lost souls. Oddities. Yet this Maud girl seemed quite charming and was clearly a good friend to her daughter. If only Freda had been to the house she could pick her brains on the matter, but her daughter seemed to know nothing of the set-up there. Now this accident was putting the kaibosh on her investigations. How vexing!

"Frances Moresby," she said to herself, "you are not a woman to be beaten," and with this she resolved to accompany her daughter and Maud back to London and to see for herself exactly what was taking place at 31, Cumberland-mansions, W.

Footnote:

1. 'Thinking' by Walter D Wintle

Friday 4th June 1915

The Lady, the Reverend and the Maid

Frances Moresby approached the Mansions from Brown Street. The chill in the air on this morning in early June was quite unexpected and Frances shivered as she stopped outside 31, Cumberland-mansions, W. Thoughts of her first attempted visit filled her anxious mind; on that occasion she had taken a detour to St Luke's across the road. The pull of the Church on that occasion had taken her unawares. Today a detour seemed appealing as Frances wasn't sure if she wanted to knock on the door and enter this unknown world. If she did so there would be no going back. With this in mind she passed by the steps for a second time and headed across Nutford Place toward the church.

The doors of the church were closed, and when Frances took hold of the large, iron handle she was unable to turn it. She walked to the right and tried the smaller door, again with no success. She turned to walk back into Nutford Place and caught sight of a robed man complete with black hat coming from the right wing of the church. She surmised that this was the Vicar and that he was leaving the priory. What fortuitous timing. She marched up to the Vicar with determination and smiles.

"Good morning Reverend, may I introduce myself? Mrs Edward Moresby, wife of the District Judge of Hastings." She extended a gloved hand. The Reverend was in no mood for social niceties - did not these people have anything better to do? He quickly remembered, however, the opportunities for wealth redistribution and hurriedly responded.

"Good morning Mrs Moresby. Do come in and tell me how I can be of assistance to you."

"Father," said Frances, still unable to shake off her early upbringing with her Roman Catholic governess, "I was hoping I could light a candle and offer a prayer for my son, Teddy, who was killed in action at the beginning of the war." After some hesitation she added, "He would have reached his twentieth year today." Frances looked directly at the Reverend, hoping to find some answers to the questions that still whirred in her head, or maybe some words of consolation. Reverend Alford stared back, expectantly. Each was seeking something from the other, and so they were both left wanting.

"My Dear Lady, I am on my way to administer to the poor and needy in my parish. You are welcome to stay. I only ask that you close the door behind you when you leave. You will find the collection box at the back of the church. Good day, madam," and with a tip of his hat he made to leave, pausing to reassure himself that Mrs Moresby was satisfied.

Frances hadn't been expecting to be left to her own devices, alone in a dark, cold church. This was not at all what she had in mind when introducing herself to this Pillar of the Community. However, Reverend Alford didn't leave room for any flexibility in this arrangement and Frances assured him that she would secure the door on her departure.

She turned to enter the church but of a sudden, on a whim, glanced back to the Reverend and asked him if he knew the lady who lived at number thirty-one across the road. She tilted her head in the direction of the window of the mansions that faced onto Nutford Place, the window where Mary had sat with Cumberland only last Monday. A dark cloud passed over Reverend Alford's face. Another of the merry band, how many of them were there? Although this one seemed to be an outsider, like himself. He calculated that Frances Moresby, judge's wife, woman of means, could be very useful to him. He told Frances that the lady across the road was Mrs Dennis, who occasionally attended his religious services, and her cronies met on Mondays, as far as he was aware. He did not, of course, use the term cronies to Frances, but this was the word he had in mind.

"A delightful meeting house, fine people, most welcoming" he told her, which only whetted Frances' appetite and left her more frustrated than before. With that, Reverend Alford turned on his heel and disappeared out of sight down Nutford Place.

Frances made her way down the nave of the church. Her eyes were attracted by the flickering candles on the left side altar and she walked toward them. She noticed that, propped up to the side of the votive candles was a board on which were written the names of people for whom candles had been lit. The most recent names were Audley Delves Thursby and Sidney Davies Sewell. She read at the top of the board "mortuus ita ut possimus vivere". The writing was immaculate, beautifully scripted; someone had taken trouble over this. Frances wondered who this might be. It seemed unlikely to her that it would be Reverend Alford; something about the man made her feel this would be considered a waste of time; she also wondered if the said Reverend would be quite this conversant in Latin. Frances made a mental note to ask Edward to translate this for her and she searched in her handbag for diary and pen so she could copy exactly what was written on the board.

Placing the diary and pen back into her bag, epitaph carefully written in the space for today's date, she thought of her own son, Teddy, dead since September last. So many bridges crossed since that time, early in the war. Perhaps she would light a candle for her son. Her hands trembled as she selected a votive, straightened out the wick and lit from the flame of another burning candle. She placed the votive in its iron holder and stepped back to survey the light she had placed to the memory of her only son. The whole experience, from reading the epitaph on the board to lighting her candle, had taken such a toll that Frances dropped to her knees on the kneeler in front of the candle display, put her head in her hands, and wept.

This was only the second time that Frances had shed a tear for her son. For six months the pain had been too intense for her to acknowledge, and life had had to be resumed. She had busied herself in war work: making teas at the soldier's canteen at Victoria station; reading to soldiers in the London Hospital and then St Dunstan's; knitting scarves and gloves and balaclavas; and most recently providing refreshments for the hay-makers in Suffolk. Work, work, work. It had been of great solace to her, keeping her going, allowing her to avoid the inevitable Truth - that she would never see her first born and only son ever again. The burial had taken place, the coffin lid screwed down as appropriate to a man of the officer class. Frances slowly lifted her head and fixed her eyes on the candle in front of her, the last remnant of the memory of her son. As she did so, a gentle voice asked, "Is there anything I can do for you madam; you don't look right; would you like my hanky madam? You look so sad, if you don't mind my saying."

Frances turned her head, startled at the presence of this young girl and ashamed at being seen at such an undignified moment. She looked at the girl, whom she observed to be from the servant class, and at this realisation Frances sat upright and erect.

"Oh I am perfectly well... thank you...I was merely taken by a sudden queerness."

Frances gathered her bag and gloves. "I am completely recovered now." She rose to her feet to make her way from the oppressive environment of St Luke's. As she stood she was overcome again, and folded to the floor.

"Here madam, let me help you to a seat." The servant girl helped Frances to the nearest pew. "Do you live nearby madam? Is there someone I can take word to so they can come for you?" Frances explained that she did not live nearby but was in the neighbourhood to see a friend across the road at Cumberland Mansions. "That's a funny thing - I work at number thirty-one. Maybe I know your friend."

"Number thirty-one? You work for Mrs Dennis?"

Lillie introduced herself to Frances Moresby and it was agreed that Lillie take her across the road to where Mrs Dennis was due to be woken from her afternoon nap. Frances suggested they wait a few minutes while she recovered herself, and so the two women from different worlds conversed together, telling one another of their lives and their hopes and their struggles in a way that would not have been thinkable six months previously. It was not lost on Frances that the death of her son in this wretched war had brought her to this place with this servant girl on this day, seeking out the secret Other Life of her husband.

"I've come here today to pray for the safe return of my big brother. He always writes regular, then his letters stopped - a fortnight since. I'm beside myself with worry I am."

Lillie saw the lady's concerned look.

"Don't get me wrong madam, Mrs Dennis is very kind: gives me time off everyday to come here and pray for him. Sometimes she even gives me a penny to light a candle. Nice lady. Lost her only son in the war."

"Her only son? I, too, lost my first-born and only son."

"Oh I am sorry Madam. How rude of me to rabbit on like this."

"No, not at all. We have all lost loved ones."

"Mrs Dennis is left all alone, except for me. That's why her friends are so important to her. They visit every Monday - oh, I must stop. Mrs Dennis wouldn't like me talking about her household like this."

"She has her husband for comfort of course?"

"It's very sad Madam. Her husband was a soldier abroad somewhere, and he died some years ago. Yes, Mrs Dennis is all alone in the world. Well she was."

Lillie trails off and retreats into thought.

No husband indeed! What was Edward really doing there each Monday?

Lillie roused herself and continued to tell Frances of her life. She liked to work for Mrs Dennis because of her kindness; "Treats me like a helper really, not a servant, very kind lady," but Lillie's lot had not been a happy one before she took up her position with Mrs Dennis. Before this she had lived with her drunken father and her downtrodden mother, with three younger sisters and her one brother who was now away in France, fighting for King and Country. Now they had changed the enlistment age to forty her mum wanted her father to go.

"He's forty, you see madam, just about young enough. If he goes my mum will get separation allowance for all the family which would be a whole lot more than my dad earns, and he wouldn't be home to drink it all away before Mum sees a penny. But Dad don't want to go; says he's too old!"

Lillie stopped and looked around the Church, wondering if there were ears listening to her every word. She turned to Frances and, seeing the concerned look in her eyes, decided to continue.

"My brother is out there doing his bit. If it's good enough for him it should be good enough for my dad."

She went on to explain that she was glad to be away from home, living at Mrs Dennis' with a small room at the top of the house, spending her days in the basement, cooking, except when she was cleaning the house upstairs. What concerned her however was that, with only her and Mrs Dennis in the house it was a very quiet life for a young girl. How was she to meet a beau if she was always stuck in the house with an older lady?

"Not that I'm not grateful you understand, but it's no life for a young girl. Still, much better than being at home with the others in all that cold and damp and noise: arguing, fighting, punching, gawd knows what."

She was very grateful to Mrs Dennis. It was just the way things were. And with all the young men away at the Front, all the ones worth knowing at any rate, she was best where she was, not missing anything really. Mrs Dennis always gave her two half-days, Wednesday and Sunday afternoons, and on these days Lillie could visit home, or go for walks, or meet her friends from younger days in the park, walking and eyeing the boys who were still here. Not so bad really.

Frances listened with genuine interest. All the young men away at the Front. Frances had never looked on it from a young woman's perspective. Maybe this was why her own daughter, Freda, was gadding about the country with no heed to tomorrow, no thoughts of finding an eligible man to marry - would there be any left at the end of it all? Of course, it all had to be put on hold for the duration of the war. And what then? Surely Freda would be so used to pleasing herself, going hither and thither on a whim, that settling down to a normal, respectable life would be very difficult. Frances had never looked at things this way before, and she was only woken from this train of thought by Lillie. "Of course, Mondays make it all worthwhile at the house. We all look forward to Mondays, me, Mrs Dennis, Wuffy."

At the sound of 'Mondays' Frances sat up with a jolt. This was the day of the meetings. This was the day the Reverend Alford had talked about. This was the day Edward was always absent from home regardless of commitments, regardless of her, his wife. Although Frances was now getting close to discovering the Other World of her husband she felt an unease, a sense of things being out of place. She hadn't been expecting such a feeling, and Frances was a woman who always took stock when unexpected feelings came into play. One could not maintain an ordered existence if one went about doing reckless things, and if she felt uncomfortable then this must be a warning sign that she wasn't to continue on this path. Perhaps she had discovered enough for today. Meeting Lillie had been a Godsend; now she knew where to find her at a similar time each day, and she knew Mrs Dennis was likely to be, on any day except a Monday, alone in the house at 31, Cumberland-mansions, W. One must allow everything its Time, and today was not the Time.

She thanked Lillie for her kindness and concern but she had decided to go home now, and to return on another day to see Mrs Dennis.

"I shall tell Mrs Dennis you called to see her. Who shall I say, madam?"

Frances was tempted to tell Lillie her name and her relationship to Judge Moresby, but thought better of it and suggested she say an old friend came to visit; she would surprise her another day.

The lady and the maid left the church together and walked

to the corner of Brown Street and Nutford Place where Frances carried on towards the Edgware Road to hail a hansom cab, and Lillie walked down the steps to the basement of the mansions.

Henry Nye

When Henry Nye arrived at 31, Cumberland-mansions, W., to enquire after his daughter Lillie he was surprised so see her walking to the corner of Brown Street and Nutford Place, so he decided to follow her. It wasn't Wednesday or Sunday, so why was she taking time off? Perhaps she was running an errand for the lady; that would be it. He would follow at a sensible distance and make his presence known at the right moment. He wasn't going home without her; she was needed at home and had no business living in this posh house with that posh lady; her place was with her mother and sisters, looking after their house and, most importantly, looking after Henry Nye.

As Lillie made her way towards the doors of St Luke's, Henry Nye was even more intrigued; his Lillie wasn't a church goer; Sunday school when she was a nipper, but that was all. Must be taking a message for the lady to the Reverend, that was it. Henry Nye decided to keep his distance and to wait around the corner where he could see when Lillie came out.

After ten minutes, Henry Nye grew impatient and decided to enter the church himself; after all, he was as likely to be in a church on a Friday afternoon as his daughter, so if the Reverend was there it would require explanations all round. At the front left of the church sat his daughter with an unknown lady - a real nob, dressed in finery. The lady and his daughter appeared to be talking. Just in front of them were the candles Henry knew people lit as a prayer; he never had understood why prayers cost money, but that was the way of this cruel world. At least the Reverend here at St Luke's was known for handing out alms from the money he collected from the toffs. That was some consolation. Henry stood completely still so that his daughter and her lady friend were not aware of his presence. So intent were they in their idle chit chat that it was easy to go unnoticed. Women! Never bleedin' stopped. Henry's heart stopped dead as both women stood and turned to make their way to the back of the church. He altered his position behind the pillar as they walked the length of the church and out through the doors at the back. He was sure they hadn't seen him, and with no other soul in the church he could begin to plan his exit without anyone seeing him. As he turned to go, from the corner of his eye he caught a glint of something bright and, turning, his eyes settled on the chalice upon the altar block ready for the next eucharist. Henry had no intention of any wrong-doing but this was too much to resist, a gift, and solid gold too. Without another another thought, he deftly made his way to the altar and removed the chalice, tucked it under the breast of his jacket and made for the exit. Once out in the open he forgot the initial purpose of his visit and made his way home, on foot, as fast as he was able without causing notice to passers by.

Saturday 5th June 1915

The Chalice

Early on the following morning Reverend Alford pulled on his robes and prepared to say morning mass. It was a dreary affair with no congregation except for the ladies who arranged his flowers, and Reverend Alford looked forward to the end of the service so he could get on with the real work of the day. He opened the door of the sacristy, made for the steps of the altar, raised his eyes and looked squarely at the altar block. Something, anything, to break up the monotony of this part of his day was an old dream long forgotten. So when he saw that the altar block was bare he was thrown into spasms of disbelief followed by eager anticipation. The chalice was gone! Where could it be? Had he transferred it to the sacristy and forgotten? In an agitated yet excited state he turned and headed back to the sacristy but found no sign of the chalice there. He returned to the altar and, seeing that even the flower ladies had failed to turn up this morning and there were no parishioners for his service, he allowed himself time to consider.

After some moments the picture in his mind returned to the previous day when the lady calling herself Frances Moresby (from Hastings he seemed to recall) had spent time in his church, closing the door behind her as she left. It seemed somewhat unlikely that a lady such as herself would steal a chalice, but one never knew with these toffs, they often thought they were free to do just as they chose. Well, not in St Luke's, not while he was vicar here. He would make his way across the street and enquire of Mrs Dennis.

———

Henry Nye sat at his table staring at the chalice.

"I don't know what you was thinking Henry Nye, I really don't! Who's gonna take that off your hands, let alone pay you for it?"

"Stop going on you old cow. It was sitting there, shiny and all, how could I resist? It's not my fault, anyone would of done it. They shouldn't have these things lying around the place. It's more than a man can bear. Anyone would of done it. Now I'm stuck with the bloody thing."

"Well you'll have to take it back" said Elsie, his wife. "Take it now, Reverend Alford is visiting round here just now so the church'll be empty. Take it now Henry."

Henry realised he had no choice and so he tucked the chalice under his jacket and headed back to St Luke's. As he turned into Nutford Place he saw someone leaving the church and, anxious not to be seen, made a snap decision to go to number 31, Cumberland-mansions, W., and see his daughter. He would deliver the chalice to her and she could take it back at a time when the church was empty.

Sunday 6th June 1915

Claridge's

Mrs Dennis had decided to break one of her cardinal rules and to meet with one of her friends away from home and on a day other than Monday. She just wanted to make sure that she would not be upsetting Emily with her plans. She had arranged to meet Emily at Claridge's for eight in the evening to discuss her idea. They could then enjoy the after dinner entertainment together, two ladies, bereft of their boys and their husbands.

The restaurant at Claridge's was opulent but comfortable, full to capacity yet calm and serene. The staff worked fast and quietly; there was no clatter of cutlery and plates, voices were generally hushed. Just a gentle hubbub and the occasional popping of a cork. Mrs Dennis took her customary seat; not that she dined here often, but in the past she had, and the staff always made sure she was booked at the same table by the window where she had sat with her late husband John. They had named their only child after his father, expecting him to follow into the 6th Dragoon Guards, which of course he had done. And so now Mrs Dennis had lost them both. It had not occurred to her as a young woman that this would be the case; she had married well, set up home, wanted for nothing, and in twelve short years everything was gone. Then, as if by a miracle, Edward Moresby had come along to begin a new phase in her life, and here she was, in her old seat at Claridge's waiting for her friend Emily Peppiatt who had the shared horror of having lost her boy.

Of course Emily had two more sons, but she had lost William all the same. Mrs Dennis was not a woman to compete in the arena of emotion; grief was grief whichever way you looked at it, and life was full of it. No, Mrs Dennis understood that everyone needed to grieve in their own way, and that is why the Monday meetings were so important to her, and, she hoped, to all those who came.

Emily arrived on the stroke of eight, punctilious and polite as she had always been throughout her adult life. As a child she had been quite spoilt, given everything she wanted, fussed over and loved by all her family and servants. When she reached adulthood and married Mr Peppiatt it was natural to her to pass on what she had been given, and so she provided the same cosy, contented nest for her own children that she had enjoyed. Their house had been full of happy boys and music. How she missed the music! William had played his piano constantly from such a young age - six years old if she remembered correctly - and the other boys had followed suit. She and Mr Peppiatt had decided to send their boys to a local school, Bancroft's, rather than take the route of boarding school. This way the boys and their music had remained in the house. Now, with the boys grown up and living independently, and William gone, there was no more music in the house. Mr Peppiatt, also William, had requested that no music be played at the service for their son in Woodford Parish Church, and this had broken her heart still further.

As she greeted Mrs Dennis and sat down, she was drawn to the pianist in the corner of the restaurant, and the lilt of the keys as he played sent her off into a dream-like state. Mrs Dennis watched carefully to see if there was any hint of sadness in Emily's reaction. Much to her relief there was none. Emily looked serene, at home, happy. This made it so much easier to broach the subject that she had in mind.

"Emily, dear, I have been perusing the newspaper as you know I am wont to do, and I have come across an advertisement placed by a Mlle Guillain. She is one of the Belgian refugees and is a concert violinist. She is offering to play in people's homes, for a fee of course, and I wondered what you would think if I were to ask her to play at the mansions one Monday."

"Oh, do go on" replied Emily, fascinated at the prospect. With such an eager response Mrs Dennis was encouraged.

"I have spoken with her, Emily, and she can bring with her a friend who plays the oboe, and between them they would like to introduce our group at Cumberland Mansions to the extraordinary beauty of music by Frederick Delius."

"I've not heard of him. Where is he from, Mrs Dennis?"

"Frederick Delius is an Englishman who has lived in Paris for some years. He has had to return to England because of the war. What makes it so difficult for him is that his studies took place in Germany and, moreover, the first performances of his work were also undertaken over there. Before the war, you understand, but it plagues him nonetheless. People don't seem willing to look beyond this."

"This wretched war! One would expect a musical recital to be above such things, Mrs Dennis."

"Quite, my dear Emily. Mlle Guillain is very keen to play, 'On Hearing the First Cuckoo in Spring'. Mr Delius composed it three years ago, and it has hardly been heard in England at all. She tells me it is a haunting piece for violin and oboe. What do you think Emily? Will our friends be offended by the German connection? And what do you think of the instruments? Will they be appropriate for my morning room?"

Mrs Dennis went on to explain that she had been careful to avoid employing a pianist because she knew how painful that might be for Emily.

Emily was deeply touched that her friend would put all this thought into her plans in deference to her own feelings. To Emily, the thought of music in Cumberland Mansions was almost too exciting to bear; thank goodness she only had to wait until Monday week.

"Please, go ahead Mrs Dennis, it will be such a treat for us all. How kind. How thoughtful." And with this Emily Peppiatt shed a tear of gratitude.

Mrs Dennis was relieved and gratified. The two ladies finished their meal and awaited the hour of music and poetry to follow before they headed home. The following day they would introduce the idea of a musical soiree to their friends at the mansions and, if all were in agreement, it would go ahead on the following Monday.

Monday 7th June 1915

Perspectives

All the friends are gathered in the garden of 31, Cumberland-mansions, W. It is an unusually hot day and Mrs Dennis has been careful to set up the table and chairs in the shade of the Turkey Oak in the far corner by the high brick wall. She is being assisted by Edward, Dr Goldberg and Colonel Sewell because Lillie is out of sorts.

"Dr Goldberg, Lillie is not herself today; she has taken to her bed. I wonder if you would be so kind as to examine her, your knowledge of minor ailments will be far superior to my own. I am at a loss what to do with her." Mrs Dennis secretly suspects it may have something to do with the visit of her unpleasant father; whenever Henry Nye appears it usually means trouble. She hopes she is wrong and that Lillie simply has a cold.

"Why of course Mrs Dennis. Just say the word and I will tend to the matter."

She continues setting the table for her friends with the help of the three men; how unlike men it is to be so domestic and interested in making the garden as pleasant as possible for the gathering. The mansions really do bring out the best in everyone.

Hampstead sits nearer the house with Mary and Cumberland. He is deeply embarrassed at not being able to help in the setting up of things. Even the nuzzling of Cumberland cannot dissipate this feeling and he feels quite useless.

"Hampstead dear, there is such a beautiful white embroidered table cloth here - feel - there is green glass tableware, and forget-me-nots in a vase at the centre of the table, just delightful! Mrs Dennis always makes such an effort for us all." When Hampstead shows no signs of interest at all Mary suggests they walk around the garden and smell the flowers, "perhaps you can guess the flowers from their scent" and so Hampstead reluctantly hauls himself up from his chair and, with the aid of his stick, his wife, and his dog he undertakes a survey of the garden. He realises that Mary is doing her best and is pandering to his every need, and with the baby due within the next two months goodness knows he should be tending to her needs. The dejection that Hampstead feels with this realisation is mortifying. He doesn't know how long he will be able to keep up this pretence. The more Mary tries to make things better, the worse they seem to get. What is to be done? And still the screeching of shells every night, the moans and groans of his comrades and friends. The man he was only six months ago was buried in the trenches in France, never to return, and the idea of Mary knowing this is too much to bear, and so Hampstead braves another day of deception.

Mary longs for the return of the man she loved. With just a little more patience and a little more time she is sure he will return to her. Maybe when their child is born it will all be as it was. Deep down Mary knows this will not be, but she will never let Hampstead know this, it would be detrimental to his recovery. And so Mary guides her husband around the flowerbeds and finally to a chair at the table that has been set so beautifully by their friends.

Rose sits next to Mary, full to the brim with anxiety at the latest horror visited upon them by the beastly Germans.

"I simply cannot sleep at night darling, what with the zeppelins and that dreadful crow sound, roaring above me. I'm on tenterhooks, wondering what destruction may be imminent. To add to my worries Tom has enlisted, Toby's hardly writing at all, I'm alone with the children... it's all so wretched!" Rose leans her head on Mary's shoulder and sobs.

"And changing my name, darling, has just made things worse." She conveys her desperation to Mary more effectively than she knows. Mary listens to this waterfall of emotion and is quite spent at the end of it all, and her relief as Hampstead takes control of the situation is tangible. Her fine, handsome husband, suffering so much himself, but able to soothe the nerves of her friend Rose. "We are quite safe, Rose, because the Germans cannot get above central London so easily; there is nothing to fear. We must stick together and reassure one another in these troubled times. Have you smelt the petunias in Mrs Dennis' wonderful garden?" and with this Rose is placated and reassured.

Maud is careful to sit away from Dr Goldberg although they do acknowledge one another's presence: all in good time, thinks Maud, all will be well. Her heavily bandaged leg is concealed by her flowing skirts, but she is unable to disguise her limp, and Dr Goldberg's heart melts at the sight. Maud sits next to Edward and tells him all about her adventure in Suffolk ending in the fall from the haystack.

"Really Edward, I feel such a prune, falling like that, and in full view of everyone!"

They both chuckle at the absurdity of it, and Edward listens enthralled as Maud describes her friendship with the wonderful Freda who is so strong and robust in health, putting herself to shame. Freda has built up her stamina over three months working at the hospital in the Pavilion at Brighton, tending to the wounded Indian Sherpas; so brave, so useful, she makes Maud feel inadequate and useless.

"My dear Maud, how could you possibly be inadequate or useless? You bring a spark to any proceedings. Why, during your absence Dr Goldberg has appeared quite forlorn."

Maud blushes crimson at this revelation, and lowers her eyes to the lush lawn at her feet. Conversely, Edward sits next to her brimming with pride at the thought of his darling Freda. He is at the point of revealing to Maud the relationship between himself and her friend when Mrs Dennis calls everyone to attention so that she can make an announcement.

Mrs Dennis rings the small hand bell that she uses to call Lillie but on this occasion it is solely to gain the attention of her guests. There is a stillness among the companions in the garden, the only movement coming from the butterflies and bees fluttering from flower to flower, and the gentle rustle of the leaves in the trees above them. There is little breeze, and the day is hot and balmy. While the friends wait for Mrs Dennis' announcement, the ladies desist from the waving of fans to cool them. Aided by Emily, Mrs Dennis explains to the friends her plan for a musical recital next Monday.

"I have contacted a violinist - one of our Belgian refugees - Mlle Guillain. This talented lady has been giving recitals in London since the autumn, and she is offering her services to private houses. She seems just perfect for one of our gatherings. Mlle Guillain has offered to bring a young oboist with her; he is from a fine musical family and he is only eighteen years of age. They will play brand new music that none of us have heard before. What do we all think?"

There is a silence while the friends digest this information.

After some moments Edward asks,

"What kind of music can we expect, Mrs Dennis?"

"I am told it is gentle and soothing and quite beautiful. It is from an English composer by the name of Frederick Delius. Although his works were written and performed in Germany when he was studying there, I am assured he is utterly English and has, in fact, been living here since the outbreak of war."

A silence envelops the garden. Thoughts of zeppelins, trenches, mud, piano fingers, screwed down lids, glowing cigarettes, teeth, whining horses, explosions, cellar steps, ships and bandages mingle in the air on this calm, warm morning. Amid the chaos and despair Wuffy chases a stray butterfly and Cumberland sniffs the air. The stillness of Mrs Dennis' guests mutes the underlying distress.

After some moments there is a general murmur of approval and it is agreed that the musical soiree should go ahead. Dr Goldberg is thoughtful. "May I request a popular tune or two following the recital, perhaps some new music from America that friends and family have sent by the American mail service. One I am particularly keen to hear is by a composer by the name of Kern, Jerome I believe, entitled, 'They Didn't Believe Me'. It's a love song and my friends tell me it's very stirring." Love song, thinks Colonel Sewell. That won't help save the Empire! These young flunkies! Why wasn't Dr Goldberg out serving King and Country? Love song indeed! But he keeps these thoughts to himself for the sake of the day and for the sake of Mrs Dennis whom he holds in high esteem.

Emily, who is sitting with Neville Thursby, is inspired. "It would be such an honour if I could have my favourite song played - you all will know Ivor Novello's rousing 'Keep The Home Fires Burning'." Even Colonel Sewell can think of no problem with this. So it is decided that the recital of Delius' work will be followed by these two popular songs and Rose boldly suggests they may all want to join in singing the Ivor Novello. Mrs Dennis is gratified and relieved that her guests are behind her in this endeavour, and she pours lime cordial, spooning the ice from a metal bowl, taking it around to her guests on her wicker tray.

Emily and Neville sit with their eyes closed and their faces to the sun. They converse in this way, at ease with the unconventional pose they both assume, a position neither would consider in any other social setting. Emily gathers her thoughts and sits upright once more as is becoming of a lady. She allows Neville the luxury of not knowing he is alone, now, in sunning himself. His breathing is still laboured and even exacerbated by the pollen in the garden today, but his cough is much improved, and although he is very thin he has an inner strength about him that Emily has not observed before.

There is a ring on the doorbell and Mrs Dennis is pleased when Edward makes to answer; so inconvenient having Lillie indisposed! Edward returns some moments later with an irate-looking Reverend Alford in tow. Before Edward is able to formally introduce him Reverend Alford addresses the gathering as a whole.

"I must see that maid of yours. Bring her to me."

"Why, Reverend Alford. How kind of you to visit us on this heavenly morning," responds Mrs Dennis, which quite takes the wind from the Reverend's sails.

"Mrs Dennis, my Dear Lady, I must see your maid. I assure you it is of the utmost urgency."

"Lillie is feeling under the weather today and cannot be disturbed Reverend Alford. Perhaps I can be of assistance?"

"Guilty conscience. Hiding something. The chalice has been taken from the church. I saw your maid with a lady by the name of Mrs Moresby in the church only yesterday. I demand to see the maid and question her."

Edward is aghast. Frances. Here. In St Luke's. Freda making hay with Maud. A stolen chalice. The whole equilibrium of his day is disturbed. The entire company is on tenterhooks. Then, to everyone's surprise, Colonel Sewell takes control.

"Reverend Alford, our hostess has explained that the maid is unwell and cannot be disturbed. We are all guests in this kind lady's home and I would remind you to mind your manners. We are, of course, concerned about a theft from your church but we cannot tolerate this intrusion. Perhaps you should be asking your Mrs Moresby about the whereabouts of your chalice."

At this point Edward can see no option but to explain his relationship to Mrs Moresby. He opens his mouth to begin his explanation but is beaten to it by Emily. "Reverend Alford, would you like to sit and partake of some lime cordial with us?" The Reverend is faced with a dilemma: if he accepts the invitation to join the happy throng he will lose face; if he leaves the house he will be no nearer to finding the missing chalice; he has no means of finding Mrs Frances Moresby as he has no idea who she is.

"A cup of tea would be welcome," he tells Emily Peppiatt, thus accepting the situation on his own terms and not losing face entirely. With resignation, carefully concealed by an outward show of decisiveness, Reverend Alford takes a seat and calculates his next move. To his consternation and bewilderment the conversation continues in the garden as if he had not arrived and his revelation had not been made. The talk is of a musical recital planned for next week. Are these people mad? Have they not heard his pronouncement of this heinous crime perpetrated in his own church? Do they not have any social conscience at all? Looking around him, Reverend Alford observes that all these people, without exception, are well dressed, well educated - at least as far as one would expect of the women - and rather genteel. They appear to pose no threat to society; in fact these are the people who keep society moving along. Yet not one of them seems remotely interested or concerned about the loss of his chalice. They would all be aware of the eighth commandment; and yet this total indifference. He can only conclude that they are hiding Lillie and planning a way to save her from the Hand of the Law. But how could this be when one of them is a District Judge? And still they drone on about their musical recital and Home Fires and Oboes.

Having made the decision to sit and partake of a drink it seems churlish to the Reverend to refuse luncheon, and so the day wears on, the talk continues, the dogs chase the butterflies. Mrs Dennis explains to the Reverend how this all began, the arrival one morning, unannounced, of Judge Edward Moresby of Hastings, the gathering of the friends, one by one, and the solace it has brought to all their lives. For a second time Reverend Alford is left wondering at the difference between the atmosphere here and that in his church across the road. So absorbed in these thoughts is he that he does not pick up on the mention of Judge Moresby of Hastings. When he finally leaves, quite late in the day, all thoughts of his chalice are long forgotten.

Monday 14th June 1915

The Recital

Isa is the first to arrive today and his hosts are taken aback to see him accompanied by his daughter, Blanch, of whom they have heard so much.

"Welcome to our meeting." Edward is tempted to correct himself as 'meeting' has a rather formal tone, but he is beaten to it by Blanch.

"Judge Moresby, delighted." She extends her hand. "Abba has told me all about his friends; I feel at home already." Edward notices that Blanch looks older than her years with sunken, dark eyes and rather thin in appearance; this blasted war, taking away Youth in so many ways. Thankfully Isa does not appear to be perturbed in any way with the appearance of his daughter, and his delight in her company consoles Edward as he thinks of his son, Teddy, who would have been approximately Blanch's age if he had survived. Life goes on, the world continues in its weary way, and the sight of a father and daughter reunited, even if only for a short time, is enough to lift Edward's spirits and bring a sense of Hope. Edward watches as Isa steers his daughter in the direction of Rose.

Dr Goldberg arrives, somewhat subdued and keen to sit alone with his thoughts. He takes a seat by the fireplace, unlit today, and opens his paper. The latest news is troubling him, and he is content to sit like this for some time perusing the paper, quite uninterrupted by the others. He reads at length before folding his paper and lighting his pipe. Six days ago now, but still the after effects, such shock, especially the patients at his practice, frightened to make the journey, cowering in their homes. So much business lost. And then the ongoing German problem.

Mrs Dennis observes Dr Goldberg and feels he will survive the difficulties of these turbulent times; he is young and self-assured; it will take its toll but he will live a full life. Mrs Dennis has, however, thoughtfully kept away from her piano in the mansions in deference to dear Emily who struggles so with the loss of William and his beautiful playing. She hopes that the violin will not upset her friend and intends that it will bring much joy to her guests this afternoon. She arranges the room with Lillie and Edward so that a corner is clear by the far window to the left of the fireplace.

"Edward dear, would you move this chair and small table into the space for the musicians and leave room for two music stands please." Edward obliges, and neither mention Lillie and her troubled demeanour.

Mlle Guillain arrives at the appointed time of two o'clock and Lillie introduces both her and a young man of eighteen years by the name of Leon Goossens. The latter has with him a case which contains an oboe; he unpacks this and sets up his music on a stand. He and Mlle Guillain request that they retire to another room to warm up. As they leave, led by Lillie along the corridor to a small room at the back of the house, the assembled group are bubbling with anticipation. Isa takes his daughter by the arm and leads her to the armchairs set out before the performance area. Blanch excuses herself with a knowing smile to Rose.

"This young boy, he will bring music to our morning. Blanch, we bring joy to our world for just a short time. Come. Sit. We drink in this jewel brought to us by Mrs Dennis."

"Such an unusual instrument, Mrs Dennis" says Emily, "I can't quite remember hearing one before."

"The young boy, as you refer to him Mr Harburg, is a very talented young man from a famous musical family, and Mlle Guillain is very keen that he is heard by as many people as possible."

All the visitors notice he is of military age, a similar age to their own sons, now gone, but not one of them speaks of this. There is a general feeling, nonetheless, that this is not quite as it should be.

The musicians return to the room, walk to their music stands and announce that they will be playing a piece by Delius entitled 'On Hearing the First Cuckoo in Spring.' Isa Harburg, Neville Thursby and Maud Burt-Marshall are somewhat uncomfortable with the knowledge that the composer of the piece they are about to hear, although an Englishman, first came to prominence in Germany and, to make matters worse, undertook his training on enemy soil. However, for the sake of their fellow guests they all remain silent.

The music begins. The solo violinist sounds somewhat lonely playing this lilting and simple melody, but when the oboe begins the sound of a cuckoo fills the room and all the guests close their eyes and are transported to their different places of comfort and repose. In all their thoughts an early morning sun rises to hail a New Day, a new beginning, a distancing from the past ten months, an enormous sense of relief.

At the end of the piece, with every eye opened and the dawning of the real day, the assembled group sit back, exhausted and spent. The intrusion of sound into their otherwise peaceful room is almost too much to bear. The silence, in contrast, leaves a vacuum that no one feels equal to filling. And so they sit, and recuperate, and ponder, while Mlle Guillain and Leon stand, uncomfortably, waiting for a reaction - any reaction. The silence is finally broken when Dr Goldberg suggests his tune by Jerome Kern.

"I've heard it sung by Walter Van Brunt and Gladys Rice - a fine fist they made of it. Grand."

Mrs Dennis has never heard a gramophone recording of anything and she is eager to hear this song herself. Dr Goldberg produces the sheet music and is closely followed by Emily who has the music to 'Keep the Home Fires Burning'.

"Perhaps we could all sing along with this one?" she asks tentatively, looking around the room for approval. The entire group smile and acknowledge this as a good idea.

The musicians decide, in an unspoken agreement, to move straight onto the first melody requested by Dr Goldberg. They do this without any announcement or indeed any words at all.

Mlle Guillain begins the soothing and restful lilt of Jerome Kern's melody which brings a sense of balance to the room, and soon Emily Peppiatt is swaying to the lilt of the tune, and Neville Thursby's breathing is less laboured. The faces around the room take on a less troubled look, and Wuffy reappears from the refuge he has sort behind the chaise longue and springs onto Isa's lap. Blanch, sitting beside Isa, is deeply touched by the bond evident between these two, her father never having shown interest in dogs or any animals before.

The musicians move with minimal pause to the second melody. Emily immediately hums along, then quietly sings, and is joined by all the women in the group in a soft and thoughtful way. By the end even Edward and Neville are singing, somewhat shyly at first, but with increasing confidence.

When the home fires have burned out Mlle Guillain and the oboist sit back and place their instruments at their feet. Mrs

Dennis and Edward distribute refreshments. The entertainers and the friends sit companionably enough, eating, drinking, resting. The customary silences at 31, Cumberland-mansions, W., are not, however, quite as comfortable for the two visitors as they are for the friends of Mrs Dennis, and after their tea and sandwiches the musicians pack away and take their leave.

Blanch has retreated to an armchair by the fireplace. She stares into the empty grate, attempting to rid her mind of duckboards and poles and human excrement. Isa looks towards his daughter from the far end of the room and watches her shudder. His instinct is to move across the room and to hold her in his arms, but a deeper instinct takes hold and prevents him from doing so. Meanwhile, Blanch watches as the soldier slips from the pole, trousers at his ankles, lets out a groan of inhuman proportions and disappears into the filth below. How else were they to relieve themselves with all the thousands of men in the nearby trenches? It had been makeshift and temporary. No one had expected an accident such as this. Blanch understands that the vision of this will remain with her always; as a spoken word once given cannot be taken back, so it is with this. Irreversible. The important thing is not to speak of it; to keep it in the mind. This way no one else will carry the burden and she will be free of that guilt at least. Furthermore, if it isn't put into words, it doesn't seem quite so appalling. She at least can live with the vision this way. At any rate, she has a chance.

The Awful Silence that Maud has felt since the disappearance of her brother hangs heavy in the air. If she tells the others he is gone, finished, then she will be able to get on with her life. To live. Telling them would make it real, irrevocable. Maud ponders on this, and the air in Mrs Dennis' room hangs heavy with thought.

Tuesday 15th June 1915

Decisions

L illie wakes early on this fine summer's morning with a plan and a purpose. She drags herself out of bed, pours some cold water from the jug on the dresser into the matching bowl, splashes her face and dabs it dry as best she can with the damp cloth hanging at the end of her bed. With a great deal of effort she pulls on her stockings, ties her petticoat, climbs into her dress reaching behind to fasten the buttons all down her back, adjusts the frilly collar, and finally adds the apron to cover her skirts in case of splashes from the many tasks ahead of her this morning.

She creeps down the stairs so as not to disturb Mrs Dennis at this early hour. Entering the back parlour she begins to lay the breakfast table remembering a second place for Judge Moresby just in case he has stayed over. She then makes her way to the scullery to light the range. Thoughts of the day ahead fill her mind and it is all she can do to get through the morning.

At midday, with Mrs Dennis preferring a late luncheon, Lillie is given time to visit St Luke's for her daily prayer imploring the return of her brother. She opens the door of the basement of 31, Cumberland-mansions, W., pulls it to behind her, and sets off across the road to the church.

⁓

Although the day was warm Lillie wore a heavy winter coat, the only one she possessed, which reached down to her ankles and looked somewhat out of place amongst her fellow pedestrians in their summer fashions. However, as a member of the servant class this went unnoticed by the people who passed her by so she was able to cross over Nutford Place to St Luke's without any interruption or delay.

She entered the church and stopped at the very back pew nearest the entrance. Here she caught her breath and prepared herself for the next hurdle in this already anxious day. She carefully opened the top buttons of her heavy coat, extricated a bundle from underneath, and wearily struggled to her feet beginning her journey to the altar at the front of the church. As she did so, a shadow moved along the far side of the church, starting at the front and moving in the same direction. Lillie stopped, rooted to the spot and on instinct swiftly bent down and placed the bundle under the pew nearest to where she was standing. With one more easy movement she turned to leave the church.

"Young lady. May I be of any assistance?"

"Oh, oh, oh no, sir, Reverend, I was just leaving. Been saying my prayers for my missing brother that's all. Must get back to Mrs Dennis."

"Missing eh?" Reverend Alford mulled this over. "I will remember your brother in my next mass. What is his name?"

"Jed, sir - er, Reverend."

Lillie had to muster all her willpower not to cast a glance back to where the bundle was jutting out from under the pew.

"Jed. Hmm. Unusual name."

"Jedidiah. It was me granddad's name. We called him Jed for short."

Reverend Alford had no time to be discussing family names.

"Very well girl, off you go! Mustn't keep the Mistress waiting."

Reverend Alford walked across the back of the church and down the side aisle to the sacristy. Frances Moresby sat transfixed by the whole episode that had played out before her. In her customary pew towards the rear of the church, but away from the entrance, her presence went unnoticed by the convenient positioning of a pillar. She had been able to observe both Lillie and Reverend Alford without either one being aware of her. She collected her thoughts and assessed the situation. From the maid's position the bundle needed careful handling and on no account should it be revealed to the Reverend. From the Reverend's angle the bundle could be a valuable discovery. She had to make a decision: was she to assist the Maid or the Reverend?

As she adjusted her position in the pew, Frances noticed, as she had not done before, that every movement was magnified, every sound amplified. The large open space created by the height of the roof seemed to bring giant proportions to every human movement and this caused Frances to feel exposed. A sense of oppression came over her quite unlike anything she had felt before and she experienced an overwhelming urge to leave this place and to rid herself of this feeling.

Making sure Reverend Alford was safely behind his sacristy door, Frances slowly and deliberately tiptoed over to the bundle at the other end of the rear pew, carefully extricated it from under the seat, steadily but determinedly walked to the altar, unwrapped the chalice and placed it back in its rightful place. She then turned and stepped calmly down the altar steps, walked directly and smartly down the centre aisle of the church and out through the doors of St Luke's.

As Mrs Frances Moresby walked into the open air a gust of

wind caught in her nostrils and filled her with relief and energy. The oppression she had felt inside the church lifted and she strode with renewed vigour along Nutford Place, past 31, Cumberland-mansions, W., and down Brown Street towards the Edgware Road. She did not hesitate and she did not look back.

Monday 21st June 1915

Separation

"I hate to let you down. You can come with me, Maudy. I'll see that all is arranged. I cannot stand to think of you here, all alone."

Maud averts her eyes from her lover's gaze. She has considered his offer, of course. It is just too much to grasp. Then there is Mother to consider.

"My door will always be open to you Maudy; just say the word. Can you understand my dilemma? The German taunts are destroying my practice, and now that the government work is drying up, I really have no choice. Do you see?"

Maud knew this day would come, but she was not expecting it to be so soon or so sudden. But there it is. They have finally got him and there is nothing to be done about it. Like the man he is, Dr Goldberg is behaving thoughtfully and carefully, explaining at length his predicament.

"I really can see no alternative, Maudy, than returning to the U.S. of A."

Maud is young with her life before her, and it seems such a bold decision to take at this point in her journey. With the war dragging on and her mother still insisting that Will may return, moving to America seems too significant and final. Sitting here with Dr Goldberg and aware of Mrs Dennis, and Edward, and darling Emily in the furthest part of the room, none of it seems quite so final anymore; there is still scope, still choices that can be made, trips undertaken.

Dr Goldberg accepts Maud's indecision with a sense of relief. God knows it is complicated enough closing down the practice and making arrangements back home; the added responsibility of Maud's welfare may tip the balance. Far better that she follow on later. The certainty he feels that she will join him in time is characteristic of the man, and it is what has brought him to this place in life. It is indeed his sense of entitlement that has made the taunts and questions regarding his bloodline so difficult to withstand. But Maud belongs in another compartment in which Dr Goldberg's confidence knows no bounds. Therefore, although he is saddened to leave her behind, he sees it as merely a temporary arrangement.

And so the day wears on, with talk of Mary's soon expected child, and Isa's new ladies' range, and Rose's diminishing dilemmas now that both her men are away at the Front, and of course Neville's ever increasing shortness of breath. What does she, Maud Burt-Marshall, have to fear? If only she can forget the sense of completeness she feels when with Dr Goldberg, she really can face anything.

Monday 28th June 1915

Change

The morning room at the mansions is full today and a feeling of change is in the air. Maud has gone to Brighton to stay with her friend Freda for the foreseeable future, or at least until she decides what to do for the best.

"Of course it never could have lasted: two different worlds, brought together by this dreary war," says Rose. Emily is not so sure, but keeps her thoughts to herself. She is attentive to Neville, whose movements are more laboured with each passing week. None of the companions have enquired directly of Neville's condition but they accept his mortality in a quiet and unspoken way.

The Colonel smokes his pipe, legs crossed, enjoying the company of Edward as they sit side by side in armchairs by the fireplace. This sort of companionship is new to Colonel Sewell even at seventy-five years of age, and he is enjoying the luxury of it. There is no judgement in this arrangement, no explicit demands. Edward, for his part, is content to pass time with the fine people in this room who share the most significant part of him: the loss of Teddy. His loss seems less bewildering when he factors in Sidney Davies Sewell, William Peppiatt, John Dennis and Audley Delves Thursby. Nothing would make it feel right, but there is a sense of common ground and mutual understanding in the room.

Isa Harburg expresses his gratitude to Mrs Dennis for extending her friendship and hospitality to him. "Without you, Mrs Dennis, there would be no Rose, and without Rose there would be no beautiful gowns. The shtof I am working with, delectable! Sheyn! I cannot thank you enough Dear Lady!"

Mrs Dennis sits back in her chair and breathes in the richness around her. Even the absence of Dr Goldberg and Maud cannot dampen her spirits: their time will come, they are still young. She remembers Mary and her imminent child, and wonders at the Perfect Completeness of Things.

Monday 26th July 1915

Beginnings

Mary's baby gurgles and splutters and gazes into his father's vacant eyes.

"How good they look together," says Edward, mesmerised by the baby's ability to look beyond the unseeing eyes of his father and into the man.

"Charming!" He pauses. "A long journey for us all. Twelve months! And still no end in sight."

Thoughts flash across Edward's tired mind, too fast to latch on to, too huge to grasp.

"We haven't settled on a name" says Mary.

"I expected he would be named after his father but Hampstead has other ideas, don't you dear. Whatever he decides I know my husband's choice will be perfect."

Hampstead is so engrossed in exploring, with trembling hands, his son's face, that he doesn't respond to his wife's words. Mary looks directly at Edward as she speaks, which causes Edward's eyes to lower so that he does not hold the gaze of this delightful, insightful creature; he is, as ever, humbled by the generosity of the young mother before him. Where did these women find their composure and strength?

Aloud, he asks, "Have you thought of a name old boy?"

Hampstead averts his head in acknowledgment and replies, without hesitation, "Teddy."

The impact this one word has on Edward is difficult to discern as it is impossible to measure the unmeasurable.

"Teddy" he murmurs, mostly to himself. "Jolly decent of you, Old Boy."

Edward walks over to the father with the child in his arms, rests his right hand on Hampstead's left shoulder, gives it a tender squeeze, and then moves over to the window seat of the morning room.

The sun falls directly on the now seated Edward, and warms his whole body, creating an equilibrium with the inner glow he feels. Already almost a year! His son would have been twenty-one this month. No key of the door for his boy; no marriage; no children. It had all been so sudden his poor mother hadn't been able to fathom it. He, Edward, had found it had led to a new life, a new circle, a new world. And now here was a new life that was to be Teddy's namesake. This little life could grow and mature, accept the key, make the vows, reproduce, live.

Edward is brought back to the present by the sound of tea cups and muted conversation. He looks around the room in wonder, and settles on the woman who made it all possible.

"Mrs Dennis. Let us raise our glasses to the boy. To Teddy."

All the friends in the room raise their glasses and tea cups.

"To Teddy!"

Mrs Dennis glances over to Edward and she holds his gaze.

Part Two

Part Two

Newspaper Clippings

KILLED IN ACTION.

DENNIS.—On Oct. 22nd-24th, Lieut. J. O. C. Dennis, 12th Battery R.F.A., beloved only son of Mrs. Dennis, 31, Cumberland-mansions, W., and of the late Colonel Dennis, 6th Dragoon Guards (Carabiniers), aged 26.

DAZZLING HEADLIGHTS.

WARNING TO MOTORISTS.

A fine of £20 was imposed by the Richmond magistrates yesterday on a motorist for riding through the town on Christmas Day with powerful headlights. The defendant, who was summoned under the Defence of the Realm Act—the case being the first of its kind heard at Richmond—was Leonard St. John Clare, motor-garage proprietor, of Richmond-road, Kingston. The constable who stopped defendant in the hew-road said that Clare remarked, " You —— fool; I very nearly killed you." After particulars had been taken defendant drove on, and when some forty yards away he relit the lamps.

Defendant denied that he lit up again. Replying to Mr. F. G. Humphreys, defendant said he did not think the regulations were justifiable if motorists were to avoid killing people. He had to attend an inquest, in which a friend of his was concerned in accidentally killing a pedestrian. Defendant further said he did not know the regulations applied outside of London.

The infliction of the penalty of £20, or in default a month's imprisonment, came as a surprise to defendant, and Mr. Humphreys remarked, " If you had been a millionaire we should have liked to fine you £10,000. The regulation made is a very proper one."

Time was allowed for the payment of the fine.

Monday 30th November 1914
Mrs Rose Muller

TOM to ROSE 915.—You cannot know how sorry, how very, very sorry. Yet all for your sake. Letters delight, charm. Mine painfully perplex? Daringly trusting love weathered ordeal take you at word bid brave for me—fortnightly or following.

EXPECTED you about noon to-day (Tuesday). May this announcement bring you. Letter waiting. Vide " Telegraph " last Wednesday. Saturday's not mine. Longing to give explanation not speaking last meeting.

UNABLE reconcile words with feeble failure in obvious duty. If explanation made at once, personally or by letter, will consider it. Don't bind myself to do more, and refuse discuss by advt.

ROSE.—After customary courtesy visit Wednesday immediately left knowing you would not be coming. All's well, nothing to fear—expected my last to infer. Curious combination responsible for long-drawn-out mistake. Forgive.

I KNOW it was my fault, but what am I to do now that door is closed? Shall willingly endure situation for you if only I may think you understand. You have guessed wrong and guessed right. 9—15.—R. ROSE.

ROSE.—I understand, and feel for you. Regret unable to comply yesterday. Shall see him to-morrow (Saturday) morning 11.15, or one day of ensuing three.—TOM.

£2 REWARD.—LOST, on Friday afternoon Dec. 10, in Hyde Park, near Marble Arch. BLACK COCKER SPANIEL, answers to name of Wuffy. Collar inscribed, T. H., 19, Norfolk St., W.—Apply 53, Seymour-street, Portman-square.

IMPORTANT NOTICE.—Owing to some unscrupulous person or persons, for motives best known to themselves, who are circulating that he is a German, Dr. GOLDBERG, of 27, New Cavendish-street, W., DESIRES to STATE that he is NOT a GERMAN, never has been one, and is in no way whatever connected with Germans. Dr. Goldberg was also the first dental practitioner to offer his services free to all Volunteers who were refused owing to the state of their teeth, and was the means of many being accepted after being attended to by him.

WILL the authoress of Thursday's and day's message communicate in first ins B. M., Box 4,883, Postal Department, Daily T

179

Thursday 7th January 1915
Mary

PERSONAL.

HAMPSTEAD.—All my BEST WISHES for a HAPPY CHRISTMAS and BRIGHT NEW YEAR. A letter is waiting containing good news. Thanks for yours. Love.—MARY.

MARY.—Sorry gave too short a notice. Meet me Monday next. Come as, under similar appointment, last we met. Promise this time if you aid sight. Love.—HAMPSTEAD.

PERSONAL.

HAMPSTEAD.—How are you? Anxious to see you. Plans have matured. Arrange luncheon same place. Letter waiting. Much love.—MARY.

PERSONAL.

MARY.—Letter awaiting you. Will call same place to-morrow (Saturday), at ten a.m. Love.—HAMPSTEAD.

MRS. DOWDALL'S New Book.

Joking
Apart

By the Hon. Mrs. DOWDALL,
Author of
"The Book of Martha."
Illustrated, 5s. net. Postage, 5d.

BLINDED SOLDIERS.

AN APPEAL TO PARLIAMENT.

To the Editor of "The Daily Telegraph."

Sir,—Will you allow me a little space in which to say something about the men who have had their sight destroyed while fighting for us? So far there have returned from the front, twenty-two men who have been incapacitated in this terrible manner, including two officers and one non-commissioned officer. Hitherto they have been sent to various hospitals throughout the country, but Surgeon-General Sir Alfred Keogh has now arranged that those who are in provincial hospitals shall be transferred to the Second London General Hospital, Chelsea, and all soldiers blinded at the front will be sent direct there in future. This excellent arrangement will render it possible to pay adequate attention to these men in the trying first stages of their affliction

Further plans for their immediate and future welfare are in process of development, and are receiving the hearty co-operation of all who have the best interests of the blind at heart, and who are specially qualified to advise with regard to them.

The most pressing question is that of their pensions. I venture to ask the members of the House of Commons to most carefully consider the case of these blinded soldiers when the question of pensions and allowances is brought before them. The members of the Committee on Naval and Military Pensions and Grants have received, most kindly, representations which have been made to them on this matter, and some of them have found time to visit hospitals and talk with blinded soldiers.

I believe that your readers will feel that the cases of these men should be treated with very special consideration. The lot of soldiers who have been permanently disabled in any way is bad enough, but I do feel that the future of these young, hearty fellows plunged into darkness so early in their lives, merits a particular degree of sympathy and attention. There will not be many of them, and it is certain that the country will not grudge any comparatively small additional sum which might be needed to place them in comfortable circumstances.

It must be remembered that a blind person has to bear expenses which do not occur in the case of those who can see. For example, he has to be accompanied by a guide, who in many cases must be paid, and who, in any event, is a source of expense when travelling.—Yours faithfully,

C. ARTHUR PEARSON, President.
National Institute for the Blind, 206, Great Portland-street. W

BLANCH.—Come home, so lonely without your dear face; been so ill since you went away. I imagined you aboard of that hospital ship which was nearly torpedoed; longing to see your dear face.—ISA.

WAITING FOR BREAD.

TO THE EDITOR OF "THE DAILY TELEGRAPH."

SIR—The letter of " F. S." draws attention to a matter which has engaged the serious attention of this society for a considerable time. Though these are troublous days, we are likely to gain advantages, that certain people, such as special constables, are being given opportunities of realising the conditions under which certain children suffer.

With reference to the children sent out in the early morning to buy cheap bread, your correspondent will be glad to know that I have recently been in communication with the committee of the London Master Bakers' Protection Society, a body, I am pleased to say, which has shown great sympathy with the proposal to keep children off the streets. Despite the many difficulties that surround the question it is hoped, with the co-operation of the persons concerned, to introduce a system which, while not depriving families of their bread, will prevent the continuance of an evil likely to have serious consequences to the health and well-being of children.—Yours very truly, ROBERT J. PARR, Director, National Society for the Prevention of Cruelty to Children, 40, Leicester-square, W.C.

KILLED IN ACTION.

PEPPIATT.—Killed in action, on the 5th day of February, 1915, William Henry Peppiatt, London Rifle Brigade, eldest son of Mrs. and the late W. R. Peppiatt, of Maglona, Woodford, aged 26. Memorial service at Woodford Parish Church, Saturday, 20th, five p.m.

with great success. A piano solo, "Deuxième Mazurka," by W. H. Peppiatt, formed the fifth item. This difficult

Frederick Thomas 'Bunny' Underhill served in the London Regiment (5th Battalion) also known as the Rifle Brigade, in October 1914. He arrived on the Western Front in the Ypres sector in November 1914. He was there with a number of school friends from Bancrofts School, Woodford Green, Essex, including William Henry Peppiatt. Below is an extract of a letter he sent to the school from the Front.

Just a card to let you know I am now out here at the Front......and am very fit and well. We are attached to one of the best Regular Infantry Brigades, and have had a lot of fighting in the trenches, etc. It is quite exciting. One soon gets used to bullets whizzing about, but I am not particularly keen on having any shells at close quarters. I know of two other O.B.'s in this Regiment (Gray and Peppiatt). I met P. Carlile a short time ago. It was quite nice to have a chat over old times. I should love a jolly good game of footer! Floreat Bancroftia.

Reproduced with kind permission of the Bancroftians' Association

186

Monday 1st March 1915
Mrs W. R. Peppiatt

BANCROFT'S SCHOOL, WOODFORD, ESSEX.
GOVERNORS the DRAPERS' COMPANY.
An EXAMINATION will be held in JULY NEXT for the
AWARD of PAY BOARDING FOUNDATION SCHOLARS, for
which boys between 10 and 13 years of age are eligible to
enter. A fee of £30 per annum is charged for each pay
boarding foundation scholar, which covers board, lodging, and
education.—For further particulars apply to the Clerk to the
Governors, Drapers' Hall, Throgmorton-avenue, E.C.

ULSTER CLUB, BELFAST.—WANTED.
HOUSE STEWARD and WIFE, acting as house-
keeper. Without encumbrances Joint salary £175 per
annum board and lodging. — Applications, stating previous
experience, with copies of testimonials (which will not be
returned), to be sent to Box 1.386, Willing's, 125, Strand
W C.

THURSBY.—Killed in action, on February 14th, Captain Audley Delves Thursby, K.R.R., only son of Mr. and
Mrs. Neville Thursby, of Harlestone, Northamptonshire,
aged 27.

Audley Delves Thursby was the son of Neville and Zoe Thursby. He had a twin sister Honor. He
was known as Arthur and was KIA on 15th February 1915 along with 54,000 soldiers of all ranks,
regiments and nations and is remembered on the Memorial at Menin Gate.

Kenneth Powell, private in the HAC,
died February 18th 1915

ATHLETE'S DEATH
AT
THE FRONT.

THE LATE KENNETH POWELL

From a Special Correspondent

Few of the many British sportsmen who have met a soldier's death will be mourned more deeply than Kenneth Powell, private in the H.A.C. His father, Mr. James Powell, of Reigate, who was the athletic monitor of his son, advises me that Kenneth died on Feb. 18. He received a bullet wound after leaving the trenches, and though borne three miles to the ambulance he succumbed in three hours. He was buried in a small graveyard. A few of his comrades who could be spared from the firing line were present. His captain is putting up a small cross so that his friends may some day pay homage to his tomb.

When the national call came, Kenneth Powell was among the first of the prominent athletes to respond. He had never done any soldiering before. Indeed, hardly a fortnight after enlisting in the H.A.C., he found himself, thanks to his sturdy physique and the selection of his officer, who was at Rugby like Powell, in training quarters at France. By November he was under fire in Flanders, and his letters home for the next two months, which I have been privileged to read, tell of the trials and tribulations nobly faced by his company during that momentous period. A glimpse of his life in the mud-invaded trenches may be given. Writing to his mother on Dec. 13 he said:

On the 9th, at night, the fifty fittest men in our company were required to go to the support trenches. Of our section only four were taken. Our trench was a line of underground dug-outs by a hedge about half a mile behind our nearest first-line trenches, where others of our battalion were stationed. M. and I shared for three days a hole 8ft long, 4ft deep, 2ft 6in wide, with 6in of mud at the bottom, and a straw cover which let in the rain. We had to sit facing each other, and I had the outside seat on a damp board, with a mackintosh sheet between me and the elements. You can imagine the discomfort to two large men, especially to their legs. We soon got covered in mud all over. As soon as I could I went out to get dry straw for the bottom, and was successful, though there were some bullets about. M. miraculously made a fire in a brazier from time to time with boxwood as fuel, and this helped us to keep warm, with soup tablets and tea. We both got choked with the smoke. Once a day, at dusk, I got relief by going to get water from a neighbouring farm; but the farm has been shelled to pieces now, which is disgusting. My way to it led by a dead cow and the remains of a French soldier, and was all under the fire of German bullets, which came over our first line of trenches, and are described as "strays" as they were not aimed at anyone, though they hurt just the same.

Monday 1st March 1915
Major Sidney Davies Sewell

KILLED IN ACTION.

SEWELL.—Killed in action in France, date unknown,
Major Sidney Davies Sewell, T.D., commanding 3rd London
Field Company, R.E., son of Col. T. Davies Sewell, 29,
Grosvenor-road, Westminster, S W., and grandson of the
late George Burt, Esq., J.P., ex-Sheriff of the City of
London.

Major Sidney Davies Sewell, Colonel Sewell's son

Major Sewell was sitting on the ground and little groups of diggers converged on him and lay waiting for the signal to withdraw. By now the enemy must have seen movements for the bullets came whining over and dropping around us quite frequently. How strange and interesting it seemed – to me the plopping of spent bullets into the ground was hardly distinguishable from the 'plops' of a tennis ball on dry turf – there was no malevolence in the sounds. True, Sapper W. Swainston had been killed by a bullet a little before but that seemed to be an isolated happening, something remote. When most of the digging party had assembled, the order to file away was given but we had not moved more than a dozen paces when Major Sewell, a tall imposing figure at the head of the party dropped without sound except the thud of a bullet and the crash of a heavy body on the soft earth.

The march back was resumed while Sgt. Blow, myself and two others made our way to a regimental-aid-post established under the shell of a farmhouse, carrying the heavily loaded stretcher across the rough broken ground. The journey seemed endless and before we reached the post, slipping, stumbling and swaying with fatigue we had fallen several times and our unconscious burden had once been tipped out of the stretcher when we fell in a jumbled heap. Arrived at the aid post, passing through the doorway covered by groundsheets to keep in the light, we came upon a normal everyday trench war scene, to our inexperienced eyes an unreal, macabre, sight. By the light of a hurricane lamp and fluttering candles, a medical officer and two orderlies were examining the wounded who were lying on stretchers or were standing with heads or arms or legs bandaged awaiting transfer to advanced dressing station. The busy M.O., diverted from his bandaging, took what seemed to be a cursory look at our burden, said, "Take him outside, he's dead" and returned to his interrupted task. We stumbled up the cellar steps, added the body to a long row of others who had finished their soldiering, and made our silent way back to our billets feeling numbed and shocked at the suddenness and absence of glory in this incident which had taken from us the dominant personality who so far had directed and led the company.

Taken from the memoirs of Samuel Charles Portman Drury published in 'Stand To'.
Used with kind permission of the Western Front Association.

189

EXCHANGED PRISONERS.—Can any of these give any INFORMATION about Captain W. M. BURT-MARSHALL, 2nd Batt. ARGYLL and SUTHERLAND HIGHLANDERS WOUNDED and MISSING since NOVEMBER 9th, from Ploegsturt Wood?—Any news of him since that date will be gratefully received by Miss Burt-Marshall, 109, Park-street, Grosvenor-square.

From a poem by Rupert Brook:-

> *Our captain's a Scotsman, what more need we say,*
> *And the foe sometimes collar him once, but no more;*
> *If you wish the best forward in Rugby to pace*
> *He is fat and short-sighted and honest of face.*
> *Neither Watson nor Beck could stand up before Peter,*
> *Then our Kaffir no half could be pluckier or neater.*

The poem refers to Rugby School, and as no Scotsman captained the School XV at this time, it is thought that Brooke was referring to the School Field XV whose captain was William Burt-Marshall. He played half-back.

Captain William Burt-Marshall, Argyll & Sutherland Highlanders, died on November 17th of wounds received in action. He was 27 years old. He was in the Rugby School Eleven in 1905 when he scored 139 runs in ten innings. He was also a well-known footballer, playing both for his school and Sandhurst. Wisden 1916 said he "died in February" (1915) but in fact he died three months earlier. He fell near the German trenches at Ploegsteert Wood on November 8th, and it was hoped that he might have been taken prisoner, but the War Office reported in February 1915 that he had died of wounds in a German field hospital at Quesnoy on November 17th 1914.

Villanelle by Roland Leighton

Violets from Plug Street Wood, sweet, I send you oversea.
(It is strange they should be blue, blue when his soaked blood was red,
For they grew around his head; it is strange they should be blue.)
Violets from Plug Street Wood, think what they have meant to me-
Life and Hope and Love and You (And you did not see them grow
Where his mangled body lay hiding horror from the day;
Sweetest it was better so.)
Violets from oversea, to your dear, far, forgetting land
These I send in memory, knowing You will understand.

DENTISTS FOR WAR HORSES.

CHICAGO, Feb. 11.

One of the peculiar war orders from belligerent nations which has come to light here is that for a special kind of cement to be used in repairing the teeth of horses in the Allied Armies.

A Chicago concern announces that a large order for such cement has recently been placed with it.—*Reuter.*

TO DENTISTS.—Kolynos Incorporated desire to thank the many hundreds of dentists who have so kindly assisted them in distributing free Kolynos Dental Cream to his Majesty's Forces at home and abroad.

Monday 8th March 1915
Miss Maud Burt-Marshall

FIGHTING MEN'S TEETH.

AN APPRECIATED FUND.

To the Editor of "The Daily Telegraph."

Sir—In presenting the first list of "personal" subscribers to the public, we desire to publish the following aims and objects of the fund:

1. Owing to many demands it has been decided to help the sailors as well as the soldiers, and in future we will deal with the sailors under the same methods as the soldiers, and the fund will be known as "The Soldiers' and Sailors' Dental Aid Fund."

2. Its objects are to keep soldiers and sailors in the Services, and to enable recruits to enter the Services, who, owing to defective teeth, would be physically unfit.

3. Its methods of dealing are through dental hospitals, dental departments of hospitals, and surgeon-dentists, who do all the fillings, extractions, &c., free; and the "Soldiers' and Sailors' Dental Aid Fund" pay for the teeth.

4. The whole of the staff are voluntary, and the offices are lent to the fund. All money, therefore, goes for the purposes of the fund.

In one dental hospital alone no fewer than 4,000 cases have been received since September to the end of December; and it is estimated that quite 60,000 men must be dealt with at once; we have already ninety-two cases in hand.

May we most earnestly appeal to the public to subscribe as liberally as possible, to enable us to deal with the long, waiting lists of applications?—We are, Sir, yours faithfully,

RICHARD BURBIDGE, Chairman.
HERBERT BARTLETT,
ARTHUR LUCAS, } Hon. Treasurers.
BETTY CONYNGHAM,
ADA ELIZABETH FLETCHER, } Hon. Secs.
36, Leicester-square, W.C., Feb. 2.

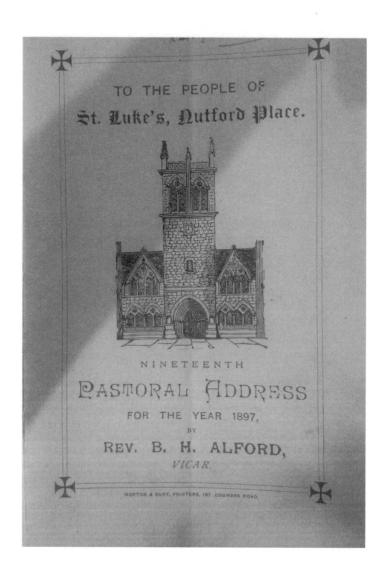

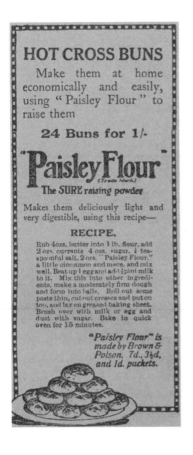

ASPARAGUS.

AN EARLY SLUMP.

Never, since asparagus was first known at Covent-garden, have consumers had so favourable an opportunity of enjoying that vegetable. To express the state of affairs in homely market language: there has been a four-day slump in asparagus. Wherever one went in the market one saw huge stacks of this erstwhile " monarch of the vegetable kingdom " on offer at extraordinarily cheap rates. And the reason? Primarily the war, because of the great disorganisation of traffic and the lessened demand for luxuries.

In point of fact, it is not accurate for the time being to describe asparagus as a luxury. During the early part of the week it was the cheapest green vegetable on the market. Whilst cabbage and common greens were dear, certain kinds of asparagus were all but given away. To put the traffic difficulty comprehensively it must be understood that the bulk of our asparagus supply at this time is derived from France. Only last week the remarks in this column were devoted to the subject of the troubles which French farmers will probably have to face owing to the war. All too soon that prophecy has been verified.

Several consignments of goods from France have arrived simultaneously. Thus, whilst some of the produce was good and fresh, other parcels were stale and unattractive in appearance. From private marks put on the packages in which vegetables are conveyed, merchants knew that some lots had been a week or more in transit. These and fresh goods were on the market at the same time. When vegetables are mixed up in such a manner trade buyers do not care to risk their money lest they suffer heavy losses. The result is that much really good asparagus has been disposed of at extraordinary low rates

RHUBARB AND BANANA AMBER.

Wipe and trim one bundle of forced rhubarb and cut the stalks or stems into 1in lengths. Stew the fruit with very little water and 3oz of castor sugar till tender, then rub all through a fine sieve and reduce a little. Next stir in 4oz of cake or bread crumbs and the yolks of three eggs. Butter a fireproof baking or pie dish, and put in the above preparation, then bake in a moderately-heated oven for about 20 minutes. Meanwhile whisk up stiffly the white of an egg and mix carefully with ½oz of castor sugar. Spread this roughly on top of the cooked fruit, and besprinkle freely with finely crushed macaroons. Return the dish to the oven for another ten or fifteen minutes so as to set and slightly brown the surface. Dish up and serve hot or cold.

CLERGYMAN TO MAKE SHELLS.

A Glasgow firm of engineers has accepted the services of a well-known Glasgow minister, the Rev. Stuart Robertson, and on Monday he will assist in making shells for the Government. The reverend gentleman will travel by the workmen's early morning train and work the ordinary hours. When questioned yesterday, Mr. Robertson said that if he made shells during the week to fire at the Prussions and shells on Sunday to fire at the devil that would be a fair division.

Monday 5th April 1915
Easter Monday

BARROW "EVER-BRIGHT" STAINLESS STEEL CUTLERY

—a marvellous invention that is of vital importance to all users of Cutlery. Never again need knives be cleaned, if you use the Barrow "Ever-Bright."

UNTARNISHABLE KNIVES

The Barrow "Ever-Bright" are absolutely rustless and unaffected by Vinegar, Sauces, Pickles, Fruit Juices or the like.

KNIFE-CLEANING MACHINES ENTIRELY DISPENSED WITH

After use simply wash as you would a china plate; they never lose their original brightness. The drudgery of knife-cleaning is no more.

A TREMENDOUS SAVING

This Cutlery effects a saving, not only in time and labour, but in knives as well, for they are no longer subject to the hard usage of knife-cleaning machines and methods.

You cannot afford to overlook this wonderful discovery. Write to-day for Illustrated Price List, with Sample (it's post free), and put it to the severest test you can think of

S. BARROW & CO., 102-104, VICTORIA ST., LONDON, S.W.

For cleaning Silver, Electro-Plate &c
Goddard's Plate Powder
Sold everywhere 6d 1/- 2/6 & 4/6

198

Monday 5th April 1915
Easter Monday

SIR E. GREY'S SPEECH.

HERR JAGOW'S RAGE.

"WAR TO THE HILT."

FROM OUR OWN CORRESPONDENT.

NEW YORK, Sunday.

A special despatch from Berlin to the *New York Sun* yesterday reports an interview given by the Foreign Secretary, Herr von Jagow, who said:

"We have it now out of Sir Edward Grey's own mouth that England was intent on completely crushing and destroying Germany. It was a frank admission to the world of what we long knew was England's motive in this war."

When the correspondent asked Herr Jagow if the German Government would reply he said:

"Sir Edward Grey's speech constitutes a renewed declaration that war means war to the hilt. So let it be. England wants it, we accept it as such, and if this human slaughter continues interminably let the world place the blame where it belongs—at the door of England, which staged and engineered the war.

"Sir Edward Grey's words must be a severe blow to those who seemed to have the hope of bringing about peace. Sir Edward Grey announces that England will not quit till Germany is completely crushed. That day is far distant. History shows that the German people are not easily crushed. Hundreds of thousands of lives will be sacrificed and much blood flow, and all because Germany dared to grow to be strong and powerful alongside England, which believed her absolute dominion of the sea was being questioned, her trade monopoly endangered, and her world dictatorship disregarded. Mere phrases will neither win a war nor conceal the cause and originator. We are thankful to Sir Edward Grey for his open avowal before the world of England's motive and purpose.

AN ANGRY STATESMAN.

199

Monday 5th April 1915
Easter Monday

BURBERRY COMPLETED SUITS

For the Elite

Successfully solve the most difficult of clothing problems—the production of suits that will satisfy the most fastidious taste, and at the same time be ready for instant wear.

Whether you require a smart Lounge Suit, a Sporting outrig, a Morning or a Dress Suit, allow Burberrys an opportunity to demonstrate how the Completed Suit idea saves time, obviates disappointment, and enables you to obtain better and more perfectly-fitting suits.

Burberry Completed Suits are far away superior to the ordinary tailoring — in style—in quality of material—in workmanship and finish— unfailingly right in every detail.

There's no risk of not being able to get a perfect fit. Burberry Completed Suits are the result of scientific anatomical mensuration, and each model is made in no less than 55 different fittings—one of these exactly fits your figure.

ILLUSTRATED CATALOGUE & PATTERNS POST FREE.

SHORT NOTICE MILITARY KIT

Burberrys keep Tunics, Slacks, Breeches, Great Coats and Warms ready to try on, so that fitting is done when ordering, and the kit completed in a few hours.

BURBERRYS Haymarket LONDON

200

FROCKS
FOR EASTER

All our Ready-made Costumes are of an exceptionally interesting character. They are copied and adapted from the most exclusive Paris models by our own highly skilled workers and are quite different from the ordinary ready to wear frock. The materials of which they are made are invariably of excellent quality, while the fit and finish are quite perfect :—

DAY GOWN in Silk Crepe de Chine, arranged with full skirt, bodice hemstitched and piped with buttons of own material. **59/6**
In black and various colourings.

Millinery of the Moment

500 Exclusive Easter Models — all at 25/9

The following Millinery announcement is one that places before Selfridge's customers the opportunity of studying the very latest conceptions of the Milliner's art, charming Hats that embody in light colours and attractive shapes, the spirit of the Easter Season. Now is the opportunity for Ladies to acquire a Smart Hat in the Latest Mode and bearing the Selfridge *cachet*. There is a varied stock to choose from, and no matter what style or shape is selected, the price is the same **25/9**

1. Wonderfully Attractive Picture HAT, with aerophane crown; ostrich feathers are arranged flat on the brim finished coloured marguerites **25/9**

No. 1

3. Charming little Trotteur HAT, in Black Taffeta with White Tagal Straw, worked in most effective way all over crown. Small wing of Taffeta and Straw arranged either side, standing out from the crown **25/9**

No. 2

No. 3

2. Becoming HAT, with roll-up brim of black silk and frills of tulle standing up all round crown; finished at side front with a lovely bunch of roses **25/9**

No. 4

4. Most Becoming Black Sailor HAT, with dainty hanging lace edge and White Satin crown trimmed with a lovely rose and foliage in front **25/9**

Small-fitting HAT, with rolled-up brim of black velvet; crown of velvet and black leghorn; plainly trimmed with belt and buckle of white petersham **25/9**

Smart Trotteur HAT, in Black Corded Silk and Tagal; black and white silk braid is worked round crown and forms an attractive pair of tiny wings at the side **25/9**

Attractive HAT for a Girl, with transparent black tulle brim and cerise straw crown trimmed wreath of small black marguerites **25/9**

Fascinating little HAT, in a beautiful shade of Purple Silk; Nattier Blue ribbon is twisted round the crown and a bunch of fruit is placed in front **25/9**

PLEASURES NEARER HOME.

From Liverpool-street and Fenchurch-street further heavy departures took place. but here the number of travellers, although more than some of the booking-clerks anticipated, was not up to the level of last year. Up to noon yesterday there were many full trains, but the rush was over twelve hours before, and yesterday's travellers appeared to be for the most part happy individuals bent upon a country walk, or an afternoon and evening with relatives or friends.

Remarkable at all the southern stations was the friendly " mix-up " of soldiers and civilians. The universality of the young men in khâki was not more apparent than the general prevalence of athletic-looking civilians in gay holiday mood and attire. Wounded soldiers there were coming back from the trenches, and men of similar mould and age going off with lady friends to the golf links.

FRANCE OR THE SEASIDE.

The ordinary cross-Channel traffic was almost confined to soldiers and to relatives and others who had obtained special permission to visit the wounded at the base hospitals at Boulogne and elsewhere. Usually this cross-Channel traffic is made up of well-to-do tourists who intend to spend Easter at one of the French seaside resorts or to go on to Paris, the Riviera, or as far afield as Rome. A certain number of tourists did venture to the Eternal City to take part in, or to witness, the Easter celebrations of the Catholic Church, but their numbers did not compare with previous years. Continental traffic was not so much small as different in its character from that of previous years.

On the other hand, the exodus to South and South-West Coast resorts was quite satisfactory from the railway point of view. At Charing-cross, Victoria, and Waterloo the crowds were so numerous on Thursday afternoon and evening that several of the trains had to be run in duplicate, and one or two of them in triplicate.

Margate, Ramsgate, Broadstairs, Deal, and Dover attracted almost, if not quite, the normal number of visitors. Many thousands made for Brighton, Folkestone, Eastbourne, Bournemouth, and Torquay, the hotels of which can have had little or nothing to complain of in the matter of patronage. At Waterloo it was stated that the bookings for Bournemouth and for the Devon and Cornwall coasts were well up to the normal.

Monday 5th April 1915
Easter Monday

MANY SOLDIERS TRAVELLING.

As at St. Pancras so at King's-cross, Euston, Marylebone, and Paddington, the platforms were dominated by khaki, which in the case of King's-cross was pleasantly varied by the tartans of Scotsmen en route for home. Quite 50 per cent. of the passengers on yesterday's mid-day express to Bradford, Leeds, York, and Newcastle wore khaki, with just a sprinkling of blue to represent the Senior Service.

At Paddington the traffic on Thursday was very little beneath the normal for the period. However fickle may be the public affection for other districts, it is firmly held by the charms of the Cornish Riviera, which drew many trainloads of jaded town dwellers away to the west.

Hampden's country, the hills of Buckinghamshire and the beauties of the Chalfonts, claimed a fair number of trippers, but traffic on the Great Central line was on the whole below the normal.

Travellers leaving Euston were mainly soldiers. There was a fair number of people whose means permitted them to take a short holiday in spite of the lack of cheap fares. Bookings to Scotland were reported to be light, but the parcels traffic on Thursday gave the staff as much as they could do. Special sleeping facilities for soldiers at this terminus were greatly appreciated by men of many regiments.

AT THE NORTHERN STATIONS.

At the railway termini north of the Thames the officials reported that, although the passenger statistics bear no comparison with those of previous years, they were far more satisfactory than the companies had reason to anticipate. In this connection the war has become its own corrective—it was owing to the war that the ordinary holiday traffic has fallen below the normal; it is due to the war that the deficiency has been to some extent made good by the transit of thousands of soldiers, who were released on Thursday from their training camps for a few days' leave.

"The people who are travelling this Easter," said an official at St. Pancras, "are those who at other times travel very little—people engaged in mechanical trades, who in these days can demand almost any wage they please. They are not going far; they cannot spare the time. But to them a trip a few miles out of London, away from the scene of their toil, has the same exhilarating effect as a Continental tour upon those in more opulent circumstances. Ordinary tourist traffic is practically dead, and the closing of the Continental tours has had no compensating effect upon the traffic to Scotland. The movement North, usually so brisk at this time, can be fairly described as negligible.

"It may also be safely conjectured that the average English traveller who knows the Riviera and the Continent generally almost as well as his own country, finds this Eastertide as strange and unreal as it is for the rest of us."

204

HEALTH & SUNSHINE.

———◆———

BRIGHTON.

Given a continuance of springlike conditions, the Easter season promises to be very successful. All the principal hotels report satisfactory bookings, and it is expected that the arrangements for the issue of special railway tickets available for the whole holiday will prove most attractive to visitors.

For some weeks the Hotel Metropole has been extensively patronised by military officers quartered in the town, and there is every indication that many of their friends will take advantage of the Easter to spend some days with them. The establishment will be the centre of much entertaining.

At the Grand Hotel there is already a considerable clientèle. For the holiday a programme of house entertainments has been prepared.

As usual there will be a full house at the Royal York Hotel, and each day the visitors will be supplemented by numerous motor parties from London. The programme includes a Cinderella dance on Saturday, and a ball on Easter Monday. A sacred concert has been arranged for Good Friday.

Similar entertainments will be given at the Royal Albion Hotel, where the bookings are unusally numerous.

At the Norfolk Hotel, Old Ship Hotel, and Blenheim House there is a brisk demand for accommodation.

In aid of the local Belgian Relief and Refugee Fund, a sacred concert is to be given to-morrow afternoon, under distinguished patronage, at the Hove Town Hall, the programme including Rossini's " Stabat Mater." Among the artists taking part are Madame Lucy Murca, Miss Florence Donovan, Miss Ethel Harman, Miss Marjorie Moore, Miss Molly Paley, Miss Hilda Mynard, Mr. Herbert Orbell, and Mr. W. A. Lauder. There will be an orchestra and choir numbering over 100, Mr. W. S. Marchant conducting.

Métropole for comfort and cuisine. Gordon Hotels.

Grand Hotel.—New lounge. Music. Excel. cuisine.

Lion Mansion Hotel.—High-class family. Fac. sea.

The Bodega, Ship-st.—Wines, spirits, cigars, grill room, and restaurant. Open Sundays, 12.30.

"Daily Telegraph " Office, 68, Kings-rd. Tel. 361.

SANDBAGS FOR THE FRONT.

NEW TASK FOR PEOPLE AT HOME

To the Editor of "The Daily Telegraph."

Sir,—Will you tell the women of England that they can themselves make defences for their loved ones at the front? What they are asking for is millions of sandbags—empty, of course. The enclosed appeal comes to-night from my brother, Lieut.-Colonel J. A. Tyler, R.F.A., at the front.

Coarse linen or canvas bags are needed. They should measure about 3ft long, by 2ft. A space should be left unsewn at one corner, for filling, and a bit of string should be tied on there, to tie up that corner, when the sack is filled.

Any sacks sent here will be forwarded without delay to the firing-line.—Yours,

M. L. TYLER.

Linden House, Highgate-road, N.W.

It is quite mild, spring weather with us now. We do not want any more mufflers or caps for warmth, but we always want sandbags, by the million; and if the kind people who have helped us so greatly during the winter with warm, knitted things want still to help, they could not do better than make sandbags for our protection. We must have hundreds of millions of sandbags in use, and we always want them. To make a nice, commodious house for a few officers in their gun position, for instance, will require some 2,000 sandbags, and the number wanted for a single battery for protection for the guns—men, officers, and telephone operators—will run into tens of thousands. A mile of trenches will require, perhaps, 100,000, and each little post, observation station, or shelter of any kind behind those trenches requires many more. Then every house, barn, or other locality occupied in the area in which shells fall for a depth of two or three miles behind our trenches ought to have its own dugout for use when necessary, into the making of which the sandbag enters. When we advance we have not time to empty our old sandbags and carry them on; we require fresh ones. But perhaps making sandbags would not be suitable work for ladies; the canvas may be too stiff.

The size of them should be about 3ft by 2ft, and the material, I should say, coarse linen or canvas—white is usual. Then the making of sandbags would not call for any special skill, I imagine, so that mere men would make them after a little practice.

Sandbags for the front are being made by the Women's Emergency Corps, 8, York-place, Baker-street, who in this way provide work for women who can secure no other employment. Orders will be welcomed.

FEAST OF PASSOVER.

This evening the Jewish community enters on the celebration of the Feast of Passover, a festival which commemorates the most notable incident in the history of the Jewish race. It is the anniversary of the redemption from Egyptian bondage, of the beginning of a story unparalleled in the annals of nations. Merciless slavery was suddenly replaced by complete freedom, and an entire people, crushed for centuries under the iron heel of a rigorous despotism, found itself boldly led forth to a new life by a powerful leader under Divine protection. The story is an old one, and the telling of it, as given in Exodus, cannot be improved upon, yet to-night, to the accompaniment of melodies hallowed by centuries of tradition, it will be told afresh, listened to afresh, and marvelled at as it has been uninterruptedly for untold centuries.

There will be the same make-believe. The youngest member of the household, in piping voice, will ask for information from its head as to the difference between this night and all other nights, as to the reason for the unleavened bread, the bitter herbs, the dipping into salt-water, and the reclining position of the master of the house. The little fellow knows the replies long before they are given; nevertheless, both he and others gathered round the festive board will listen with intense interest to the answers as they are recited in ordered manner. He will hear of the descent of Israel into Egypt, of the slavery of their ancestors, their embittered lives, the arrival of Moses, the miracles, and the final deliverance. There will be gratitude in every moment of the crowded evening, and none will be more welcome to the ceremony than the stranger.

There will be a certain measure of sadness on the present occasion, for Jews, like others, have sent their sons in thousands and tens of thousands to take their proper places in this devastating war, yet there will be a special significance in the celebration to-night, and from many a lip there will ascend the fervent prayer that there may be a speedy liberation from the slavery of a despotic militarism, and that the principle of the freedom of little nations may again be publicly proclaimed even as was the case with the Israelites of old.

207

Monday 5th April 1915
Easter Monday

PRISONERS IN GERMANY.

HELP FROM HOME.

The following statement was issued by the War Office:

As the result of articles and notices which have appeared in the Press, considerable sums are being remitted to the Prisoners of War Help Committee for the benefit of British prisoners in Germany. The committee gratefully acknowledge the help which is thus being given, and the money will be expended in relief of such urgent cases as are brought to their notice, or will be held in reserve for future needs.

The number of parcels which have been, and are being sent day by day through the Post Office or through the agency of this committee are ample evidence that the prisoners' wants are in no way overlooked by their relatives or by the public in this country. The committee are concerned to give every support and encouragement to regimental or county organisations, believing that the most effective way of giving aid without overlapping is through such agencies, which have the best means of ascertaining the real needs of individual prisoners.

For months the Church Army has been exerting every effort, with the assistance of the public, to alleviate many of the inevitable sufferings of our prisoners of war in Germany. The comforts sent vary from the most nutritious forms of food to the every-day necessary comforts of socks, shirts, braces, &c. A collection of these articles that are so much needed are being provided for by the Church Army. Selfridge's have devoted a window in Orchard-street, for the next day or two, to the display of many of these comforts as supplied by them to the Church Army.

Monday 12th April 1915
Hampstead

SOLDIERS' AND SAILORS' TEETH.

OFFER OF HELP.

The hon. operating secretary of the Soldiers' and Sailors' Dental Aid Fund, 36, Leicester-square, W.C., writes:

"The notice of the London recruiting campaign in *The Daily Telegraph* has been brought to our notice. May we ask for space to say that we are prepared to remedy at once one of the reasons for not joining the Army, i.e., teeth. We will gladly supply our forms for distribution at any of the meetings, and on the filled-in forms being returned to us, together with the recruiting officer's letter, we can get to work immediately.

"On one urgent occasion we supplied a soldier for the front with false teeth in twenty-four hours."

"CURSE OF TOOTHACHE."

The need for the Fund is eloquently voiced in the following three extracts from letters received from men serving in the Army:

"I have served in the Cameron Highlanders for twelve years (and served with them through two campaigns—Sudan, 1898, and South Africa), holding four medals, with eight bars; I re-enlisted on Sept. 1 this year, and when my turn came to proceed to the front I was rejected owing to my teeth only, which makes me feel rather sore to be left behind. Now, would you consider my case, as I am looking to be with the old corps again, and try my luck once more?"

"After being sent to the front and serving three months with the Expeditionary Force in Belgium and France, I was unfortunately forced to report sick, and was sent home convalescent, through having defective teeth."

"I am attached to the Essex Regiment, and have been obliged to have my teeth extracted. As my continuance in the Service depends upon my having same replaced, may I be permitted to ask for some financial assistance?"

What the officers think of the fund may be gathered from the following: "Having just come back from four months with the Expeditionary Force, I well know what agonies many of our men had to suffer from toothache, and anything that will cure or alleviate this awful curse is well deserving of support."

OUR TEETH.

THE IMPORTANCE OF MASTICATION.

GOOD SOUND TEETH SO VERY ESSENTIAL.

Dr. Goldberg, the American Dental Specialist, of 27, New Cavendish Street, Harley Street, W., gives some very important facts concerning the teeth, and tells why so many are victims of decaying and aching molars. He says : "The teeth are but sentinels of health ; the grinding stones of the mill of nourishment and proper digestion. Lose them, and all sorts of physical ailments must naturally result, especially derangement of the digestive organs."

The dental chair should have no terrors for the patient nowadays. Science and discovery have brought dentistry to such an art that pain is unnecessary even in the most delicate operations. Speaking from experience, consequent of my own practice he added : " I have yet to experience that complete loss of confidence and expectancy of pain so commonly related "

Now, disease of the teeth is a most important thing to humanity. As Dr. Goldberg says : Our teeth are the sentinels of our health, and if incapable of doing their duty, then disease and illness must necessarily pass them by and ravish the entire constitution.

SOUND TEETH AND MASTICATION.

The importance of proper mastication is so very evident that little need be said here on the point. Food not properly chewed and ground into a pulp before being swallowed puts a strain on the stomach that must naturally result in dyspepsia, anæmia, and various forms of stomach trouble. One has only to think for themselves to realise the importance of sound teeth. In point of fact, we have the important revelation that more than three thousand men were invalided home during the Boer War on account of defective teeth, while thousands desirous of joining Lord Kitchener's Army have been rejected for the same reason.

To ask the cause of this great prevalence of bad teeth, speaking generally, lack of knowledge briefly summarises the situation, but from experience the writer's belief is that dilatoriness on the part of the adult accounts for 80 per cent. of the decaying molars and toothless gums among the population, and this dilatoriness is frequently caused by an unnecessary fear of pain supposedly experienced by a visit to the dentist.

Now this is wrong. Modern dental science is a totally painless art. Invention, discovery, and knowledge acquired by the dental practitioner have made it so.

Monday 12th April 1915
Hampstead

...cannot have made to so.

But to revert to sufferers and the gradual decaying of the teeth. They seem to lose sight of the fact that once the enamel of the tooth is broken the inside of the tooth quickly decays, and, of course, as soon as the nerve becomes exposed pain sets in. The natural instinct is to have such teeth extracted. It is a toss up between toothache and fear of pain being caused by the cleaning and filling of such decayed teeth in the early stages of decay.

But did one only take such surface decay in time, even when only a small pinhole is observable on the outside, which indicates a far greater cavity inside, pain would never be experienced, and the dentist would be able to turn what is a quickly decaying tooth into a perfectly sound tooth capable of lasting a lifetime. There are cases, when teeth already extracted need replacing by artificial dentures, and in this Dr. Goldberg may well be called London's foremost dental specialist. For it is undoubtedly his wonderful method of Bridge Work that made his reputation in this country some ten years ago. His unique methods have made his services greatly in demand amongst ladies, and especially those of the theatrical world.

Plates, of course, are sometimes necessary, and when they are, perfect conformity to the mouth—a perfect fit—is absolutely essential; while lightness with strength and durability are, of course, important considerations.

The fact that Dr. Goldberg represents all that is best in the science of dentistry in the U.S. of A. speaks eloquently of his ability and accounts for his very large practice. His parlours are at 27, New Cavendish Street, Harley Street, London, W. Telephone: Mayfair 2022.—*Advt.*

214

BROKEN HEALTH.

A graphic account of the conditions prevailing among the civilian prisoners at the Ruhleben camp, supplied apparently by an inmate, was sent to Mr. Page by the Foreign Office on Jan. 19. The following is an extract:

There is a canteen, where at exorbitant prices such luxuries as sugar, white bread, condensed milk, butter, chocolate, cigars, &c., can be bought by those who can afford it. Those who cannot afford to buy these luxuries are in a very bad plight. They are not actually dying of starvation, but they can only just keep themselves alive and no more. About eight at night we begin to go to " bed " as best we can, and at nine there must be dead silence. All this as related here does not sound so very terrible, but in practice for those who have to go through it it is " hell."

Six men abreast in a space of about 10ft 6in means that they are packed like sardines in a box, and no one can move. They are supplied with only one poor blanket each, and those who have none of their own are in a sad plight. If one man in the line attempts to turn he disturbs all the others. Young men in the full vigour of life may be able to stand it, but for elderly men it simply means, if not immediate death, then certainly a shortened life and broken health for the rest of their days. The coughing which starts shortly after they have all turned in, and which is apparently caused less by colds than by foul air and the dust, is awful to hear.

Let us just take a few names quite at random. There is Private HYSLOP, for example, of the Gordons, who succeeded in getting through with " a most urgent message " after six of his comrades had been killed in the attempt. Yet even that was not heroism enough for a single day, for at dusk he acted as guide to " an Officer's position, a place of danger, situated only fifty yards from the enemy's trench." Those few lines of print mean that the medal which Private HYSLOP will wear shines bright with the gallantry of the six nameless dead as well as with his own. Or there is Private FRENCH, of the 4th Middlesex, who at a critical moment, when a German bomb had been thrown into our trenches, " with consequent great destruction and confusion," at once took charge, had the parapet manned, rapid fire opened on the enemy, wounded collected, and the fire in the dug-out extinguished, all with the greatest promptitude. We hope that Private FRENCH is a sergeant by this time. It is men such as he who are the backbone of an army. Again, there

"LURE OF DRINK."

SHIPBUILDERS' PROPOSAL.

A deputation from the Shipbuilding Employers' Federation have arranged to meet Mr. Lloyd George in London this week to discuss the question of restricting the sale of intoxicants in areas where munitions of war are produced. Shipbuilders favour complete, rather than partial, closing, with compensation to license-holders, which, they say, would be earned twice over by increased output. To prevent preferential treatment they are willing to have clubs closed, and cellars sealed till the end of the war.

DRUNKENNESS IN ENGLAND.

Among the lower orders the woman has the hardest lot, for she suffers much from the intemperance of the men. Drunken women are, indeed, a common sight in England. What they drink is simply fusel oil, whether it be named gin or brandy or whisky. There are ladies who, failing anything else, empty their Eau-de-Cologne flasks. Such an atmosphere of spirits may well have produced the Suffragette.

The Germans have been reproached for their thirst, but the good German beer never harms them. The noble vine that grows on the Rhenish hills does not produce its fragrant essence for a nation of drunkards. It has bred dreamers, fiery geniuses, and philosophers. It has flowed in Auerbach's cellar for the most brilliant of all Germany's poets. When the German opens a bottle of wine he does it with a certain festive feeling that he is drinking to his friends, and, it may be, to the woman he loves. When, on the contrary, the Englishman settles down to drink seriously, the hostess gives the ladies a sign to leave the table. . . .

PUBLIC-HOUSE CLOSING.

DRASTIC REGULATIONS.

An order has been issued by the military authorities for the later opening and the earlier closing of public-houses in Lancashire, Cheshire, and certain other parts of the North of England. From Monday next the public-houses will not open till 10.30 a.m. on week-days, and they will close at ten p.m. On Sundays they will only open between 12.30 and 2.30 p.m., and 6.30 and 9.30 p.m, Local orders are not superseded, provided the hours of opening are not earlier and closing are not later than the hours now prescribed. The orders have not caused much surprise.

In Birmingham the justices have made an order that after Monday next the sale of intoxicants is prohibited before ten a.m. and after ten p.m. each week-day.

The General Officer Commanding the Western District has ordered that on and from Monday next all public-houses shall close except between 10.30 in the morning and ten at night, and on Sundays except between 12.30 and 2.30, and between 6.30 and nine at night. Time is thus taken off both morning and evening facilities. Local orders are not superseded, provided the hours do not start earlier or end later than those prescribed.

ESTATE DUTIES

OF

OFFICERS KILLED IN ACTION

The ever-growing list of officers killed in action directs attention to a matter of great importance to their lineal descendants—the extent to which their estates are subject to succession duties. Inquiries having been received on the subject, it may be well to state the position as it stands at present.

The Finance Act of 1900 made certain provisions in regard to the remission of death duties in the case of persons killed in war. Under that Act the Treasury could, if they thought fit, remit, or, in the case of duty already paid, repay, up to an amount not exceeding £150 in any one case, the whole or any part of the death duties if the total value of the property for the purpose of estate duty did not exceed £5,000.

This concession only applied to the widow or the lineal descendants of the individual killed. Having regard, however, to the very large number of young unmarried men who are daily sacrificing their lives in the country's cause, it became necessary to enact that, as respects the present war, the concession should apply to property passing to lineal ancestors as well as to property passing to widows or lineal descendants. This extension was duly made at the end of August in the Death Duties (Killed in War) Act, 1914.

QUICK SUCCESSIONS.

There have been several cases during the present war where the death in battle of a man who had recently inherited an estate has meant a quick succession in the same estate. In normal times this is regulated by the Finance Act, 1914. Under that Act, land or business passing a second time within one year have the estate duty reduced by 50 per cent., within two years by 40 per cent., within three years by 30 per cent., within four years by 20 per cent., and within five years by 10 per cent.

It is thus conceivable that under this Act greater benefits may accrue to legatees than under the Emergency Act, which allows merely the deduction of £5,000 for the purpose of estate duty. Where this proves to be the case the older Act may be invoked in order to obtain the greater benefit.

As regards quick successions in the same estate, consequent upon the death in the war of different members of the same family, no duty is payable in the case of the second death, whether the property passes on that second death to a lineal descendant or not.

I.L.P. AND THE WAR.

CONFLICTING VIEWS.

RECRUITING QUESTION.

From Our Special Correspondent.

NORWICH, Tuesday Night.

To-day's sitting of the Independent Labour Party conference has revealed some indications of disagreement with the anti war policy of the party and of the active opposition to recruiting by its members. Delegates from the North-East Manchester branch spoke in support of the active recruiting efforts of Mr. J. R Clynes, Labour member for the division and a member of the Independent Labour Party. Even more suggestive was the revelation of the numerical insignificance of party as represented in the conference on the recruiting resolution. The CHAIRMAN (Mr. F. W. Jowett, M.P.) decided that the vote should be taken by card, and it was publicly stated that each vote represented fifty members. The total votes recorded were 243 for the resolution and nine against. This means a membership of only 12,600 persons represented and voting in the national conference. At the opening of the sitting a letter was read from Mr. James Parker, M.P. for Halifax, explaining that he was unable to attend the conference, as he was busy attending recruiting meetings. " I have been doing work which I consider my duty," added Mr. Parker.

STRAND CORNER HOUSE.

A NEW RESTAURANT.

In some respects the most notable, the Strand Corner House is the latest demonstration of the enterprise of Messrs. J. Lyons and Company. The evolution of the modern restaurant, in its impetuous career, has already made the old-fashioned, dingy London coffee-house a mere memory. It has gone, and the Strand Corner House is the youngest of its successors.

The Corner House in Coventry-street was opened only a few years ago. Its popularity doubtless suggested the new Strand establishment, which is admittedly an embodiment of the same policy. The main idea is in the words of the management, to "provide everything in the way of refreshment that the public may require from the seven o'clock breakfast to the eleven o'clock theatre-supper, and to do this in irreproachable style, surrounded by every comfort and at reasonable charges."

The chief frontage of the new building is in the Strand, and the structure stretches riverwards along the west side of Craven-street. Its style is of the Early Rénaissance period, and internally the arrangements are such as to secure for the customer elegant surroundings, with prompt and efficient service.

ATTRACTIVE SURROUNDINGS.

The main entrance from the Strand leads into the show-room, where pastries, chocolates, sweetmeats, and dainties may be purchased and consumed. Behind is the entrance to the ground-floor of the café, and, this reached, the extent of the premises is at once realised. An elliptical well, roofed with stained-glass, pierces three floors, and, yesterday, at a special private inspection, to which many guests were invited, each floor was flooded with sunlight, and the walls and pillars, being of veined white marble, warmed with touches of crimson, an air of cheerful comfort and elegance is secured.

The café, which is fully licensed, is one of the largest in the world. With 600 waiters, cooks, and attendants to minister to them, 1,200 guests can find seating accommodation. This is secured by adding ground and upper floors, to which electric lifts convey customers.

In every way the "Strand Corner House" has the atmosphere of all that is best in the Continental type of café. The visitor may sit, with every comfort around, watching from the windows the world of London pass to and fro, meanwhile entertained with the latest popular selections, rendered by an excellent string band, for music all day has been arranged for. On every floor there is a separate kitchen and the service department. Here everything is arranged with a view to securing rapidity of service and the most hygienic conditions.

THE FAMILY WINE MERCHANT

Sir—As a family wine merchant, I am anxious to know what is to happen to the members of this particular branch of the trade should the Chancellor of the Exchequer's drastic measure be brought into force, and our premises closed for the duration of the war.

Those of us with branches have paid large sums to the revenue for license duties, part of which is unexpired: Will these sums be returned to us? Our spirit stocks represent considerable amounts paid on account of duty. If the Government prohibit the sale will they refund the duty on stock in hand, or, allow interest on same? Further, are we expected to pay rent, rates, and taxes, or our creditors during the time we are compulsorily closed down? Those of us whose entire capital is invested in this perfectly legitimate business, and who also possess large families—what is our position?

Are we to see those for whom we are morally and legally responsible starved, because a small proportion of workm in the north cannot use alcohol with discretion?—Yours faithfully,

EDWIN G. WATERS (D. Waters and Son).
Brighton, April 3.

ENEMY SUBJECTS.

LEAVE TO RETURN HOME.

The American Embassy has reason to believe that there are still in this country German and Austro-Hungarian subjects who might obtain leave to return home, but who have not yet obtained it owing to lack of information. For the benefit of such individuals the Embassy gives the following notification of the classes of persons whose requests to be repatriated are considered by the Home Office. The following classes of German and Austro-Hungarian subjects may apply for permission to leave Great Britain:

1. Women of any age.
2. German men under 17 or over 55 years of age.
3. Austro-Hungarian men under 18 or over 50 years of age.
4. Austro-Hungarian men between 18 and 50 years of age whose physical condition renders them totally unfit for any kind of military service.
5. German or Austro-Hungarian physicians, surgeons, and ministers of religion.

Persons in any of these classes who desire to leave the country should

(a) apply to the Home Office (Permits Department), and,

(b) according to their nationality, communicate with either the German Division, 9, Carlton House-terrace, S.W., or the Austro-Hungarian Division, 18, Belgrave-square, S.W., for any further desired information.

The Austro-Hungarian Division organises from time to time parties, which are personally conducted, to Vienna or Buda-Pesth. These parties, the dates of which are announced in advance, are specially adapted for the safe repatriation of older people, women, and children.

MOTOR CARS.

ALDRIDGE'S, ST MARTIN'S-LANE, London
(one minute from Leicester-square Tube Station).
W. and S. FREEMAN, Proprietors.

MOTOR AMBULANCE.
NEXT WEDNESDAY, 14 April, at about 2.30 o'clock,
Messrs. W. and S. FREEMAN will SELL by AUCTION a
DENNIS 4-STRETCHER MOTOR AMBULANCE.
The proceeds of sale to be devoted to the provision of a
motor field kitchen.—On view.

The MOTOR AUCTION on WEDNESDAY NEXT, com-
mencing at twelve o'clock (cars at 2.30), will also include
1911 MERCEDES live axle Landaulette.
1912 UNIC Landaulette.
1913 PILAIN Interior-drive Coupé.
1913 STUDEBAKER Touring Car.
1911 TALBOT Touring Car.
And other late model 2-Seaters, Landaulettes, &c., Acces-
sories, Stepneys, Tyres.
Catalogue on application.

MADAME TUSSAUD'S.

Thousands visited Madame Tussaud's Exhibition yesterday, and throughout the day there was a long queue of people anxious to gain admission. The exhibition just now includes many trophies from the war. Interest in a relic is increased if the spectator can touch it, and the visitors to Madame Tussaud's are permitted to handle and examine German swords and rifles and a large number of other trophies which have been taken from captured German trenches. One of the latest additions to the collection is a German sword bayonet, with its cruel saw edge. The large model of the Dardanelles, which has been placed by the side of the great war map this Easter, was inspected with close attention, and the continuous free display of war and other pictures in the Cinema Hall was equally attractive.

BLINDED SOLDIERS' HOSTEL.

QUEEN ALEXANDRA'S VISIT.

Queen Alexandra, the Princess Royal, Princess Victoria, and Princess Maud (daughter of the Princess Royal) were present at the concert given yesterday afternoon at the Blinded Soldiers' and Sailors' Hostel, St. Dunstan, Regent's Park, N.W. The institution exists for the benefit of officers and men of both services who have lost their sight in the war. Here the men become accustomed to their altered mode of life, and, besides being taught to read and write in Braille, are given instruction in suitable occupations.

The Royal party were received by the Hon. Arthur Stanley and Mr. C. Arthur Pearson. Queen Alexandra wore a black velvet coat and skirt, trimmed with silk embroidery, and a black jetted toque. The Princess Royal and Princess Victoria were also in black. Princess Maud wore a coat and skirt of russet-coloured Duvetyn and a black velvet hat. Queen Alexandra brought with her two baskets, decorated with red, white, and blue ribbons, containing a number of bunches of primroses, which her Majesty distributed among the men. The audience included Lady Isobel Gathorne-Hardy, Lady Victoria Primrose, Lady Garvagh, Lady Roxburgh, the Right Hon. W. and Mrs. Hayes Fisher, and Mr. and Mrs. Tennant.

That the programme should be provided by the students at the Royal Normal College for the Blind was a very happy thought. To begin with, no better entertainment of its kind could have been arranged, for there are many talented, well-trained musicians at the college, and they were naturally delighted to give their services in such a cause. Moreover, it gave a practical illustration of what those who have been deprived of their sight can accomplish. For the blind pianoforte soloist, Mr. William Edwards, A.R.C.O., who played Chaminade's " L'Automne " very skilfully, and the blind accompanists, Miss Elsie Buscall, Miss Mabel Davis, Mr. A. J. Eyre, and Mr. Sinclair Logan, who acquitted themselves most admirably, are all pianists of no small accomplishments. The excellent choir, too, though unable, of course, to avail itself of the guiding baton of a conductor, was never at fault, even in the most complicated passages of Holbrooke's " Footsteps of Angels " and Granville Bantock's very elaborate arrangement of " Annie Laurie," but sang these, Eaton Faning's " The Miller's Wooing," Coleridge Taylor's " Viking Song," and other part songs with admirable unanimity as well as with great sympathy and understanding. Both from the technical and from the artistic point of view their performances were most excellent.

To the soloists, too, the warmest praise must be given. Miss Isabella Vass caught the happy spirit of German's " All the world awakes to-day " very successfully. Most charming, too, was Miss Elsie Buscall's singing of Landon Ronald's " Sunbeams." Mr. Andrew Fraser, a baritone with a particularly good voice and a real sense of style, gave interpretations of Roger Quilter's Shakespearian songs that had a real artistic value; while Mr. Ernest Littlewood, a very capable bass, gave Mendelssohn's " I am a Roamer " with great aplomb and humour. At the close of the programme Queen Alexandra warmly congratulated all those who took part in it on the great success that they had achieved.

Monday 26th April 1915
Reverend Alford

CARE OF BLIND SOLDIERS.

WAR OFFICE INTEREST.

It is officially announced through the Press Bureau that the Secretary of State for War has approved of the arrangements which have been made for providing additional accommodation at the Blinded Soldiers' Hostel, at St. Dunstan's, Regent's Park, London, N.W., to an extent which will enable 120 men to be cared for and trained there.

These arrangements include the erection of spacious workshops, besides those already in use, and considerable additions of a temporary character to the house.

The War Office approves of the work of the Blinded Soldiers' Care Committee, and is satisfied that this organisation will meet the needs of all those who may be blinded during the war.

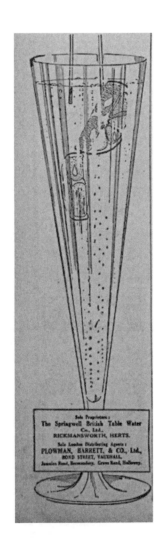

RESULT OF POST-MORTEM.

One of them died shortly after our arrival. A post-mortem examination was conducted in our presence by Lieutenant McNee, a pathologist by profession, of Glasgow University. The examination showed that death was due to acute bronchitis and its secondary effects. There was no doubt that the bronchitis and accompanying slow asphyxiation were due to the irritant gas.

Lieutenant McNee had also examined yesterday the body of a Canadian sergeant who had died in the clearing station from the effects of the gas. In this case also very acute bronchitis and œdema of the lungs caused death by asphyxiation.

A deposition by Captain Bertram, 8th Canadian Battalion, was carefully taken down by Lieutenant McNee. Captain Bertram was then in the clearing station suffering from the effects of the gas and from a wound. From a support trench about 600 yards from the German lines he had observed the gas. He saw first of all a white smoke rising from the German trenches to a height of about 3ft. Then in front of the white smoke appeared a greenish cloud, which drifted along the ground to our trenches, not rising more than about 7ft from the ground when it reached our first trenches. Men in these trenches were obliged to leave, and a number of them were killed by the effects of the gas. He made a counter-attack about

Monday 10th May 1915
The Lusitania

Surgeon-Major Frederic Warren Pearl (1869-1952) was travelling on the Lusitania with his wife Amy Lea, children Stuart, Amy, Susan, Audrey and the children's nurses Alice Lines and Greta Lorenson. During the sinking, Warren and his wife became separated from their children and their nurses, and spent much time looking for their children until the ship sank from beneath them. Of their party, he, his wife, Stuart, Audrey and Alice Lines survived the Lusitania sinking.

Used with kind permission of Mike Poirier / NARA collection

	Major F. Warren Pearl Saloon Passenger Saved
	Image credit: US National Archives/Michael Poirier.
Born	Frederic Warren Pearl 26 August 1869 Bradford, Massachusetts, United States
Died	2 January 1952 (age 82) London, England, United Kingdom
Age on Lusitania	45
Ticket number	46071

PEARL	Master	Stuart Duncan Day	Saved	5
PEARL	Miss	Audrey Warren	Saved	03-months
PEARL	Surgeon-Major	Frederic "Frank" Warren	Saved	46
PEARL	Mrs.	Frederic Warren (Amy Lea Duncan)	Saved	34
PEARL	Miss	Susan Whitewright	Lost	1.5
PEARL	Miss	Amy Whitewright Warren	Lost	2.5

235

If any SURVIVOR of the R.M.S. "LUSITA-
NIA" saw anything of Mr. and Mrs. ALAN DREDGE
during the voyage, and especially at the time of the disaster, he will confer a great favour by COMMUNICATING
with Clive Davies, 2, George-street, Mansion House, E.C.

LUSITANIA SURVIVORS.
Will any PASSENGER who was ACQUAINTED with
Mr. WALTER WRIGHT, first saloon passenger, kindly
COMMUNICATE with Mr. J. McDowell, Dunlop Rubber
Co. (Ltd.) Aston cross, Birmingham?

If any SURVIVOR of the R.M.S. "LUSITA-
NIA" saw anything of Mr. and Mrs. ALAN DREDGE
during the voyage, and especially at the time of the disaster, he will confer a great favour by COMMUNICATING
with Clive Davies, 2, George-street, Mansion House, E.C.

WILL any SURVIVOR from the LUSITANIA
who spoke to Mrs. N. WICKHAM (second-class
passenger) during the day of the disaster, either before or
after, kindly COMMUNICATE with Mrs. Ida Taylor, 21,
Comeragh-road, Barons-court, W.?

LUSITANIA.—Will any PERSON or RELA-
TIVE or FRIEND of persons saved by SHIP'S LIFE
JACKET ("Boddy" Life Jacket) kindly write us, giving
any testimony they can regarding its qualities as life
preserver? They may save another life by doing this.—
BODDY LIFE SAVING APPLIANCES (1914) (Ltd.), 4,
Broad-street-place, London, E.C.; 601, Tower-buildings,
Liverpool.

£5 REWARD.—Whereas some person or persons are CIRCULATING that our client, Dr. H. GOLD-BERG, of 27, New Cavendish-street, W., is a GERMAN, we hereby state that he is in no way connected with or descended from Germans, and we will pay the above reward to anyone giving information of any person or persons spreading such report. Proceedings will be taken WOOLFE and WOOLFE, Solicitors, 29, Duke-street, Piccadilly.

THE DAILY TELEGRAPH, THURSDAY, APRIL 29, 1915.

AN APPEAL FOR RESPIRATORS.

The War Office has issued the following :

As a protection against the asphyxiating gases being used as a weapon of warfare by the Germans, supplies of one or both of the following types of respirator are required by the troops at the front. Either can be made easily in any household.

First, a face piece (to cover mouth and nostrils), formed of an oblong pad of bleached absorbent cotton wool, about 5½in. by 3in. by ½in., covered with three layers of bleached cotton gauze, and fitted with a band, to fit round the head and keep the pad in position, consisting of a piece of half-inch cotton elastic 16in.

long, attached to the narrow end of the face pad, so as to form a loop with the pad.

Second, a piece of double stockinette, 9½in. long and 5½in. wide in the centre, gradually diminishing in width to 2½in. at each end, with a piece of thick plaited worsted about 6in. long, attached at each end, so as to form a loop to pass over the ear.

These respirators should be sent in packages of not less than 100 to the Chief Ordnance Officer, Royal Army Clothing Department, Pimlico. The photographs show :

[Photos.] (A) COTTON WOOL AND GAUZE.   (B) STOCKINETTE.   [C.N.

These photographs are not official, as the exact pattern has not been determined by the Army authorities, but Pattern A was made up by Messrs. Burroughs and Wellcome to the

War Office description. As stated in our article on Page nine experiments are in progress with a view to perfecting the official pattern.

HAY FOR THE ARMY,

WORKERS WANTED.

Yet another method whereby civilians can help towards fulfilling the military requirements of the country presents itself, and that is in connection with the important department dealing with the supply of hay to the Army. Before delivery at the various depôts and ports the hay has to be pressed into bales, and for this operation a machine called a "baler" is used. Seven people are required to keep it working, and of these three must be experts. The other four only require the assets of health and strength. Two are required to fork the hay from the stack to the baler, and two to attend to the binding apparatus, which is quite simple. All the equipment required is a pair of goggles, a rough suit, and a pair of stout boots. The baler is hauled to a new farm practically every day, so that the occupation provides great variety of scenery.

Colonel H. Godfrey Morgan, military member, Organising Committee, Farmers' County Committees, informed a *Daily Telegraph* representative that 500 persons were required immediately for this work, and hundreds more would be wanted. The pay is 2s 6d a day, irrespective of the working of the machines or not, and 3d is allowed for every ton completed. Parties now at work are earning as much as £2 10s a week each person. At present a lot of the work is being done by farm hands, but these are much required for expert work on the farm, and it is hoped that by the help of civilian volunteers a lot of these men could be released for their important duties. It is suggested that persons owning motor caravans or cars might make up picnic parties, and spend several weeks at a time on this baler work. Motor-caravan owners will be allowed 1s 6d a ton for hauling hay to the stations. The counties where help is most needed are Hampshire, Durham, Northumberland, Cumberland, Yorkshire, Devon, Somerset, Norfolk, East and West Suffolk. East Wales also wants help, but Kent, Sussex, and Surrey need none. All persons, men or women, engaged in this work will receive a military badge. Applicants should apply to Major Smith, 4, Whitehall-place, S.W.; Telephone 3,738, Victoria.

Monday 24th May 1915
The Garden

MAY TULIPS.

As the earlier spring flowers pass away we look forward to the coming of the bolder objects for the garden border, the harbingers of an early summertime. There is no waiting, but rather one continuous chain of flowering plants as the days and weeks go by. Some of the most beautiful of bulbous plants are at their best in May—among them the delightfully fragrant poet's narcissus and its new hybrids. The double-flowered narcissus poeticus is always valued, and succeeds best when deeply planted in moist soil.

A good deal of damage is done to plants by watering them overhead. Unless the why and wherefore is understood it is always safest to water the soil instead of the foliage.

Then the month of May is quite rich in its dower of tulips—not those earlier sections of the race that we know as "bedding" or "early-flowering cottage," but that greater and incomparable host of Darwin varieties, all of which are essentially "May flowering." Nothing can equal in brilliancy or richness of colour a bed or border planted with a mass of gorgeous tulips showing their full beauty in the month of May. It is one of the most striking in the whole host of garden attractions. Tulips lend themselves for effect in a great number of ways, presenting the most delicate combination of colours when arranged in tasteful design. They will thrive in any good garden soil, and we have seen them planted as late as January and give a splendid result.

When placed in beds or borders the bulbs should be put in as recommended for hyacinths: if poked into a hole made with a dibble they are frequently not a success: like

241

THE C.O. of a REGIMENT of KITCHENER'S ARMY, living some eight miles from camp, owing to there being no C.O.'s quarters, asks a PATRIOT to PLACE a MOTOR CAR at his DISPOSAL.—Write S., Box 6.466. Daily Telegraph, 161, Piccadilly, W.

A RESERVE BATTALION of the NEW ARMY, likely to remain in its present quarters for some time, requires SHRUBS and PLANTS to make its surroundings more pleasant, attractive, and homely.—Write R. F., Box 6.467. Daily Telegraph, 161, Piccadilly, W.

WILL anyone give GRAMOPHONES and GRAMOPHONE RECORDS for DESPATCH to the CONVALESCENT BRITISH SOLDIERS in FRANCE?—Please send to Cox and Co., Harrington House, Craig's-court, Charing-cross, S.W.

CARDS FOR INDUSTRIOUS MEN.

Sir—May I be allowed space in which to reply to " J. M. D."? This gentleman apparently holds the opinion that this country is governed by a wise and beneficent autocracy. If he will carefully read the newspapers for the past month (*The Daily Telegraph*, for instance), he will find that such is not the case, and any attempt to introduce Russian police methods would be immediately visited with calamitous results.

I need only remind J. M. D. that any card system having for its object the Governmental tabulation of the workers, and emanating from the historic enemies of the workers—the employers—would, in all probability, bring the men out on strike more quickly than any other method I have heard suggested. J. M. D. evidently does not know the hard lives of the munition workers on the Clyde, and elsewhere, or the dour and surly spirit that unites them.

The remedy that appears to me as being more in keeping with the times is: Better housing, better wages, better conditions, and the abolition of over-time. By skilful co-ordination of the work in progress all these reforms could be carried out, and result in a temperate working-class.—Yours, &c.,

April 5.   TRADE UNIONIST.

COUNCILLOR'S ACTION.

At a meeting of the Paddington Borough Council yesterday the Mayor stated that he had received a letter from Councillor E. M. Meyer assenting to a suggestion that for the present time he should absent himself from meetings of the Council. The letter read:

" Dear Mr. Mayor—I am obliged for the courteous terms of your letter. I have lived in this country since 1872, and renounced my German nationality in 1877, a year before I was naturalised. I have always been true to my oath of allegiance, and have endeavoured to be a good citizen to my adopted country. At the same time, I appreciate that it is useless as an individual, however loyal I may be, to stand out against the wave of feeling which has been aroused by the dastardly outrages of which the Germans have been guilty."

CARE OF BLIND SOLDIERS.

WAR OFFICE INTEREST.

It is officially announced through the Press Bureau that the Secretary of State for War has approved of the arrangements which have been made for providing additional accommodation at the Blinded Soldiers' Hostel, at St. Dunstan's, Regent's Park, London, N.W., to an extent which will enable 120 men to be cared for and trained there.

These arrangements include the erection of spacious workshops, besides those already in use, and considerable additions of a temporary character to the house.

The War Office approves of the work of the Blinded Soldiers' Care Committee, and is satisfied that this organisation will meet the needs of all those who may be blinded during the war.

THE PUBLIC TRUSTEE.

TWO SONS KILLED IN ACTION.

Much sympathy will be felt in the community for Mr. Charles John Stewart, the Public Trustee, who has lost two sons at the front, as well as a son-in-law. His wife, Lady Mary Stewart, whom he married in 1884, is a daughter of the late Earl of Norbury, and they had two sons and three daughters. One son, Captain and Adjutant Gerald Charles Stewart, was in the 10th Hussars, and Second Lieutenant John Maurice Stewart, had also joined the Army after the commencement of the war. One was killed in action recently, and now Mr. Stewart has received news that the other has also been killed in battle. His eldest daughter married last year Lieutenant Colin Campbell, Scots Guards, and that officer has likewise lost his life at the front.

Monday 24th May 1915
The Garden

AT THE ZOO.

A PLEASANT DAY.

One almost needed coloured glasses to look comfortably at the vivid crimson and white of the flamingos in the Zoo yesterday, and the macaws, swinging splendid and uproarious on their perches under the elms, were rainbow-hued. Seldom has there been a Whit Monday of clearer air or more metallic sunshine, and, cheap railway tickets being unobtainable for the moment, and the tramways into the country in abeyance, the public went to the Gardens in something approaching record numbers. The paths were thronged; many of the houses, especially those where the monkeys held reception from noon till night, and the bird of paradise's private palace next door, were unapproachable. "It makes me quite hot to look at them," the little bonnet-monkey said of the crowding visitors to his friend the brown capuchin over the way. "Yes; and only three nuts and a button from the lot of them," answered the latter, taking the articles meditatively from the pouches in his cheeks. "Times are nothing like what they were before Dr. Chalmers Mitchell double-wired our cages and put glass round the bottom of them; mean jealousy, I call it!" and he turned reflectively to hunt for the holiday flea in the wanderoo, which is quite a game preserve in this direction, and hires himself out to sporting neighbours on the topmost benches of the cage.

A MERRY PICNIC.

It was not a day for seeing everything in the Gardens, even if such an adventure could have been thought of by the most energetic. It was too hot in the sun for one thing, and the great, kindly crowd was too thick to permit of it for another. But it was a memorably happy day in the shade of the big elm-trees, piled right up to the pale blue sky overhead with tender green leafage, and the wide lawn, between the fish-house and the bears, was the scene of a giant, ten-hour picnic, a feast that began so early that surely some of the feasters must have brought their breakfasts with them, and went on, constantly replenished from the teeming commissariat close by, until the shadows of the elms were long as church steeples on the green sward, and even the patient elephants, who had carried

RESPIRATORS.

NO MORE REQUIRED.

Yesterday afternoon the Press Bureau issued the following announcement:

Thanks to the magnificent response already made to the appeal in the Press for respirators for the troops, the War Office is in a position to announce that no further respirators need be made.

It is no exaggeration to say that this intimation on behalf of the War Office came as a complete and pleasant surprise—tinged, perhaps, with just a little sense of disappointment—to the countless willing needlewomen who had energetically thrown themselves into the work of providing respirators for our troops in the field. There was surprise because the announcement was totally unexpected. It fell like a bolt from the blue. There was disappointment, too, because the official intimation deprived numerous enthusiastic households and energetic work parties of a golden opportunity of rendering a much-needed service to our gallant soldiers.

SPLENDID PUBLIC RESPONSE.

In truth, the response to the War Office request for respirators has been wonderfully prompt and cordial. No sooner had the military authorities made known the need for contrivances to protect our soldiers against the murderous gases so barbarously employed by the enemy than respirators came rolling in literally by the thousand. It has been estimated that by Wednesday evening—and the appeal was published only that morning—some 2,000 had reached the Royal Army Clothing Department at Pimlico. By the first parcels post delivery there came no fewer than 110 consignments. As

Sunday 6th June 1915
Claridge's

CLARIDGE'S HOTEL, TO-MORROW (SUN.), 9.30 p.m.
AN HOUR OF
MUSIC and POETRY AFTER DINNER.
Tickets, 10s. 6d.

Monday 14th June 1915
The Recital

VIOLINIST.—Mlle. KIMEY GUILLAIN (of
Brussels), pupil of Ysaye, is in LONDON.—For engagements
and terms for lessons apply 8, Duke's-lane, Kensington, W.